RESTITUTION

By

Kristy Shelton

Published by Innovo Publishing LLC
www.innovopublishing.com
1-888-546-2111

Providing Full-Service Publishing Services for
Christian Authors, Artists & Organizations: Hardbacks, Paperbacks,
eBooks, Audiobooks, Music & Film

RESTITUTION

Library of Congress Control Number: 2016957961
ISBN: 978-1-61314-363-6

Cover Design & Interior Layout: Innovo Publishing LLC

Printed in the United States of America
U.S. Printing History
First Edition: November 2016

Dedication

To my daughter, Alex, who inspires me greatly.

Endorsements

"Kristy Shelton's *Restitution* crackles with energy from start to finish. I found myself sneaking back to it throughout the day to see what surprising turn was around the corner. Shelton has managed to weave together lovable, dynamic characters who not only find themselves embroiled in a global crisis but also wrestle with their most important relationships. It's equal parts thriller, romance, and faith journey. At its core, *Restitution* explores the nature of faithfulness with an honesty that few Christian books manage and provides a picture of modern marriage that gives us all hope. I loved it and I'm confident you will too."

—Jenny Runkel, co-author of *ScreamFree Parenting* with Hal Runkel, LMFT

"Restitution is the compelling account of ordinary people forced into an extraordinary situation. Throughout the story one is invited into moments of intrigue and life-altering decisions. You will be captivated by this spellbinding story of God's grace and mercy in a world turned upside down."

—Andrea Popham, Student Teacher Supervisor, David Lipscomb University

"*Restitution* captured a piece of my imagination I never knew existed and I found myself unable to put it down. The mystery, intrigue, and hope for restored lives kept me turning page after page. Discovering a new genre to explore with characters that I easily related to broadened my perspective and challenged me to seek God's will for our lives, even when things do not seem to be going as planned."

—Catrina White, Teacher, Greater Atlanta Christian School

Acknowledgements

It is with a grateful heart that I acknowledge those who have helped me with this book.

To Andrea Popham, Catrina White, and Janine Irwin, colleagues and former colleagues, sisters and friends, thank you for taking the time to read and critique my manuscript. I appreciate your honesty and fearlessness in sharing your opinions. I found it amusing when it came time to review the epilogue, of which I wrote two very different scenarios. Janine was adamant about one, Andrea was adamant about the other, and Catrina was adamant about neither! Well, for what it's worth, there *is* no epilogue. I hope you're all happy! At least you know what *might* have happened. I love each of you dearly.

To Jenny Runkel, high school English teacher and respected colleague, thank you so much for saying "Yes" in the school parking lot to reading my manuscript at the absolute busiest time of year—the week before school started. I felt deeply honored to trust it in your hands. You have no idea how much you bolstered my confidence with your insightful comments.

To my husband, Cliff, thank you for understanding my need to write. And just as importantly, thank you for finding other things to do while it's happening. You're the best!

To Dr. Bart Dahmer at Innovo Publishing, I'm grateful for our continued relationship through publishing. I truly believe God sent me to Innovo in 2010.

To my editor, Rachael Carrington, I appreciate your comments and enthusiasm for this latest adventure. You have been a joy to work with, and I hope we will have many more opportunities in the future.

And most importantly, all thanks and glory and honor goes to God, whom I adore.

>>Chapter 1

SEPTEMBER 2027

H ey, Babe. I just heard the news. Do you want me to come to the hospital?"

Karissa tamped down the sudden irritation Marc's term of endearment spawned. How hard was it for him to call her by her name? Rolling her eyes through a shuddered breath she admitted something to herself that she could never tell Marc—she needed him right now. "Yes…please," she said quietly.

"I'm on my way. I'll see you in twenty."

He sounded out of breath, like he was running.

"Wait! Marc?"

"Yeah? I'm here."

"There's a lot of press outside." Karissa stared down the hall at the bulging crowd near the hospital entrance. "The police are here too. Just show them who you are and they'll let you through."

There was such a long silence Karissa thought she had lost the connection. "Marc, are you still there?"

"Yeah, yeah." She heard his door slam and the sudden blast of the tech screen. "Off!" he yelled, then apologized for the noise. "What really happened?"

"Not now, Marc. I'll tell you what I know when you get here."

Quickly she dropped the connection. She didn't really want to see Marc in the first place, but of all the people who had ever been in her life, her estranged husband was the most levelheaded of them all. He could help her make sense of this horrific situation.

A team of medical personnel passed by at a frenzied pace. They disappeared inside her mother's surgical suite. *Oh, God, what now?*

Tears spilled over her lashes. The confusion running unleashed through every nerve of her body threatened to overwhelm—

"Oh, no!" She groaned out loud, seizing her phone again. "Voice call only...Ally." *Come on, come on. Answer.*

"Hi, Mom. What's up?"

"Ally, honey, listen to me..." Karissa's voice broke, and she closed her eyes tightly, releasing another stream of tears.

"Mom, what is it? What's wrong?"

Karissa took a deep breath and leaned her forehead into the cold wall, then used the calmest voice she could muster. "Honey..." She shook her head—*this can't be done on the phone.* "I'm sorry, I forgot to pick you up from soccer practice."

"Oh, is that all? The Bentley's brought me home. We figured you had to work late again. I'm fine...just getting my homework done. What's all the noise?"

Karissa glanced down the hall again and quickly headed to the other end. "It's nothing. Is that better?" She closed the door to a small waiting room near the nurse's station. "Listen, Ally, no screen, okay? Only homework."

Ally giggled. "Okay."

"Promise me."

"Mom," she said, laughing this time. "I promise, but what's the deal? I don't have that much and when I get done I wanna watch the next passage of *The Kinsman.*"

"No!" Karissa fairly shouted, then cringed inwardly. "I'm sorry, I...I've just got a lot going on right now at work. I'm having trouble concentrating." An idea suddenly came to her. "Hey, your dad's coming over tonight. He really wants to spend some quality time with his girl. I just wanted to make sure you didn't get distracted by anything. Get your homework done and he'll be there by seven or so."

"Okay, Mom. I'll call him and see if he wants to go to dinner."

"No—"

"Mom, what's really going on?"

"I mean, um…look, he wanted to surprise you. I guess I kind of spoiled that. Sorry, honey."

"It'll be fine," she said. "I'll act surprised."

Poor girl, she had no inkling of the major surprise she would have to deal with tonight. There would be no *acting* involved.

"Listen, I just wanted to check on you to see if you're okay, and I really am sorry I missed picking you up."

"No problem. I'll see you tonight."

"Okay, sweet girl. I…I love you."

There was a short pause. She knew her daughter must think something was wrong for sure. Karissa rarely said those words to her anymore. The cheery voice on the other end replied, "You better!" She could picture her daughter's mischievous grin. "And Mom, for the record, I love you, too."

"You better," she said as lightheartedly as possible.

Almost twenty minutes to the tee, Karissa watched a policeman at the hospital entrance scan Marc's face. When his picture and ID popped up on the officer's screen, he stepped aside to let Marc squeeze through, then immediately closed the temporary barrier to keep everyone else out. Her husband's presence brought a smidgen of confidence that she'd be able to survive whatever was coming.

"Kari, I got here as soon as I could." Marc reached for her, but she kept her arms wrapped tightly around her waist. He briefly pulled her to his chest, then stepped back. "I've been watching the news all afternoon. I couldn't believe it when they released your mom's name."

Karissa shook her head, cursing under her breath. "What could she have been thinking?"

"Let's not go there now. We don't have all the facts." His brow furrowed deeper. "Is she going to make it?"

"I don't know. I haven't heard anything yet."

"Mrs. Gale?"

Karissa turned sharply from Marc to see two men and a woman approaching, all wearing dark suits.

"Yes?"

"FBI, Ma'am. We need to talk." One of the men touched her elbow. "Please, come with us."

She took two steps, then suddenly turned back to Marc. "He needs to come with me. This was…*is* my husband, Marcus Gale."

"Sir, please come with us."

Marc matched his wife's stride and put a protective hand on her back. She leaned in close to tell him about Ally. "She's expecting you by seven. You're going to have to break the news to her somehow."

He swallowed hard, but said nothing.

Saint Francis' hospital administrator appeared at the end of the hall motioning them toward an open door. "You'll have privacy in my office. Let me know if you need anything else," she said solemnly.

Karissa felt dazed. *This can't be happening.* How would she ever be able to defend what her mother had done?

>>>

"Hey, Cupcake! How's my girl?" Ally gave her dad a breathtaking smile and melted into his arms. He didn't want to let go. How had thirteen years gone by so fast?

"I'm glad you're here. I was thinking we could go to our favorite place on the coast for dinner. Mom doesn't like Papa Joe's Seafood. This is our chance."

Marc took a deep breath and ran a hand through his dark hair. This was going to be harder than he thought. Maybe they could drive out to the coast and have a nice dinner before he broke the news to her on the beach. "Good choice," he said, forcing a smile. "You might want to grab a jacket for a little walk on the sand. Does that sound good?"

"It's a plan," Ally called over her shoulder, taking the stairs two at a time.

Marc sighed deeply. He hated this arrangement—he was missing too much of Ally's growing up. He was missing Karissa too, but what could he do except go along with her headstrong, self-centered plans. It was slowly killing him. He had no clue how to win back her favor or, to be honest, how he had lost her favor in the first place.

Ally broke into his thoughts as she ran down the stairs, skipping the last three altogether. When Marc opened the front door he felt his heart collide with his sternum. Cars jammed the street in front of the townhouse. Reporters were descending onto the lawn like a gaggle of geese. Even a small aircraft hovered over the driveway.

"Get back inside," Marc said roughly. He took his daughter by the shoulders and turned her back into the living room. Slamming the door, he swiped the automatic locking system.

Her eyes were wide with fright. "What's going on, Daddy?" Then worry captured her features. "Where's Mom?"

"Your mom is just fine, she'll be home soon. Let's go upstairs and talk." He wanted to get as far away from the crowd as possible.

Marc took her by the hand and felt her trembling. Oh how he wished they were walking alone on the beach. The falling dusk and sound of the waves would've created a more peaceful environment to give his daughter the terrible news.

Her bedroom wasn't a bad second choice, though. Ally had decorated her room in cream and blue colors. One entire wall she'd dedicated to all of her favorite things—a popular band, pictures of friends, soccer team photos, and a poster of wild horses running in the ocean surf. His eyes moved to her dresser where family photos lined the entire length of the mirror. Lingering on the one of Kathleen with her granddaughter taken on Ally's thirteenth birthday, he felt his throat tighten. This conversation was going to be harder than he thought.

Father and daughter sat down uncomfortably on the edge of the bed and stared at each other. Marc raked his fingers through his hair—he needed something to do with his hands while he rummaged through troubling thoughts.

"Daddy, I know Mom was keeping something from me when I talked to her after soccer practice. What's going on?" Ally kicked off her shoes and swirled to face him, sitting cross-legged on the bed.

"Baby, something really bad happened today. It's been on the news all afternoon."

"Oh, you mean that Russian guy getting killed? I heard about that at school." Her brow knit tightly and she tilted her chin slightly to the right—something she always did when she was trying to figure things out. "So what does that have to do with us?"

Marc reached for his daughter's hand and covered it in both of his. "Your Granny K was involved. She was driving the car that—"

Ally immediately withdrew her hand. "That was Gran? How could that have happened?" Suddenly tears spilled down her cheeks. "Daddy, please tell me she's okay. Please…"

Marc scooted toward her on the bed and took her into his arms. He dropped his chin onto the top of her head. "She's been in surgery all afternoon. When I left the hospital I still hadn't heard her condition."

Ally sniffled, then leaned back against the soft pillows on her bed drawing her knees to her chest. There was a long silence before she asked about the people outside the townhouse. "Who are they?"

"Reporters, most likely. Everyone's trying to get a story." He gently rubbed his hand along her arm. "But don't worry, I'm not going to let any of them get to you. I'll take care of all that stuff." He had no idea how he was going to handle it, but there was no way any of those guys were getting near his daughter.

"Is Mom still at the hospital?"

"Yeah, I left her there. I don't know when, or if, she's coming home tonight."

"Can we call her?"

Marc instantly tapped his wrist band. "You bet."

Karissa's face popped up on the screen within seconds. Her eyes were red and watery. As soon as she saw Ally she chastised her husband. "Marc, what are you doing?"

"Babe, Ally just needs to know you're okay."

His wife turned her face away for a moment, obviously wiping away tears. When she looked back Marc was the first to speak. "Hey, why don't I give you two a little time alone. I'll go downstairs and make us some sandwiches." He gently pulled the back of Ally's light brown ponytail and projected her mom's call to the bedside table screen. As he stood, he gave his daughter an *I love you* sign and headed to the kitchen.

> > >

Marc came up off the couch gripping his old metal softball bat with both hands. His knuckles turned white as he drew it back, ready to swing if necessary. Karissa jumped back into the dark kitchen and let out a screech.

"I'm sorry, Kari," Marc said softly, tossing the bat onto the plush cushions. "I must've fallen asleep."

"Is it safe?" Karissa's sarcastic tone told Marc he would need to tread lightly. She stepped into the warm glow of the living room lamp, throwing her bag in the chair. Her normally neat, unwrinkled appearance had been commandeered by havoc. "It's bad enough I have to sneak into my own house, for heaven's sake."

"What time is it?" Marc asked, smoothing down the back of his hair.

"Two-thirty. I'm going to bed."

Marc's mouth dropped open. "Wait a minute...can you tell me a little of what's going on? How's Kathleen?"

"I don't know," she said, with almost no emotion.

"Well...what are the doctors saying?"

Karissa turned her back to him and headed for the stairs.

"Kari, don't do this—"

"Keep your voice down, Marc. I take it Ally is asleep," she whispered harshly.

He followed her to the stairs aware that his voice had not been raised. "Just answer my question and I promise I'll leave you alone."

"It's complicated."

"Try me." His eyes pleaded with her and she momentarily dropped her ire.

"If she's still alive..." Karissa's expression turned to something akin to agony. "They're keeping it a secret."

>>Chapter 2

At five o'clock in the morning Marc had three screens going at once—a built-in screen on the glass coffee table, his hand-held tablet, and the TV on the opposite side of the room. He was trying to glean as much information as possible. It wasn't that difficult. Every media organization was covering the story like a plague. *The Los Angeles Times* was heralding a war between Russia and the United States. The two countries had already been skating on a slippery precipice for decades. Could this be the nudge to send them hurtling into the abyss? *If so,* Marc thought, *the world as we know it is about to unravel.* He needed coffee in the worst way.

Scenes from the Ocean Terrace restaurant dominated the TV screen. Kathleen had taken their family to dine there on many occasions. It was her favorite place, not only because of the incredible seafood, but because of its remarkable atmosphere. Dining areas were built directly into the side of the cliff, on terraces overhanging the ocean. Stairways zigzagged between each level. If customers preferred an indoor meal, they were treated to a large dining area underneath the bluff, well above the pounding Pacific surf. Marc had witnessed several spectacular sunsets while dining with his family on one of the terraces. Apparently, Russia's Deputy Prime Minister, Pavel Vasiliev, had been sitting on the terrace directly below Kathleen's parking spot yesterday morning. What Marc couldn't seem to understand, nor could the authorities investigating the scene, is how or why she had crashed through the parking barrier and fence above.

CNN began profiling the life of legendary coach, Kathleen Raines. That coffee would have to wait. Marc bumped the volume up a bit, but not so loud to wake Karissa and Ally. There would be no work or school for any of them today. A long, private conversation with Karissa was in order. He hoped she was getting some much-needed sleep. They were going to have to navigate through a tangled mess.

Scenes of Kathleen's three volleyball national championships at Pepperdine University splashed across the TV screen. Marc leaned back on the couch feeling a heavy weight settle onto the center of his chest. He and Kathleen had always been so close, sharing the same profession, and loving the same woman—her daughter.

He sensed another presence in the room and turned his head to see Ally standing in the doorway from the kitchen. She was mesmerized. Quickly, Marc swiped the story away.

"No, stop! I want to see."

He stared at her for only a second, then swiped it back. He wanted to see, too.

"Come 'ere." Marc opened his arm to Ally and she didn't hesitate to snuggle up to his side on the couch. Together they watched Kathleen's life portrayed on the screen. Pepperdine's President spoke of his coach's impeccable character and love for her players. She was an icon at the university, still very much involved with the school since her retirement four years ago.

Ally wiped her eyes on the sleeve of her robe. "Daddy, we have to go see her." She put her feet on the floor and sat up out of his arms. "Let's go now. I've already figured out how we can sneak out without anyone knowing."

Marc shook his head, but before he could speak, she pressed on like a train without brakes. "We'll call a cab to pick us up on Grayson Avenue, in front of the Bentley's. All we have to do is go through the back gate into the Fowler's yard. No one will ever see us. Please," she begged. "I have to be with—"

The signal on the table screen chimed. Someone was trying to call.

"Do you recognize that signature, Ally?"

She shook her head slowly. Marc hesitated. The reporters were still hanging around outside. What if it was one of them? Then again, what if it was the FBI? He made an abrupt decision and swiped *reveal*. To his surprise, the caller wasn't cloaked.

The hospital administrator he remembered from last night was on the other end. She had obviously been without sleep—dark circles surrounded her eyes. "If you want to see her, it has to be now." Marc's pulse quickened as he watched her nervously glance over her shoulder. "Don't wait…do you understand?"

"Yes. But can you tell me—" The screen went blank. As soon as Marc had acknowledged her request, she cleared the call.

Ally sprang off the couch and ran for the stairs. "Come on, Daddy. We have to hustle!" Before disappearing into her bedroom, she yelled down, "You wake up Mom."

Marc's blood pressure skyrocketed. It would be easier sneaking past the press outside than waking up his wife. But he knew it had to be done and he didn't want to stop his daughter's progress. Blowing out a deep breath, he headed upstairs.

Softly knocking, he opened the door and stepped inside Karissa's immaculate bedroom. Her clothing from last night lay crumpled on the easy chair in the corner—totally out of character for…

His wife turned over on her back, drawing her left arm above her head. He allowed himself five seconds to stare at her natural beauty. With her silky brown hair tousled across the pillow, he ached to be lying beside her every morning. Moaning inwardly, he shoved the distraction aside.

"Kari?" He moved closer and touched her leg. "Kari, wake up."

Her eyes opened slowly and she tapped the headboard with her knuckles. "5:23?" She sat up letting the sheet drop to her waist. Marc tried to keep his eyes on hers. "What are you doing in here?"

"The administrator from Saint Francis Hospital just called. She said if we want to see your mother, we have to come now."

Karissa vaulted into action with the same intensity as her daughter. "Go wake up Ally," she yelled from the bathroom. "She needs to be with us."

"I'm already awake, Mom." Ally swept into the bedroom pulling her mom's jeans and a blouse out of her closet.

"Oh, thank you, sweet girl." Karissa flew back into the bedroom, throwing off her gown.

Marc cleared his throat and turned toward the door. "I'll wait downstairs." His pulse was still galloping when his wife and daughter appeared in the living room. Karissa grabbed her bag from where she'd thrown it last night and commanded them to follow her out the back door.

Dew clung to their shoes as they trekked across the small backyard. Marc kept his head ducked in case anyone was watching the fence line, but there was nothing they could do if there was an overhead drone. By the time they were all in Karissa's car where she'd parked it at the curb last night, the sun was just cracking the horizon. She sped along the backstreets heading toward the freeway on manual control. Karissa preferred to be in charge of her car's navigation, just like everything else in her life. Rush hour traffic was already in full swing and she whispered a curse word.

"Mom!"

She glanced over her shoulder at Ally in the backseat. "Sorry, honey. I'm working on it."

Marc and his mother-in-law had tried for years to get Kari to clean up her language, especially for Ally's sake. Apparently his daughter was taking over the crusade they had lost.

There was still an army of reporters and a heavy police presence at the hospital. An aircraft hovered over the scene. Karissa kept a wide berth and drove into a tunnel. Marc asked her where they were going.

"Last night my car was brought to a private entrance below the hospital. I couldn't have made it home otherwise."

She rushed them to an elevator near their parking spot and slid her hand across the sensor multiple times. Finally, the door opened and all three stepped inside. There was only one button to push and Karissa pounced on it like a cat. When the door opened, the hospital administrator turned sharply from where she'd been pacing.

"Don't say a word," she cautioned. "Follow me."

Marc mentally confirmed his earlier deduction. Amy Burke was still wearing the same gray suit he'd seen her in last night. She was tall and slender, most likely in her fifties, and very much in charge. They almost had to jog to keep up with her.

"In here." Ms. Burke opened a door and stepped back, ushering them inside.

The room was small and dark, the overhead light deliberately mute. It was so full of technical equipment and blinking monitors Marc almost felt claustrophobic with four people inside.

Ms. Burke kept her voice low. Her expression relayed the gravity of the situation. "I will deny any knowledge of meeting you here today if you are discovered. Do you understand?" She didn't wait for a response. "In a few minutes Kathleen Raines will be brought into the adjoining room." She pointed toward another door. "She's being administered several neurological tests. The room has to be cleared while the tests are being run and it will not be monitored on Ocu-Vision. No one will see you. There will be no harm to you, but your presence will essentially botch the test. This may be the only chance you'll ever get to see your mother again."

Karissa's eyes clouded with tears and she couldn't hold back the stream.

Amy Burke briefly held her gaze. "They're planning..." Abruptly she cleared her throat. "Actually, I don't know what they're about to do. All I know is that you may never get a chance to see your mother after today. I'm not willing to let that happen. You have every right to see her."

"Is she going to make it?" Marc asked.

Ms. Burke turned a sympathetic expression toward Ally and Karissa before locking eyes with Marc. "Honestly, I don't know if she'll make it through the day. The prognosis is not good." She looked back at Ally. "I'm really sorry." Ally leaned into her dad.

"Now here's how this is going to work. As soon as you hear me knock twice on the door from the hallway, you go straight into the testing room. One of you set an alarm for six minutes." Marc immediately activated his wrist monitor.

"At the end of six minutes, come back into this room." The three nodded their agreement. It was all so cloak and dagger.

"What about the tests?" Karissa asked.

"I'll make sure they're administered again. Don't worry about that part." She nervously glanced at the door and took in a deep breath. "Under no circumstances are you to stay in that room more than six minutes, and," she leveled her gaze at them, "do not leave *this* room until I come for you. Understood?"

"Yes," they all breathed in unison.

Amy Burke checked her wristband to monitor the hallway, then slipped outside the room leaving them huddled together.

> > >

Karissa felt like a caged animal. She was finding it difficult to stand still in the tight quarters. Finally, she reached for Ally and pulled her close. "How are you holding up, sweet girl?"

Ally looked into her mother's face with a hint of fear in her eyes. She swallowed hard before answering. "I'm okay."

"You know we're not going to let anything happen to you. Don't worry about any of this. Like Ms. Burke said, we have every right to see Granny K."

"I know, but what if we get caught?"

"We're not doing anything wrong. They're the ones keeping Gran from us, so we'll be fine."

Ally stepped back from her mother. "Why are they doing this, anyway? Wasn't all of this just an accident?"

"Sure it was," Karissa told her with as much confidence as she could rally. "I'm sure that's what all these tests are for. They want to see if Gran had some kind of seizure or stroke or something before…" Her words trailed off. The FBI had pressed her hard last night, trying to find an angle. Anyone who knew her mother would know this was a horrific accident, pure and simple.

Karissa drew in a sharp breath at the sound of two knocks on the hallway door. Marc pushed himself away from the wall where he'd been leaning and quietly opened the door to the next room. Karissa stepped into the darkened room first. Kathleen lay on a steel table wearing only a flimsy gown. Her first thought was to find a blanket to cover her mother. It seemed inhumane—not even a pillow beneath her head.

Slowly, all three stepped up beside the table, none with dry eyes. Despite the mesh cap around her head lighting up with rhythmic pulses, Ally gave her grandmother a lingering kiss. She pulled back sniffing and wiping away the moisture she'd left on Kathleen's cheek, then leaned back down to her ear. "I love you so much, Granny K." Ally's shoulders began shaking. "Please don't leave me…please…"

Karissa fought hard to keep her composure. The last thing she needed to do was break down sobbing when this could be the last few minutes she would ever spend with her mother. She lifted Kathleen's flaccid hand to her chest, feeling the sting of regret, or was it guilt? Hard to say; both emotions were insidiously bound within her heart. For many years Karissa had held this woman at arm's length, only letting her into tiny compartments of her life. She had worked so hard not to *be* like her—not to *think* like her. She closed her eyes and silently prayed—something she hadn't done sincerely in perhaps two decades. *Oh, God, if you're still listening to me…*the words fell flat. They wouldn't even form in her heart. She felt so helpless and alone.

Aware that she was the only one still standing with Kathleen, Karissa gently laid her mother's hand back on the table and turned around. Marc was holding Ally in his arms while she quietly wept. His eyes were full of sympathy in the dim light and he whispered, "Thirty seconds."

She turned back for one last look, then gently kissed her mother's cheek. "I'm sorry, Mom," she whispered, mere inches from her face. "Truly, I am." Marc laid his hand on Karissa's shoulder, but she turned away from his touch and told him, "We need to get back in the other room."

Amy Burke was already waiting for them with the hallway door open. "Come now," she urged. "Ocu-Vision is off line in this hallway for two more minutes. Hurry!"

Just as before, all three hastened their steps down the hall to the private elevator. Ms. Burke swiped the sensor before earnestly addressing Karissa. "Please don't contact me." She checked her wristband, then emphasized her directive as the door slid open. "Ever!"

Karissa didn't know what to say. This woman scared her to death. "We won't," she replied meekly, feeling like a scolded child. A second before the elevator door closed, Karissa attempted to say thank you, but Ms. Burke had already disappeared down the hall.

>>>

The moment the threesome entered the kitchen, Karissa heard the front door alarm blaring. She sighed heavily. "Ugh. What now?"

Marc headed to the front room and tapped the door access screen. The same three FBI agents from last night were standing on the front porch holding up their badges. He called to Karissa that he was letting them in. As he swiped the door open, several reporters stormed the front porch, jostling one another and shouting questions. One agent turned around to repel the onslaught while the other two slipped inside.

Agent William Sykes stepped forward, dropping his badge into his lapel pocket.

"Agent Lang will stay outside. We have a few questions for your daughter."

"Oh, no you don't," Karissa ordered. "You put me through hell last night and I will not allow you to do the same to my daughter."

"Mom," Ally said quietly, touching her arm. "It's okay."

Agent Amanda McAlister smiled at Ally, then turned a steely gaze toward Karissa. "You have no choice, Mrs. Gale. This has to be done. I'll take good care of your daughter. Please don't make this more difficult than it has to be."

"I'm not letting you question her without me...without *us*." She gestured toward Marc who moved to Ally's other side. Both parents flanked their daughter in a demonstration of solidarity.

Agent Sykes took off his jacket and neatly hung it on the back of a chair. "Mr. and Mrs. Gale, you two will be staying with me. Do you have a private room for Agent McAlister to question your daughter?"

When neither of them spoke, Agent Sykes lightly rested his hand on the weapon strapped to his waist.

"My Mom has an office in the back," Ally offered sheepishly. Both parents stared at her in dismay.

"Surely she doesn't have to do this alone," Marc interjected. "She's only thirteen."

"That's why you're going to watch the interrogation with me." Agent Sykes made himself comfortable on the couch, swiped the table screen, and entered a code.

Agent McAlister signaled for Ally to lead the way while Marc sat down on the other end of the couch and Karissa nervously took a chair. They watched intently as Ally and Agent McAlister sat down facing one another in Karissa's office.

Agent McAlister took a round object out of her bag and pressed it into the palm of Ally's right hand. "Do you know what this is, Ally?"

"I think so. Is it a truth detector?"

"Yes it is," the agent replied. She smiled again, obviously trying to put her subject at ease. "The detector will remain green as long as you're telling the truth. Would you like to test it just for fun?"

Ally grinned. "Sure."

"Okay, I'm going to ask you two questions. I want you to tell the truth on the first one and a lie on the second one. What is your full name?"

"Allyson Kathleen Gale."

The agent's mouth tilted upward as she nodded toward the truth detector. "Very good. Now, tell me how old you are."

Ally didn't hesitate. "Fourteen." Instantly the truth detector glowed red in her hand. "How does it know?" she asked.

"The acute sensor in the palm of your right hand instantly picks up your heart rate, blood pressure, and detects the opening of sweat glands, along with seven other indicators. It has a 96.9% accuracy rate. So let's start for real…how old are you?"

"Thirteen." Ally looked at her palm and smiled again.

A full hour later Agent McAlister followed Ally back into the front room. Karissa stood up and hugged her daughter, then decided she had a few questions of her own. She wanted to know what was happening to her mother and if they really thought she had intentionally planned such a terrible act.

Raising her chin to create an air of authority, she said, "I want to know if I'm allowed to see my mother now?"

Agent Sykes, with deliberate ease, lifted his jacket off the back of the chair. His eyes met hers and his left one twitched slightly. His next words sent a chill of fear all the way up Karissa's spine. "You already have."

>>Chapter 3

Cream puff was the nickname Marc gave Karissa's sofa. He considered sleeping on the floor but decided the couch was the lesser of two evils. He wasn't about to let his wife and daughter be alone during this ordeal. Putting up with a backache was the least of his worries. Before school every morning he ran five miles on the beach with his high school boy's cross-country team. All of the stiffness in his back usually worked itself out by mile three. He never ran with the team in the afternoons. His forty-year-old knees couldn't handle the pounding on the trails and pavement anymore.

This morning, taking long strides near the surf, he replayed everything in his mind from the previous days. Despite visiting the hospital on three different occasions, no one in the family was given permission to see Kathleen. Even her condition was not being released. For all they knew, she might already be dead. Karissa's meltdown on the third visit hadn't exactly helped their cause. Thankfully, Ally was in school and didn't have to witness her mother's angry outburst. Marc had to actually restrain his wife from physical contact with one of the nurses. By the time he got her outside the hospital, she was apologizing profusely, but the damage had been done. Two police officers threatened her with an arrest warrant if she ever stepped onto the hospital premises again. To make matters worse, a video of her tantrum surfaced on social media and had gone viral before the end of the day. No matter how utterly frustrating this situation had become, they were going to have to lay low and let this play out on the international stage without them.

Marc wracked his brain for possible solutions hour by hour. He found it as difficult to teach his high school history classes as it was to sleep at night. He was a patient man, but there were times the frustration level was so high he wanted to rip someone's head off. Fall break was in two weeks. He hoped to get Karissa and Ally out of the spotlight soon. But for now, he was working behind the scenes to glean information. Even Karissa didn't know he was meeting with a Los Angeles police detective this afternoon. One of his teaching colleagues made the arrangements for him and he hoped the detective could shed more light on the situation. The FBI was of no use. They had refused to return their calls or even allow them past the front desk at the field office in Los Angeles.

At three-thirty, Marc announced the afternoon workout to his team, then left his assistant coach in charge of practice. He was meeting Detective Owen Kristoff at a small coffee house outside of Malibu. Driving his jeep along the coastal highway, he wondered if there was any cause for concern about the detective's obviously Russian last name. What was he getting himself into?

When Marc entered the coffee shop the only customers were two women sipping lattes and a group of college students studying in the corner. He decided to wait outside on the covered deck. After forty-five minutes passed he realized this was probably a colossal waste of time. Blowing out an exasperated breath, he spoke into the analog band on his wrist, "Fifteen-minute alarm." One hour was all he could stand to wait.

Twelve minutes later a car pulled into the parking lot and a tall, middle-aged man stepped out. His white dress shirt was unbuttoned at the collar to accommodate a loose tie. Walking inside to the counter he didn't bother to remove his sunglasses, and he ordered a large black coffee. When Marc came in, the detective lowered his sunglasses and shook his head. Marc immediately froze. *Now what?*

Detective Kristoff paid for the coffee, headed to his car, and backed out of the parking spot. He idled there for a moment, appearing to check his tech screen. When Marc walked out front, the detective lowered his window. "Leave all of your electronics in your vehicle and get in."

Marc immediately locked his wristband in the jeep, all the while praying he was doing the right thing. The detective said nothing when he got into the front seat, not even after setting the navigation screen and heading out onto the highway. He merely checked data on his phone, occasionally looking up to make sure they were still on course.

After a couple of miles, Detective Kristoff's car turned onto a sandy road and Marc remained silent but tense. Pulling beneath a canopy of trees, the detective touched the screen, turning off the car, and got out. He walked around to Marc's side of the car and shook his hand when he got out.

"Sorry for the secrecy, but I'm taking precautions for your sake and mine." He grinned. "You can relax, Mr. Gale. I understand your need for information."

Marc didn't realize how hard he'd been breathing. He tried to relax, but something in the way the detective used his name made him uneasy.

"How can I help you?"

"Well…first of all, it's been a week since the accident and no one will give us an update on Kathleen. We don't even know if she's still alive. Why are they keeping us in the dark?"

"What else do you want to know?"

The detective's question caught him off guard. Was he ignoring Marc's plea for information the same way the hospital and the FBI were? He tried again. "Uh…well, I'd really like to know how Kathleen's car ran through an area that had been blocked off and why she didn't stop before heading over the side of the cliff."

"What else?"

Marc gulped, feeling the perspiration break out on his forehead. "Is our family in some sort of trouble? Are we going to need a lawyer…I mean, my wife is a lawyer—a corporate lawyer, but…" He wiped the sweat off his brow with the back of his hand. "I just want to protect my family."

Detective Kristoff removed his sunglasses and leaned back against the car. "You really are in the dark on this." He glanced up the road toward the highway, then back at Marc. "Look, I'm going to give you a little information, but if you let any of this leak, your family will be at risk. Do you understand?"

Marc rubbed the back of his neck, suddenly wishing he hadn't asked for this meeting. The last thing he wanted to do was put Karissa and Ally in danger. Even so, he heard himself saying, "I understand."

"Kathleen Raines is still alive. She's no longer at Saint Francis Hospital. They're fairly certain she's not going to ever regain consciousness, but her body is in remarkably good shape."

"Where is she?" Marc interrupted. "Can we see her?"

Kristoff shook his head. "That's all you're going to get as far as Coach Raines is concerned. I don't know much more than what I just told you. But if you or your wife start making waves about where she is, you're going to be in deep trouble." He set his sunglasses on top of the car and hooked both thumbs into the pockets of his slacks. "I know I don't have to tell you what a precarious situation your mother-in-law has put our country in. She killed the so-called *Peace-maker of Russia*. He was here on a diplomatic mission to help smooth out relations between our two countries. If I were you, I'd be running as far and fast as I could to distance myself from her. I'm not saying that lightly—I mean that with all seriousness."

Marc could feel the heat rising up the back of his neck. "What should we do?"

"Don't talk to anyone about this—not even other family members or close friends. Keep your mouths shut and you may make it through this unscathed. The Russians are going to demand restitution, and you don't want your family anywhere near when that happens."

Marc thought he was going to be sick. He bent at the waist and grabbed his knees with both hands. Detective Kristoff moved his feet just in time. He reached into the car and grabbed the napkin he'd been given with his coffee.

"Here," he said, handing it to Marc.

"Thanks," Marc whispered, thoroughly embarrassed.

The detective moved to the rear of the car. Marc followed him, apologizing for being such an idiot.

"I'm going to tell you one more thing, it's the reason why the FBI and the Russians are watching your family so closely."

Those words sent Marc into deeper distress. Kristoff grabbed his shoulders to keep him steady. "Relax, they didn't surveil you today. I made absolutely sure before I met with you. That's why I was so late—I was watching you and checking tech for nearly an hour. You don't have a brain chip, do you?"

Marc shook his head. "No, I don't want anyone in my family to have one."

"Well, that means they have to track you the old fashioned way."

Marc nodded his head nervously.

"Coach Raines didn't have a heart attack, or an aneurysm, or a stroke, or *anything*. The only damage to her brain was caused by the accident when her car flipped over the cliff upside down onto the Russian Deputy Prime Minister and his body guards." Kristoff cleared his throat. "Here's what I'm trying to tell you…investigators are exploring the possibility that Kathleen Raines drove her car over that cliff on purpose."

Holding back the nauseating reaction was no longer possible. Detective Kristoff sidestepped again as Marc proceeded to lose the remaining contents of his stomach.

Stopping by his apartment in Malibu, Marc decided to take a shower. He needed to figure out how to relax before going to the townhouse. He couldn't stop checking his rearview screen on the way home. Was the detective telling the truth? Was Karissa being tracked at work in LA, and even worse, was Ally being watched at school?

After shoving a few more clothes in a bag, he grabbed a water bottle out of the refrigerator and sat down in the sparsely decorated living room. "Oh God," he prayed aloud, "please lead me. I don't know what to do or who to trust. Help me know what to tell Karissa and Ally." His mind and body felt so weak—even his hands were shaking. He quickly set the water bottle on the table and leaned forward. Before Marc knew it, he was on his knees, begging God to protect his family. At the end of the prayer he felt better, but wasn't sure what to do with the strange combination of dread and peace roiling in his gut. He was counting on the Lord to help him sort it all out.

Marc was an hour later than usual getting to the townhouse. "Where have you been?" Karissa chastised. His countenance immediately dropped. Even though she was the one who pushed for the legal separation, his wife was acting like he still belonged there. She could make him feel like such a heel at times.

"I'm sorry, Kari. I stopped by the apartment to shower and pick up some extra clothes. You could've called." Something had Karissa scared—he could see it in her eyes. "What's wrong?"

Her sarcastic laugh nearly grated on his last nerve. He needed help processing what he had learned this afternoon, but his wife was doing her dead-level best to make it worse. "Why don't you ask your daughter," she squawked, pointing toward the stairs.

Marc's heart skipped more than one beat. "What happened?" he asked, hanging on to his last remnant of composure.

She turned her back and headed for the kitchen, apparently unwilling to give him the slightest hint. He wasn't about to stick around to pry answers out of Karissa when she was so angry—or was she scared? Maybe a little of both. He took the stairs two at a time and walked down the hall to Ally's closed door.

Knocking cautiously he ventured, "Hey, Cupcake, can I come in?"

"Not now, Daddy."

He leaned his forehead into the surface of the door. "Uh...I don't think I can go back downstairs to your mom without seeing your pretty face," he spoke softly.

After a long pause, Ally's door swung open. She was sitting on her cushioned window seat with a stream of sunshine caressing her tanned skin. She had punched the app on her tablet to unlock the door. Marc walked across the room, pointing to the other end of the seat. "May I?"

Ally shrugged her shoulders, never moving her gaze from the backyard. She clasped her knees tightly to her chest. Marc knew his daughter better than anyone else, with the exception of Kathleen. *Oh, God, please help Kathleen.* He decided to sit quietly and wait her out. That tactic worked one hundred percent of the time...at least it had up to this point.

After a prolonged silence, Ally shoved her face into her legs and began sobbing uncontrollably. Marc's heart shattered. All he knew to do was hold her, but when he reached for her, she surprised him by crawling into his lap. Suddenly she was five again.

"Shhh, Baby, I've gotcha." He kissed the top of her head and gently rocked her in his arms. "It's okay," he whispered. "Let it all out."

> > >

Several minutes passed while Ally spent the last portion of fear and anxiety in her daddy's arms. She had tried to be so strong and brave for her mother, but that wasn't working anymore—especially after what had happened at school today. It was only her second day back after the accident—apparently her teachers and classmates had no qualms about giving their opinions and voicing criticism.

She needed to talk but wasn't sure she could tell her dad what had happened in social studies class this afternoon. Thank goodness it was the last period of the day. As soon as the bell sounded, she had darted out of the building and ran all the way home—four miles without stopping. The bus would've been a gossip trap. At least her dad could be proud of her running accomplishment today.

Ally untangled herself from Marc's arms apologizing for the mess she left on his shirt.

"What? This?" he joked, pointing to a few wet blotches. "I like the decorations."

His goofiness made her laugh. She took the tissue he offered and sat down on the window seat to face him again.

"Dad, I think we're handling this…situation pretty well. It's really hard, but I think it would be a lot worse with some of my friends' parents."

He grinned. "Thanks, Cupcake. I'm pretty proud of the way you're handling everything, too." His eyes narrowed slightly. "So…what happened at school today?"

Ally took a deep breath and looked into her dad's unimpeachable brown eyes. "Do you remember Connor, who came to my birthday party last year with Lexi?"

Marc nodded. "The one with the really blonde hair? Tall, kind of thin?"

"Yeah, that's him." Ally shook her head, taking in a deep breath through her nose. "Today in social studies he swiped a video onto the main screen up front. It was Mom throwing her fit at the hospital."

"What did your teacher do?"

"He didn't know whose screen it was, apparently Connor was cloaked, so Mr. Donaldson just let it finish. I thought I was gonna die. I know everyone's seen it already, but I felt completely humiliated with the whole class staring at me."

"I'm really sorry, Babe."

"Oh, it gets worse. I have no clue who did it. Lexi swears it wasn't Connor, but right after the video, a picture of Gran popped up with the word *terrorist* flashing on the screen. Mr. Donaldson checked everyone's device, but he thinks it was someone in cyber class."

"Do you want me to talk to him? I can head over to the middle school tomorrow during my planning—"

"No," Ally interrupted. "I don't want you to do that. If that's the worst of it, then I can handle it. I just don't understand why people have to be so insensitive. Maybe they're just scared."

Marc raised his brow. "Smart observation. I think our whole country is on edge right now. No one knows what's about to happen." He reached over and squeezed her knee. "Hey, listen, we need to lay low for a while, you know, not make any waves or do anything to draw attention to our family. Keep ignoring all the press and don't give them anything to talk about."

She gave him a lopsided grin. "Tell Mom that."

"I know, I know. I've been working on a plan for fall break. I'd like to take you and Mom camping up in the mountains. My grandfather used to take me to a secluded camping spot in the San Gabriels. It would be perfect. What do you say?"

Ally nodded hopefully. "I'm in! But what about Gran?"

"Baby, she's in God's hands right now. Let's leave her there and trust that He's taking good care of her for us."

That calmed Ally's nerves and the touch of a smile returned. "Fall break can't get here fast enough."

>>Chapter 4

"Count me out." Karissa couldn't think of anything worse than a camping trip right now.

"Mom, come on!" Ally pleaded. "We need to get away from all of this. Please."

Karissa finished her last bite of salad and shook her head. "You two can go if you want, but I've got too much going on to head into the wilderness." She picked up her plate and water glass. "Besides, I don't like camping. Remember?"

Heading into the kitchen Karissa was thankful for the arrangement she and Marc had made during their first week of marriage sixteen years ago—whoever cooks doesn't have to clean up. She was free and clear the rest of the evening and planned on getting a little extra work done in her office. To her chagrin, Marc followed her down the hall.

"Kari, can I talk to you in private?"

Inwardly she bristled. Karissa was looking forward to a little alone time. When she sat down at her desk, Marc took the easy chair by the window—the one where Ally had endured a long interview with Agent McAlister.

"Marc, if you're here to chastise me about some camping trip, save your breath—"

He didn't let her finish. "That's not why I'm here. I have something I need to tell you."

Karissa closed the office door with the tap of her finger on the glass-top desk. Marc had been acting strangely at dinner and now he looked like he was flailing in the ocean, maybe even drowning. She wasn't sure she wanted to hear what he had to say.

With an uneasy exhale he started in. "I met with a Los Angeles police detective this afternoon."

She could literally feel her heart moving into the next gear. "Did he question you about Mom?"

"No, it wasn't like that. The meeting was set up for me—I felt like we needed more information." He leaned forward, resting his elbows on his knees. "He confirmed that your mother is still alive, but she's been moved to another location."

"Where?" Suddenly Karissa's temper flared. "How could they move her without telling us?"

Marc sat back and raised a cautionary hand. "I feel the same frustration you do, trust me. But if we start asking questions about Kathleen, our family may be in danger. The detective told me we're being watched."

"By who?" she cried.

"The FBI, and maybe even the Russians. Apparently they didn't find anything wrong with your mom—there seems to be no physical reason for her to have driven her car off the cliff." He cleared his throat nervously. "They think...well, it appears that she did it on purpose."

Karissa was at a loss for words, except for inappropriate ones. It took everything she had to hold them back. Finally, she blurted, "That's ridiculous. Everyone knows Kathleen Raines would never do such a thing. What else did he say?"

"That was about it, really. He suggested we distance ourselves from your mother—you know—try to stay out of the limelight. That's why I want us to get away over the break."

Karissa completely ignored his camping innuendo and switched gears. "I had a meeting of my own today with two of Mom's friends."

"The ones she eats with every other Wednesday?"

"Yes, Liz and Carolyn. They met me downtown to talk. I actually spent most of the morning with them. They've been grilled by the FBI more than once."

"Were you planning on telling me about this?" Marc asked.

"Yes..." she said defensively. "Eventually."

"Kari, we don't need to be holding anything back from each other right now. What did they say?"

With an exaggerated sigh, Karissa began telling him how frightened her mother's two friends were. They had been meeting at Ocean Terrace restaurant for lunch twice a month for nearly two years. They had no idea that the Deputy Prime Minister of Russia was going to be there that day. According to the news reports, it had been an unexpected stop on his diplomatic mission.

"You know how Mom is about being on time—they said she was always the first one to arrive." Karissa couldn't count how many times she'd heard her mother say, *if time is important, then be on time.*

"When Liz and Carolyn arrived at the restaurant, the place was already in chaos. They had no idea what had happened to Mom." She closed her eyes briefly, remembering their distraught tears. "They both want to see her. They begged me for information about her. I wish I'd known what you found out this afternoon so—"

"No, don't, Kari!" Marc was suddenly animated. "You can't give them the slightest details—not even the fact that the doctors didn't find anything physically wrong with her before the accident."

Something in Marc's tone nearly unhinged her. "Are we in danger?" she whispered, trying to hold back tears.

Marc squeezed his fists tightly. She watched his knuckles turn whiter by the second. He was obviously suppressing a great deal of anxiety. "What are you *not* telling me?"

"Listen, Babe, this is really important. We can't talk to anyone, and I mean *anyone*, about this. We could accidently set off a chain of events that could cause a war. I don't have to tell you how devastating that would be."

Suddenly Karissa felt overwhelmed by such an odious state of affairs. It seemed impossible to escape their connection with her mother, but that's exactly what Marc was suggesting. How could her mother have led them down this precarious path? Karissa felt like their entire family had been plunged over that dreadful cliff along with Kathleen. The bitterness inside her began clawing its way back to the forefront, ravenously eating its way through her heart. And she hated herself for it.

>>>

"Do you think Mom misses us?"

Marc stared at the back of his daughter's ponytail, bobbing side-to-side as she tread the rocky path ahead of him. The last twenty-four hours had been such a welcome relief from the nerve-wracking drama they'd been forced to endure in the city. After much begging and cajoling, Karissa still refused to join them in the wilderness. Fearing for her safety, Marc paid for a hotel room near her office in downtown Los Angeles for the week. It was a pretty good chunk out of his paycheck—one that his wife could've more easily afforded—but he insisted on her taking the precaution while they were gone. They even left under the cover of night trying not to be followed by the press or FBI. So far he and Ally had only seen a couple of hikers, and that had been before arriving at their campsite in the mountains.

"I'm sure she does, Cupcake." Marc knew down deep Karissa wouldn't be missing *him*, but Ally was another story. He felt certain she would be thinking about her daughter constantly throughout the week.

Marc steered Ally toward a shady spot where they could spend a little time fishing. Finding boulders side by side, they promptly threw a line in the water. "Maybe we'll catch enough for dinner tonight," he remarked, hoping the trout would seek out their shiny lures.

Ally smiled but said nothing as she reeled in her line for another cast. She was unusually quiet and Marc wondered what was on his daughter's mind. He concentrated on the peaceful setting and the occasional zip of their lines, reminding himself to stay silent.

It was a good ten minutes before she put a voice to her thoughts. "Dad, are you moving back in with me and Mom?"

A deep sigh escaped as he cast his line into the middle of the river. How could he answer such a personally confusing question? He opened his mouth and closed it again, wondering how much to share with her. Ally would be fourteen soon, she was already turning into a beautiful young lady. He glanced at her knowing she was old enough to have this conversation, but all he could see was his innocent little girl on the other end of that fishing pole.

Telling her the truth could only damage the close relationship she shared with her mother. He and Karissa had made a pact not to make the other look bad in Ally's eyes. Marc didn't plan to be the one to break that pact...yet, what could he say in response to his daughter's query?

"Just for now, Cupcake, until all of this blows over."

Ally's eyes were intently focused on his. "Do you not want to come back, or is Mom the one keeping you away?"

Oh, Lord, help me. Marc prayed for a fish to jump on the end of his line—anything to keep from having this conversation. He hurt for his daughter, though. She deserved to know what was going on in this family. Resolved to take a stab at it, he reeled in his line and set the pole on the rocky bank. Ally did the same.

"I *do* want to come home, sweetheart. My biggest desire in the world is for us to be a family again. But—"

"It's Mom, isn't it?"

He briefly looked away making a hasty decision to be transparent with his girl. After everything they'd been through during the last month, he couldn't bear to keep any more secrets from her.

"Yeah, Cupcake, Mom just needs some time to find herself."

Ally's eyes clouded with tears. "Did you do something?" she whispered. "You know, Kylie's dad—"

"Oh, no, sweetheart," he interrupted. "Nothing like that happened. You don't have anything to worry about where that's concerned."

She took in a deep breath, obviously relieved that her dad had not been unfaithful. But Ally's eyes suddenly grew round and Marc could see exactly where her mind was going. He threw up a hand to stop her thoughts dead in their tracks. "It wasn't your mom, either. There's never, *ever* been anyone else for either one of us. And if I have my way, there never will be."

Father and daughter spent the rest of the afternoon talking and fishing, laughing and crying, until both were able to come to some sort of peace with their current family situation. Marc knew he would have to gently break the news to Karissa when they got home. She was going to be angry about their conversation, maybe even mad enough to kick him out of the townhouse. He would respect her decision if it should come to that, but there would be a hefty price to pay if Ally decided to go with him.

> > >

"Come on, Cupcake, there's something I wanna show you."

Ally tugged on her Pepperdine volleyball sweatshirt as the evening chill chased away the afternoon warmth. She was always ready for an adventure, even at dusk. "Where are we headed?"

"There's a place my grandpa used to take me to back in the 90s when we camped up here. You're gonna love it, but we need to get there before dark." Ally grabbed her headlamp for later and followed her dad.

They walked along the level path by the river for a while before coming to a fork in the trail. Marc looked over his shoulder as he branched off to the right. "This is pretty steep in some places, but nothing the two of us can't handle." She could see his wink, even in the waning light, and loved his confidence in her.

He was right, it was a hard climb to the top of the mountain, and Ally savored every step of the way. Both of them were breathing hard by the time they reached the spot her dad was looking for.

"Okay…this is where we need to be extra careful."

Ally watched as her dad moved to the edge of the rocky bluff, then worked his way down to a lower ledge. He held his hand out to her and she latched hold like moss on a tree until she was safely at his side. Reaching into his pack, he pulled out a blanket and spread it along the ledge. Marc sat down with his back against the rocks, stretching out his long legs. Ally noticed his boots nearly hung over the edge. She nestled down beside him feeling the cool breeze and looking out over the forest of pines far below.

Father and daughter silently basked in the beauty of the ethereal moments between day and night. Spoken words would've ruined its significance—they both knew it. Gently the last hues of orange and pink vanished, and a dark, velvety blanket spread out all around them. That's when the enchantment began. Ally's mouth dropped open at the spellbinding array of stars, dipping to touch the earth like an umbrella of splendor. All she had to do was reach out her hand to touch one—they seemed to be within her grasp.

Ally wasn't sure how long she'd been mesmerized by the night sky before she slowly switched her gaze to the man who had introduced her to the extravaganza. He was staring at her instead of the stars, and she giggled.

"Dad, this is the most amazing thing I've ever seen."

"I was hoping you'd say that." He trailed her eyes back to the heavens. "My grandfather showed me this wonder when I was ten." His voice took on a quieter tone. "It's where I found God."

"How could you not?" Ally wondered aloud. The Creator was more evident here than anywhere she'd ever been. She could literally feel His presence.

"Your great-grandpa taught me about God's grace while watching these very same stars," he said. "It stuck with me."

Ally had heard so many stories about Grandpa Gale from her dad. She would've loved to know him. Now she wanted to hear his wisdom for herself. "What did he tell you?"

"He told me that God's grace is breathtaking beyond words—just like these stars. And that God shows us His loving kindness even though we don't deserve it. But he also taught me that even though it's available to all people, not everyone will accept it."

Ally found herself thinking about her mom, realizing she'd never had one significant spiritual conversation with her. She had learned about God from her dad and Granny K and the church they attended. She was reminded of the youth group retreat last year when she gave her life to Christ and was baptized in the ocean with two of her friends.

"Dad?"

"Yeah, Baby?"

"Does Mom know about this grace?"

Such a long silence fell between them that Ally had to look over at her dad. He seemed to be struggling—she could see his jaw muscle tightening and relaxing. Finally, he put his arm around her, drawing her close, and answered quietly, "No, Baby. Not yet."

>>Chapter 5

On more than one occasion Karissa had been accused of being a workaholic. Rather than perceive that as a fault, she took pride in her intense work ethic. With Ally away on fall break she could now give all of her energy to the new merger deal she'd been working on for the last two months. Not even her mother could disturb her. She sat back in her chair suddenly full of regret. How could such a thought darken the door of her mind? But like a bullet out of the chamber of a gun the notion couldn't be taken back. She berated herself for being such a horrible daughter.

Swiveling her chair toward the glass wall, Karissa peered out at the sparkling lights of downtown Los Angeles. It was a spectacular view from the fourteenth floor. She had always found the city fascinating at night and loved being in her office after most of her co-workers had gone home. Since her hotel was merely two blocks away, she vowed to stay at work later than normal. Ten o'clock was about the time some of the firm's partners left for home each night. Karissa hoped to be one of them by the time Ally went off to college.

She had been moving upward in the firm at a steady pace. An office with a view like this was proof that very little stood in her way. Marc had been in her way once, but not anymore.

Marc. A melancholy shroud settled over her, and suddenly working till midnight held little appeal. On impulse, she shut down the work screens, including the holographic designs of the merging corporation headquarters, and gathered her belongings. Most of the offices were empty as she walked by, leaving Karissa feeling much the same way.

"Ms. Gale! Working late again, are we?"

She turned to see Randall Thomas striding toward her, the two thousand dollar suit he wore perfectly fitted to his broad shoulders and trim waist, still looking as neat and crisp as he had that morning. Of the three managing partners in the firm, Randall was the driving force. In his early fifties, he'd been married three times with as many divorces. Women were attracted to his dark looks and he knew it. Randall's confident swagger usually made Karissa a little uneasy. She wasn't particularly looking forward to being alone with him in the small confines of the elevator.

Karissa glanced at the bold lettering on the wall as they waited— Thomas, Tanner & McGill. Gale would look very nice among those well-respected names.

"Speculating whose name will go up next?" he asked.

Karissa felt the heat rise to her cheeks. How could he have known what she was thinking? Thankfully the door slid open and he gestured politely for her to precede him into the elevator.

"You know, Karissa, we have to be so careful when it comes to choosing partners for the firm." He stood uncomfortably close. She could feel his warm, minty breath on her ear. "A scandal of any sort could ruin us."

"Of course, I understand completely," she agreed, wondering where this was going.

Instead of continuing along that line, Mr. Thomas changed the tack in conversation altogether. "How about joining me for a drink tonight? I'd like to hear how things are going in your personal life. The last few weeks have been quite an ordeal for you, I'm sure."

While many men at the firm were drawn to Karissa, she had carefully discouraged it. Their attention was flattering but easily repelled. Randall Thomas, on the other hand, was an entirely different animal. He held all of the power—her job depended on his opinion of her.

When the elevator opened to the main floor, he possessively took her elbow and walked her into the lobby. She got the distinct impression he wasn't going to take no for an answer.

"Mr. Thomas, I really appreciate the offer, but I'm not feeling well tonight. In fact, it's the reason why I'm leaving earlier than planned."

His condescending smile was enough to make her sick, almost keeping her from being a liar. Still, he held her elbow and led her outside to the waiting car, a silver Jaguar luxury sedan. His driver stood beside the backseat door as it opened automatically.

Karissa's feet refused to move any farther. "I'm very sorry, but I can't."

"Don't worry, Karissa, I'm not forcing you to have drinks with me. I'll take you to your hotel. I can't have you walking alone, at night…" A shadow crossed his features. "And not feeling well. What kind of a gentleman would I be?" He smiled benignly while ushering her inside.

"Derek, take us over to the Carmichael Hotel. That's where Ms. Gale is currently staying."

"Just until my daughter…and husband get back from their camping trip," she interjected. "We felt it would be better for me to stay in the city while they're away." Her answer sounded weak, even to her.

Only a couple of minutes passed before the car was pulling up to the Carmichael entrance. Randall Thomas stepped out of the vehicle first, then offered his hand. She had no choice but to take it as she exited the car.

"I'll walk you up to the room…especially since you're not feeling well."

He was toying with her and Karissa knew it. Randall Thomas wanted to see what she was made of. Well, he would find out tonight.

"That won't be necessary, Mr. Thomas," she said firmly, sliding her hand out of his. "I'll see you tomorrow. Thank you for the ride." She quickly headed into the hotel lobby without a backward glance, all the while sensing his prowling eyes on her every move.

Finally inside the room, Karissa dropped onto the edge of her bed, feeling exhausted. She had worked nearly as hard to repel Randall Thomas tonight as she had on the merger all day. Kicking off her heels and throwing her jacket on the chair, she leaned back against the plush pillows along the headboard. Whether meaning to or not, Mr. Thomas had given her a great deal to think about.

One thing was certain—she would never sleep her way to a name on the wall. If that's what Randall had been insinuating tonight, then so be it. She had always felt strongly about not giving her body away, most especially for a job. Karissa had been very open with her daughter on that subject as well. She and Marc had both kept themselves for each other, which saved them a lot of heartache and doubts in the early years of their relationship. She hoped Ally would do the same.

Marc. Why did he keep hijacking her thoughts tonight? Having him sleep at the townhouse for the last month had been a blessing. She and Ally both rested easier knowing he was downstairs on the couch. But how long was he going to stay? They had never actually talked about it. In fact, she only spoke to him when absolutely necessary. She didn't want to encourage him where their marriage was concerned.

Hoping to get Marc off her mind, she thought about Randall Thomas' reference to her personal life—a calculated barb on his part. Of that, she was certain. *Message received, loud and clear.* Karissa wasn't willing to play her boss' flirtatious games, but she *was* willing to do whatever it took to separate her name from Kathleen Raines. She didn't have a clue how to do it yet, but she was confident in finding a way.

Ally and Marc were due home in two days and Karissa immersed herself even deeper into work. Randall Thomas had made it a nightly habit of stopping by to offer her a ride to the hotel, but she had politely refused each time. The roguish glint in his eyes told her he knew what she would say before he even asked. Still, he persisted.

Tonight, he had actually come into her office, slid around her desk, and sat down on the edge. Looking down from his perch, his eyes continually roamed below her neck, making her more than a little uneasy. Even so, she firmly refused to give in to him. She knew her plucky resolve was probably what kept him coming back. He was a man who loved a challenge. But his unwelcome attention suddenly made her miss home for the first time this week.

It was eleven-thirty when she waved goodnight to the security guard in the lobby and started her walk to the Carmichael. With several downtown hotels and restaurants in the area, the streets were far from empty. Karissa felt safe walking the short distance every night. But tonight, something had her senses on high alert. More than once she glanced over her shoulder, unable to shake the feeling that she was being followed.

Relieved when the lights of the Carmichael Hotel came into view, Karissa took one last look over her shoulder. That's when she saw him out of the corner of her eye. He hadn't been following directly behind, but on the other side of the street. Now the stranger was sprinting across traffic to catch her before she made it inside.

"Mrs. Gale, we need to talk."

Karissa's first instinct was to run, but her heels were an aggravating hindrance. And where did all the people on the sidewalk suddenly go? Even the doorman to the hotel had stepped inside. Knowing she couldn't make it to the lobby in time, she turned to face the man head on. At least she wouldn't go down without a fight.

When he took her arm, she aggressively yanked away from his grasp and he stepped back, throwing his hands in the air. "Whoa, whoa, whoa. I'm not going to hurt you."

For the first time Karissa noticed the man was wearing a suit with a leather bag slung over his shoulder. Not exactly the image of a rapist or robber. He didn't even look like the straggly reporters that had constantly hounded her every move up until recent days.

"What do you want?" she asked bluntly, trying to catch her breath. Seeing him relax his guard, she tried to bolt for the hotel lobby again.

"No, wait! Please, Mrs. Gale." He started to reach for her arm again but immediately dropped his hand when she turned a scowl on him. "I...I have an offer for you—"

"Not interested," she said. "Leave me alone." She was within a few feet of the door. Almost home free.

"It's about your mother."

Karissa stopped dead in her tracks just as the Carmichael doorman appeared. She turned slowly to face the man who had stalked her here. "What about my mother?"

47

The young man blew out an anxious breath before introducing himself. "My name is Dr. Steven Utley. I've been calling you for the past two days. Have you listened to any of my messages?"

"*Doctor?* How old are you, anyway?"

The Carmichael doorman stepped up beside her. "Ma'am, is the gentleman bothering you?"

"Uh." Karissa paused for several heartbeats, unsure of what to do. "No," she finally said. "He's not bothering me." Tucking a loose strand of hair behind her ear, she nodded to the doorman. "But thank you for your concern."

Bowing slightly, he stepped back, still keeping an eye on the situation.

"What exactly did your messages say?"

Dr. Utley cautiously glanced around to see who might be listening. "I don't think this is something you'll want to discuss…out here." He pointed toward the lobby. "May we go inside?"

The lobby was too public and her room too private. "There's an automated coffee bar around the corner," she offered. "We can talk there." Without waiting for his approval, Karissa led the way. Her stomach was in knots by the time they chose a booth at the back of the bar.

Steven Utley slid into the seat across from her and pulled the leather strap over his head. "I'm sorry I scared you back there. It's just that…well, it's been so difficult to get in touch with you, and this is such a timely issue."

Karissa cut to the chase. "What do you know about my mother?"

"A lot, actually. I've been monitoring her for the past two weeks."

"Where is she? What's her condition?"

Just then a robot waiter appeared beside their table. "Order please."

Karissa felt like knocking the thing back to where it came from. Besides, coffee would keep her awake all night. On second thought, she blurted, "Small coffee, house blend, one cream, one sugar." She had a feeling that after this conversation there would be little hope of sleep.

"I'll have the same," the doctor said.

Karissa demanded to know what was going on. Her choice of words made it quite clear that she was tired of being kept in the dark.

"Have you heard of UISC—Universal Intergalactic Space Corporation?"

"Never. What does that have to do with my mother?"

Dr. Utley planted his elbows on the table and clasped his hands. "We have an offer for you that would not only make restitution to the Russians but could possibly benefit all of mankind."

Laughing in this young doctor's face felt like the only appropriate response at the moment. He must be mad. She held her tongue, however, waiting for him to explain.

A small door slid open at their table and Steven reached for both coffees, setting one in front of her. "I'm sorry to tell you this, but your mother will never regain consciousness. Her brain injury is too severe. But, I'm sure I don't have to tell you this, her body is more like that of a forty-five-year-old, not a sixty-four-year-old."

Kathleen had been one of the best all-around athletes in her high school during the early 80s. The world of athletics had been much different in those days. She had actually lettered in four different sports—volleyball, basketball, softball, and track—before choosing to attend Pepperdine University on a volleyball scholarship. Even now she held her own on the sand courts at the beach where she was a regular. Her mother never seemed to grow old, and Karissa told Dr. Utley just that.

"She does have a few broken bones and a minor neck injury, but we want to use her body, while it's still functioning at such a high level, on an experimental space flight."

This time she couldn't hold back a laugh. It all sounded ridiculous. "Where? You mean like around the earth, or the moon and back?"

Steven cleared his throat before answering. "Mars."

"Excuse me? After the disaster two years ago, you want to send my mother to Mars?"

Karissa was referring to the twelve people who had died in a crumpled heap of metal trying to land on the red planet in 2025. A private space exploration company had teamed up with NASA to land the first colony on Mars. While it had been a colossal disaster, several other space agencies rushed to perfect their rocket's landing systems.

"We've learned from their mistakes. Our corporation is taking the lead on this experimental voyage. We're not trying to land an entire colony, just one person."

Confusion was written all over Karissa's face. She took a sip of coffee before asking the obvious. "So why don't you send one or two experienced astronauts to try out your little *fool-proof* system?"

Dr. Utley hesitated for a few seconds, his icy blue eyes taking on a warmer hue. "Because for now, a return trip is impossible. Once the craft lands on the planet's surface, it will be unable to take off again."

A deathly silence fell between them. Karissa felt her chest tighten—she wanted nothing to do with this. "No!" she blurted. "That's not going to happen." Grabbing her bag, she prepared to leave.

Steven Utley raised his hand, trying to keep her there. "Please, don't leave. You need to hear me out. I know this is hard, but you're going to be held responsible for the death of the Russian Deputy Prime Minister, and—"

"Me!" Karissa dropped her bag back on the seat. "You don't know what you're talking about." Her voice shook; she was on the verge of losing it.

"I do know. Dealing with the Russian government is like dealing with a sly fox. Most people believe it was just a freak accident—even the Russians have found no credible evidence to the contrary. But they're forcing everything to their advantage. They have the upper hand."

"But holding me responsible for something my mother did? That's preposterous."

"Now that General Sokolov has taken over the Deputy Prime Minister position, it's a whole new ballgame. He's a warmonger—definitely not the diplomat that Vasiliev was. By threatening you, they're essentially holding our government hostage. They want their pound of flesh."

"How can sending my mother into space possibly rectify the situation?"

Dr. Utley let down his guard a bit, sensing Karissa had switched back to her fight not flight mode. "The Universal Intergalactic Space Corporation is a multi-national organization. Believe it or not, we have astronauts from Mexico, India, Japan, you name it, and of course, Russia.

This will become a joint operation between our two countries. And if it works—"

"If!"

"*When.* I meant to say, *when* it works, the Russians will essentially be able to claim the prize for conquering Mars…along with the US, of course." Steven Utley took his first sip of coffee, keeping a close eye on his tablemate. "There's another aspect to the mission I haven't told you about yet."

Karissa let out a tiny groan. "What is it?"

"You know how I said this mission could possibly benefit mankind? Well, something happened to The Twelve the closer they got to Mars. They began to realize health benefits in deep space. One of them had suffered asthma on Earth, but all of his symptoms disappeared before the landing. I won't bore you with the other cases. But trust me, there were several instances of, for lack of a better word, healings."

"And you want to see how my mother's body heals in deep space." Her tone was flat. It wasn't a question.

"Exactly. I'll be the lead doctor, along with Dr. Dmitry Yashkin. We'll be able to research her body's regeneration process in deep space. It'll be a monumental study. By the time we have the capability of actually starting another colony on Mars, we may be able to heal thousands here on Earth with what we learn."

Karissa wished she could feel Dr. Utley's enthusiasm, but she couldn't. Her mind was going through information overload. The very fact that the Russians were using her as a pawn unnerved her. But there was something else—something that alarmed her beyond sanity. Feeling her throat constrict with unexpected emotion she put her fear into words. "What if deep space heals her brain? Did you stop to think about that one, Doctor?"

>>Chapter 6

Marc took Karissa's arm and led her to the opposite corner of the room where no one could hear their conversation. An army of lawyers and executives surrounded the conference table at Universal Intergalactic Space Corporation headquarters. The FBI maintained their presence in the room, along with a California state Senator and several Russian officials. It was hard to feel privacy in the glass-incased room.

"We can find another way, Kari. Are you sure you want to do this to your mother?"

She did this to herself, Karissa wanted to scream. Holding back an onslaught of emotions she breathed deeply through her nose and let it out slowly through tight lips. With as much patience as she could muster, Karissa whispered, "I have no choice. Unless UISC makes restitution, my life will be completely ruined." Her back immediately straightened and her signature chin in the air, *I've got everything under control* attitude flared. She stuck her hand out to Marc.

"What?" he asked quietly.

"Give me the pen," she demanded in a hushed tone.

He shook his head in disbelief and surrendered the stylus.

Without another glance she turned and walked back to the conference table. "Show me where to sign."

The UISC lawyer briefly stood, giving Karissa a somber smile. "This will take a few minutes. We have several screens to go through." He gestured toward a chair at the table and she promptly sat down.

After Mr. Drayton reviewed the first document, he opened the signature line on Karissa's screen. Her hand stilled for only a moment above the line, then she dropped it ominously onto the screen and scribbled her name.

"Now a palm-scan beside your name, please."

Karissa complied.

Marc watched from across the room with a feeling of dread. After her first signature he turned and silently left the room.

> > >

"You did *what?*" Ally cried, dropping her school bag onto the kitchen counter.

Karissa summoned a calmness she knew she didn't possess and explained the restitution process by sending Gran's body into deep space. Saying it out loud sounded almost ludicrous, even after signing a slew of documents all morning.

Ally's eyes were wild. "How could you do such a thing? I'll never get to see her again!"

"Calm down, Ally."

"No! I will *not* calm down. You have to undo this…this…horrible thing you've done."

Karissa made a move toward her daughter, but Ally threw her hands up, backing away. "What kind of daughter does that to her mother?" she spewed.

Every bit of self-restraint seeped away as Karissa's pride took a hit. "This was the only way!" she shouted. "If I didn't do this our lives would be ruined. I'd never make partner and you wouldn't have one dime to go to college. We wouldn't be able to—"

Ally didn't let her finish. She grabbed her bag off the counter and ran up the stairs sobbing.

"Allyson! Come back here!" At the slam of the bedroom door, Karissa's words trailed away along with her confidence. What *had* she done? This morning she was so sure of her decision, but Ally's adverse reaction was causing her to vacillate between conviction and doubt.

Marc had yet to come back to the townhouse. He would have to be the one to deal with their daughter. Karissa straightened her shoulders letting a mudslide of guilt drop to the floor. None of this was her doing—it was all her mother's fault. She would not bear the burden of responsibility—not one iota.

Dr. Utley had made it very clear, Kathleen Raines would not be waking up from her coma. Not even deep space would make an impact on her brain. He wanted Karissa to know that if her mother remained in the hospital here on earth, the family would eventually be making a decision to terminate life support. In some ways, her mother would end up a hero if she made it all the way to Mars, an eight-month journey.

The family had an opportunity to see Kathleen before her voyage into space. Ally's little explosion had kept Karissa from telling her about their visit tomorrow. *Leave that one to Marc, too.* A flicker of jealousy skidded through her mind—just one more chunk of resentment to throw onto the ever-growing heap.

> > >

Breathing in through his nose and out through his mouth, Marc siphoned every bit of tranquility from the sand at his feet and ocean in his view. He reveled in the solitude, watching the sun lower itself toward the horizon. He'd been sitting in the sand all evening, unable to go back to the townhouse. If he left the beach at all, he would sleep in his own apartment tonight. Marc was a forgiving man, but Karissa had done the unthinkable. Being in the same room with her right now wasn't an option.

It was so like his wife to make a hasty decision. That was her modus operandi, and she'd gotten away with it all of her life. She never seemed to think about consequences or how her decisions affected other people. A thought suddenly hit him between the eyes like a raging migraine. He brought his knees up and lay back in the sand feeling the sharp pain all the way through his core. *That's what she did when she married me.*

They had met at USC in a senior level English class during the fall semester. Marc had noticed her right away—long, silky brown hair, creamy chocolate eyes, and shapely tan legs. She had chosen the seat next to his, not hiding her intentions to get to know him. Soon she was hanging out at the USC indoor track meets, cheering him on in the 800 meters and mile run. By February, barely four months into the relationship, Karissa started talking marriage, and Marc, falling hard, had given her a ring in April. They were married the first weekend of June.

Hurting like never before, Marc closed his eyes and a small stream of tears leaked out through the corners. He'd been working so hard to win Karissa back, and now, he wasn't sure he really wanted to. Somewhere in the back of his mind he'd kept hope alive. Is this what it felt like to lose it? If so, he'd rather walk into the ocean and end it all tonight.

"Ally," he whispered aloud, and sat up. *Oh, Lord, I didn't mean it. Please forgive me.* Tomorrow, at sunrise, Marc knew he would renew the fight—grasp for hope once again—aspire to save his family. But tonight, he was resigned to wallow in despair.

Giving the back of his head a good rub, he watched an older couple stroll by in the last remnant of light. Marc stood up brushing off the clinging sand particles, and made a decision to walk in the opposite direction, away from the lights dotting the shoreline. He allowed the sadness to sift through his very being, mourning the loss of Kathleen deeply. He felt closer to her than his own mother. Kathleen had been the one to renew his faith in God only weeks before his marriage to Karissa. Since then, she had been his spiritual mentor, and Ally's too. And now—

More tears slipped down his cheeks and he stopped to stare into the night sky. Mars was up there somewhere, millions of miles away. The scientists at the space center had told them today that the launch window was fast approaching. They wouldn't be pointing Kathleen's spacecraft directly toward Mars; the engineers were aiming at a broad orbit around the sun, using its gravity like a slingshot. It would save both fuel and time. He calculated the months in his head. By the time this school year ended, Kathleen could be lying peacefully on Mars. Her body, however, would not remain entombed there forever. Somewhere amidst mission control's countless instruments was a red toggle called the *cremation switch.* Her ashes would remain encased within the spacecraft as a memorial to all of the pioneers that followed. How ironic. Kathleen was one of the most down-to-earth people he had ever known.

"Dad? Are you there?"

Marc looked at his wristband and stared at his beautiful daughter. She looked so much like Karissa it was uncanny. Ally was the only one he had left communication open to tonight. He could be here for *her* and no one else.

Swiping *reveal,* he answered, "Yeah, Cupcake. I'm here."

"Sorry, Dad. Did I wake you up?"

"No, I'm actually on the beach right now."

"Can I come?"

Marc was thankful to be covered in a shroud of darkness, choosing not to go infrared. He didn't want Ally to see that he'd been crying. As much as he'd love to have her company any other time, he had to be alone tonight.

"Not tonight, Baby. I just need a little time to myself." He hesitated a moment. "I...uh...won't be coming back to the townhouse tonight."

A tear shimmered on her cheek. "So this is it, isn't it? You're not gonna stay with us anymore?"

Marc cleared his throat, feeling more like sobbing than talking. The heat behind his eyelids was mounting. "Honestly...I don't know. Maybe it's time."

Ally blinked and a flood of tears followed.

"Hey, Cupcake, I haven't made any decisions—now's not the time to think about that. Why don't we have a long talk tomorrow, you know, when everything doesn't seem so dark?"

Nodding through a shuddered breath, Ally bravely answered, "Okay."

"Listen, I'll be over in the morning to pick you and Mom up to go see Gran. I've already programmed my cyber lessons and gotten you excused from school."

"Thanks, Dad," she said quietly. Her eyes were so forlorn it broke his heart. "Is there any way we can stop this?"

"No, Baby, there's nothing we can do." He had to get off the phone before he sent Ally into further distress. "I'll see you in the morning." Closing his eyes tightly he managed to utter, "I love you so much, Cupcake."

"I love you too, Daddy."

Marc watched until the screen went blank, then he dropped to his knees on the sand and wept uncontrollably.

> > >

"Where were you? I could barely sleep last night."

If this was her mom's way of getting her dad to come home, Ally seriously wondered what was wrong with her. *She's totally lost it.*

"Are you ready to go?" Marc asked, ignoring the reprimand. He'd clearly been up all night.

"I'm ready," Karissa snapped, "but I'm not getting in the car with you. You look like—!"

"Mom!" Ally yelled.

"Hey, let's get something straight before we go." Ally had rarely heard her dad raise his voice, but he obviously wasn't going to put up with her mom's shenanigans today. "What we're about to do is *not* about us, it's about Kathleen—Granny K." He looked pointedly at Karissa. "We're going to show her the kind of respect she deserves. I know that might be hard for you, but that's what we're going to do. Maybe when we get past all of this you can get the professional help you need."

Ally stood dumbfounded. Never in her whole life had she heard him say anything remotely unkind to her mother. She didn't know whether to head outside and give them privacy or join in the fight.

Karissa seemed to be momentarily at a loss for words, but it didn't take long for her to recover. "Don't try to fix me, Marc." She grabbed her bag and headed for the door. "I'm not broken."

"That's just it," Marc said, watching her go. "Until you admit you're broken, you won't be able to have a meaningful relationship with *anyone*—much less God."

Ally knew her mother hadn't heard that last part—she was already storming outside toward her car. She prayed silently that her dad's words, as hard as they were to hear, would somehow get through. She also prayed that her mom would not make a scene when they said goodbye to Granny K.

> > >

The car held an awkward silence both coming and going to the space center. Marc felt bad about airing out his feelings in front of Ally, but he wasn't in the mood to put up with Karissa's selfishness. Later, when he observed her surprisingly affectionate farewell with Kathleen, all of his previous anger melted away. He blamed *himself* for the argument they'd had that morning.

The swish and whir of Kathleen's life support system still echoed through his mind three hours later. Before they were taken to see her, the program director, Dr. Carter Dunleavy, led them through the mission control center. They had been introduced to several members of the team as preparations were being made for this historic mission. The flight director, Nathan Cruz, had made it a point to put their minds at ease, letting them know that he would do all in his power to take care of Kathleen. It was his job to make all of the decisions relevant to the mission, and he assured them that everything was proceeding as planned. Her spacecraft had been tagged, *Pioneer and Kathleen, the Pioneer Woman.*

Eventually, the family was led into the space agency's huge medical lab. Kathleen was laying inside a shallow capsule the size of a hospital bed, wearing a surprisingly soft protective suit. Everything she needed for living in space was within her suit. All of the built-in sensors were synchronized perfectly with the capsule's intricate functions. The suit would provide oxygen, nutrients, and muscle stimulation. It was designed to provide the lab on Earth with endless medical data. If it hadn't been for the oxygen tube running into the corner of her mouth and one in her nose, she would've appeared normal, as if she were peacefully sleeping. And truth be told, she was.

After Ally's tearful goodbye, Marc took Kathleen's hand and brought it to his lips. Oh, how he would miss their long conversations and good-natured banter. Kathleen had been such a steady influence in their lives, at least, in his and Ally's. Karissa had never gotten over the past and had missed out on the love Kathleen so freely offered. If she were to awaken now, she would've been stunned. Karissa lay gently across her mother's body, drawing her into her arms. Marc had never witnessed such affection from Karissa before. He was left baffled by the open display of tenderness.

Now, back at the townhouse, Marc made his way to the couch. As uncomfortable as it was, he was actually looking forward to passing out on it this afternoon. Karissa and Ally headed for the kitchen to make a light lunch, the tense atmosphere from earlier had thankfully dissipated.

Slipping off his shoes, Marc felt the grogginess behind his brow and decided to lie down for a moment. When he awoke, someone had covered him with a light blanket and the shadows in the room told him it was late afternoon. He had slept all the way through lunch and more.

When he pushed the blanket back and sat up, Marc realized he wasn't alone in the room. Karissa sat in the easy chair to the side of the room, her legs curled up beside her. She'd been watching him sleep, of that he had no doubt. Her red-rimmed eyes also told him she'd been crying. He was relieved that his heart still went out to her. He wanted to hold her.

"Karissa." He said her name with tenderness and held his arm open to her.

She sat completely still, obviously trying to decide what to do. *Don't overthink it, Babe. Come on.*

Finally reaching a verdict, she stood and said quietly, "Your lunch is in the refrigerator." Then she resolutely left the room.

Marc's hand dropped to his side, and he leaned his head back on the couch—utterly destroyed.

>>Chapter 7

JUNE 2028

MARS CONQUERED! - ONE GIANT LEAP FOR WOMANKIND! - FIRST MAN ON MARS IS THE PIONEER WOMAN!

The media blitz billowed out of control like a California wildfire, and the Gale family landed right in the middle of the blaze. Marc and Ally seemed to discover ways to escape the public's attention, but Karissa found herself in the forefront. Everyone wanted an exclusive interview with the daughter of Kathleen Raines.

Randall Thomas strolled into Karissa's office unannounced and closed the door. "Let's talk," he said, sitting down in a chair facing her desk. He reached over and patted the chair next to his, summoning her to his side.

Karissa hesitated. She knew he was trying to put her in a vulnerable position, but when he patted the chair a second time, it was clear she would have to submit. His eyes indulged in her every move.

"It's quite a media circus downstairs in the lobby," he said. "Our firm feels the responsibility for added security."

Letting out a deep sigh, Karissa apologized. "You know I never wanted this."

He turned in his chair, purposely touching her leg with his. "I know you didn't ask for any of this, but we need to get ahead of it. We can work all of this to our advantage with a solid plan."

"What do you suggest?" she asked, crossing her legs the other way. The glint in Randall's eyes told her he was very much aware of the discomfort he was causing. It only seemed to egg him on. He put his arm on the back of her chair.

"We have a partner meeting in my office in an hour, and we'd like for you to be there."

Karissa found the excuse to stand and move back around her desk. She touched the glass desktop pulling up her morning schedule. "I'll need to clear an appointment, but that shouldn't be a problem."

"Good," he said, rising to his feet. "I'll see you at 10:30." He opened the door, then turned to face her again. "By the way, plan on leaving your car here tonight. My driver and I will personally see that you get home safely."

The pace of Karissa's heart quickened as she watched him leave. He hadn't waited for a response. There was no doubt Randall Thomas was planning to use this situation to his advantage. He was holding all the cards and they were lining up neatly in his hands. He was subtly letting her know that a name on the wall would come with a price. And for the first time in Karissa's career, the lines began to blur.

> > >

"How do I look?"

"Mom, you're gorgeous."

Karissa dropped a light kiss onto Ally's forehead. "I knew I could count on you," she said, giving her daughter a shaky smile.

"Mrs. Gale? We're ready for you." The assistant to Jonathan Montgomery motioned with her arm toward the set.

"Break a leg, Mom," Ally teased. "You're gonna do great."

"Thanks, sweet girl."

Karissa's eyes briefly landed on Marc's and he gave her an assuring nod. "I'm praying for you," he said quietly.

If that was supposed to calm her nerves, it failed miserably. She turned and walked to the plush chair facing her host. She hoped her makeup didn't look two inches thick like Mr. Montgomery's. Of course, he had been in the news industry for over thirty years—there were more than a few wrinkles to hide.

Immediately Mr. Montgomery put her at ease. "May I call you *Karissa?*"

"Of course," she said, sitting on the edge of her seat.

"Karissa, I want you to sit back and get comfortable. Pretend it's just you and me. Concentrate right here." He held up an index finger between wide-set gray eyes, the crinkles at their corners hardly noticeable beneath the heavy makeup.

"I see your daughter is here today. She looks just like you. How old is she?"

"Fourteen. She'll be going into high school this fall."

Their conversation continued for a couple of minutes, and by the time Mr. Montgomery's assistant started counting down the seconds, Karissa felt completely at ease. It was an odd feeling considering this interview would be broadcast live all over the world. The law firm had chosen LNB Network, not only because of its highly regarded international reputation, but also because Jonathan Montgomery and Randall Thomas were longtime friends. Karissa was fairly certain that Randall had manipulated how this interview was about to progress. He had told her the night he'd taken her home that the firm was going to profit exponentially from the worldwide exposure. He had also hugged her at the door. And she had allowed it.

"Tonight, her silence is broken," she heard Mr. Montgomery saying. "It has been nine long months without a direct word from the Gale family, so I want to start off by thanking you, Karissa, for this opportunity to speak about your mother."

"It's my pleasure," Karissa heard herself saying. She concentrated solely on his eyes, coercing a smile from within.

"Let's start by talking about the accident, if you don't mind. What was that like finding out your mother was involved?"

"Obviously, I was shocked. We had heard the news about Russia's Deputy Prime Minister at the law firm where I work. We were all keeping up with the details. When I received the call later that afternoon, I thought it was a joke."

"So you rushed to the hospital to be with your mother?"

"Yes, but of course she was in surgery, so I wasn't able to see her."

Mr. Montgomery uncrossed his legs and leaned forward slightly in his chair. "As shocking as the incident was, how difficult was the investigation?" He raised his brow. "For a while, the FBI believed Kathleen Raines may have acted out of free will—that she somehow intended the outcome."

Karissa let out a nervous laugh wishing she didn't have to defend her mother, but she would do so vigorously if need be. "Anyone who knows my mother knows how ridiculous that theory is. My family and I were most grateful when it was finally ruled an accident."

"Still, there is a sort of mystery behind it all—and of course, she will never wake from the coma to tell her story."

"No," Karissa said softly, "she will never wake up." She could feel the heat behind her eyes and hoped desperately to hold back her emotions.

From off the set Marc watched Karissa's interviewer closely. Jonathan Montgomery appeared to be getting the emotional response he desired. Why would he want to break her down so early in the interview? What would be the purpose, unless it would somehow make Karissa seem more sensitive toward her mother's plight? There was speculation that Coach Raines and her daughter had been estranged. He hoped Karissa was prepared to face the current line of questioning with integrity. It would hurt Ally to the core to hear her mother lie—and truth be told, he didn't have the stomach for it either.

Mr. Montgomery slowly began to turn the screw. "Tell me about the decision to sign your mother over to UISC. How did your family handle the news?"

She cleared her throat, feeling part of her composure slip away. "It was as difficult for my daughter and husband as it was for me. Believe me, I didn't want any of this to happen. But, I was convinced that it really was in the best interest of everyone involved, and even for the medical advancements that are being made. It's hard to believe that her body is on another planet, but I was told that we would eventually have to make a decision to take her off of life support. In a sense, it was like donating her body to science—"

"While she was still alive," Mr. Montgomery broke in.

"Yes, I guess that's what makes this such an unusual situation."

"In a moment, we'll talk about the incredible fact that Kathleen Raines is the first inhabitant of Mars, but for now, I'd like to know more about the relationship you had with your mother."

Karissa felt the muscles tighten in her neck. "What would you like to know?" she asked nervously.

"Let's start when you were young. I understand you were quite an athlete yourself. Why did you choose to walk away from volleyball, the sport your mother coached, before your senior year in high school? That had to have caused some hard feelings."

Apparently Jonathan Montgomery had done his homework well. But this was a path Karissa was unwilling to take. Hashing out her childhood before billions of people would do nothing but make her look like the villain. Her mother was obviously unable to defend herself against anything she might say. It only took a split second to decide not to bite.

"I'm sorry, Mr. Montgomery, but I'd rather keep my relationship with my mother private. Like most people, there are things I'm not proud of growing up, but that simply has no bearing on the current circumstances. My mother and I loved each other—that's all that needs to be said on the subject."

"Perhaps you'd like to enlighten us on your father."

Karissa wondered how she could have been so ill prepared for his line of probing. These were not even close to the questions she had been given ahead of time. Walking away from the interview was obviously not an option, but her past was none of Jonathan Montgomery's business—not to mention the entire world's. Still, she needed to toss out a morsel in hopes that he would be satisfied and move on.

"My father and I were very close. I guess you could call me a daddy's girl. Sadly, he was involved in a fatal car accident when I was twelve."

"I'm sorry for your loss at such a young age. As you say, you were a daddy's girl and suddenly you were left with a very ambitious mother. Did that become a problem for you?"

Despite the bright lights of the studio, Karissa searched for her family off the set. She saw Marc staring intently into her eyes. He was trying to infuse as much positive energy into her as possible. Taking in a deep breath she said, "I'm sure you remember what it's like being a teenager. You don't want anyone telling you what to do or how to do it. I took the loss of my dad very hard, and probably made my mother pay for it by walking away from something she held dear." She sat up a little straighter in her chair. "But we were able to put all of that behind us and move on with our lives. We had a very good relationship." *Lies, all lies*, her subconscious screamed.

Seemingly satisfied, Mr. Montgomery altered course, and within thirty minutes, the interview was over. Karissa felt a monumental wave of relief as she shook his hand and made her way off the set. She had hoped for a congratulatory hug from her daughter but grudgingly accepted one from Marc, instead. Ally stood with her arms crossed at the waist and Karissa tried to read her sober expression.

"Sweetheart, may I have a hug?"

For a moment, Ally hesitated. Karissa hoped no one on the busy set was paying attention. She wanted everyone to perceive them as a perfect family. Frightened that Ally might say something to blow their cover, she forced a cheerful smile and drew her daughter close. Thankfully, Ally gave in to her hug, evidently willing to play along…for now.

"Thank you both, for your support!" Karissa's voice was overly loud, as she turned Ally toward the private exit where a chauffeur waited to take them home. LNB had sent a private car in order to get Karissa and her family to and from the studio for the exclusive interview.

Ally and Marc maintained silence all the way home. When they walked into the townhouse Karissa could literally feel the awkward tension. Marc strode into the kitchen, leaving mother and daughter alone in the front room. No doubt he intended to give them privacy, but Karissa had hoped they could forget about the interview and move ahead. She had done what was necessary to get through the questioning. Now it was time to put it all behind them.

Karissa was relieved when Ally headed toward the stairs. But just as she put her foot on the first step, her daughter froze. "Mom," she said, not looking over her shoulder. "What really happened between you and Gran?"

She watched her daughter slowly turn around and felt the aggravation of ripping open a deep wound. "It was nothing, sweetie. That's all in the past and we don't have to think about it ever again."

"Well, it's too late for that. I need to know."

Ally came back into the room and plopped down in the chair, crossing her arms again. Karissa inwardly cursed Jonathan Montgomery's name. How dare he mess with her past?

"Ally, there's nothing to tell. You heard what I said in the interview. I was just closer to my dad, that's all."

"Mom, you lied to Mr. Montgomery about your relationship with Granny K, but I can't handle you lying to *me*."

Karissa noticed her daughter was close to tears, but she couldn't accept responsibility that it might be her fault. Nonetheless, she would have to choose one of two options—either, do what comes naturally and walk away, or sit down and face the music. She would find no peace, either way. Too tired to escape, Karissa resigned herself to the couch, vowing to get this over with as quickly as possible.

"Here's the honest truth," she said, a little more harshly than intended. "It was a Sunday afternoon and we'd just come home from church. My parents went into their bedroom at the other end of the house and shut the door. I was too far away to hear what they were arguing about, but both of them were yelling at each other. The one thing I remember hearing loud and clear, was my mother telling my dad to get out. She had made him so mad, he didn't even bother to tell me goodbye." A lone tear slid down her cheek, and Karissa instantly brushed it away. "That very night," she said angrily, "the police showed up at our door. Daddy had been killed in an accident, and I have... *never*... forgiven my mother for what she did."

Suddenly, Karissa stood up, bitterness compelling her to run away. She narrowed her eyes, unable to hold back the shocking pronouncement. "As far as I'm concerned, she *killed* my father."

Ally's eyes grew wide with dismay, and there was not one thing Karissa could do about it. Once the wound had been opened, the blood horrifyingly gushed out. Without so much as a backward glance, Karissa quickly escaped into the darkness of her bedroom. Tomorrow, she vowed to smooth things over with Ally, but tonight, she would voluntarily wallow in acrimony.

>>Chapter 8

Olivia Cole sipped her third cup of coffee while sifting through a mountain of data being transmitted to her screen in the mission control center. As assistant flight biomedical engineer, Olivia worked the night shift. In her early thirties, the slender blonde had been fighting her way through a man's world, trying to prove daily that she had earned her chair at the space agency. It wasn't easy. People tended to judge her by her looks, deciding somehow that beautiful and intelligent didn't mix. She hoped that paying her dues on the night shift would eventually lead to a research job in the lab…while the sun was shining.

During the day, either Doctor Utley or Yashkin monitored the seemingly small station near the back of the control center, while the other worked in the medical lab testing data. A host of others worked throughout the space center at night, but only two other assistant engineers worked the control center. They were barely within shouting distance inside the cavernous room. Donald Graham kept a close watch on Kathleen's environmental control systems and Viktor Belkin maintained all ground and satellite networks throughout the night. The colossal screen at the front of the command center mirrored Olivia's monitor.

Only one other person had access to the control center at night, and that was sixty-two-year-old Mason Hill. He worked for California Industrial Cleaning Services. As the longest tenured employee, Mason was the only one allowed behind closed doors at UISC. A clause in his cleaning contract specifically forbade him to share information about the space agency with anyone on the outside, a stipulation he strictly adhered to. He couldn't afford to lose this job. His wife had been diagnosed with ovarian cancer last year. Medical bills were beginning to pile up. He had already been looking for ways to supplement his income during the day. It was hard, considering the amount of time he needed to help take care of his wife's needs.

Tonight marked Kathleen's twentieth night on the planet's surface. A day on Mars was 39 minutes longer than that of earth, so if they were counting Martian sols, she hadn't quite reached twenty. Either way, no one had expected Kathleen Raines to make it this far.

Olivia's brow furrowed deeper every time she recorded a muscle twitch. Earlier in the night the fingers on Kathleen's right hand had drummed out a twitchy rhythm. The action took all of four seconds, but nothing like that had happened before. It was almost like her muscles were starting to revive. Already her heart was beating stronger than it had before the mission began. Olivia was tempted to sleep in the lounge at the end of her shift so she could help monitor the intricate brain scan the doctors would be performing later in the afternoon. The scan could only be done one time, and both Utley and Yashkin believed the time was now. As impossible as it seemed, there was some kind of activity going on in Kathleen's brain.

At exactly ten minutes past four in the morning, Kathleen's entire body shuddered. Olivia let out an involuntary squeal and within seconds Donald Graham was standing agog at her station. "I saw that!" he said excitedly. "What's going on?"

Olivia didn't bother to look up. "I'm not sure." She zoomed her camera lens in for a closer look. "If I could only do that brain scan, maybe we could pick up some kind of activity going on."

"But that's impossible," Donald said. "There's no way her brain could—"

His words were cut short when Kathleen's right arm bent at the elbow, propelling her hand partially off the bed. It immediately dropped back to her side.

Stunned, Olivia looked up at Donald Graham for the first time. "Did you see that?"

Eyes wide, Donald confirmed the movement.

Olivia grabbed her phone to call Dr. Utley but was unable to give the voice command. Kathleen's eyelids began twitching uncontrollably.

"She's waking up!" Olivia cried.

All of a sudden, Kathleen's right hand ascended to the tube in her nose and yanked once, then twice. On the second try, the tube floated snake-like above the bed, still attached to the open capsule.

"Oh, no, no, no!" Olivia watched in horror as Kathleen yanked on the breathing tube inserted into her mouth. "Donald!" she screamed, giving the environmental control officer a forceful shove. "Flood the compartment with oxygen. NOW!"

Donald took off at a sprint to his station, still watching the gigantic screen up front. Kathleen was yanking and gagging while sputum discharged from her mouth and nose. The thick liquid hovered sickeningly around her head. Within seconds he was on his station computer, reprograming the environmental system inside the spacecraft.

"Hurry up!" Olivia yelled louder than before. Kathleen's face was turning a light shade of blue. The intubation tube was now completely free from her lungs and throat. The weights inside the lining of Kathleen's suit kept her hand pinned to her chest, still grasping the tube. Olivia was amazed at the power she had displayed in using her right arm and hand. The muscle stimulation exercises must have been working.

Every bell and whistle was going off on Olivia's panel—warning lights lit up the dark control room. She feared they were going to lose Kathleen. "Donald!" She screamed. "Talk to me."

Sweat trickled down the side of Donald's face as he confirmed a normal oxygen level inside the entire cabin. He looked up at the screen in the front of the room. Kathleen's breath came in gasps, but her limbs lay completely still—the bluish tint to her skin had disappeared. He opened the communication system at his desk to talk to Olivia. "What's happening?"

Olivia finally got her panel under control, completely shutting down the ventilator system. Hastily checking Kathleen's vital signs, she answered breathlessly, "Her heart rate is elevated, blood pressure up, but…she appears to be taking air into her lungs. How is that possible? It would take days to wean her off the ventilator."

Donald continued to monitor the oxygen levels in the compartment. "Was this some kind of freakish reflex reaction or something?" When Olivia didn't respond to his question, he looked up at the giant screen in the front of the room. His mouth gaped wide in awe. Kathleen's eyes were open and remained open for a long moment. Slowly her lids closed for a few seconds, then opened again. Her brow crinkled slightly.

"Kathleen?" Olivia's voice remained low and soothing, which took a great deal of self-control. "Kathleen, can you hear me?"

Her eyes closed tightly this time, the lines in her forehead possibly indicating pain.

"Kathleen, you're going to be okay. If you can hear me, please open your eyes."

Kathleen's eyes immediately opened. A look of confusion strained her features. Olivia thought she heard a tiny grunt. It was a low inarticulate sound. "Don't try to talk right now, you won't be able to do that for a while. Just listen to my voice and stay relaxed."

Olivia continued a steady stream of encouragement, reassuring Kathleen that everything was going to be fine. At one point she muted her com system to tell Donald to contact Doctors Utley and Yashkin, then immediately continued to bolster Kathleen's peace of mind with soothing words and phrases. Eventually, Kathleen appeared to drift off to sleep.

Viktor Belkin, the satellite technician, entered the control station after his thirty-minute break, unaware of the previous turmoil. He passed Olivia's station on the way to his desk and joked with his heavy Russian accent, "All quiet on the Western Front?"

"Hardly," Olivia quipped.

Viktor stopped and turned around. "What do you mean?" he asked in his native Russian.

She pointed toward the big screen. "See anything out of the ordinary?"

It only took a moment for Viktor to notice the tubes were missing from Kathleen's mouth and nose. "Bozhe moy," he murmured under his breath. "What is going on?"

"Sleeping Beauty woke up."

"Impossible." Viktor's features grew dark. "Did she say anything?"

Olivia looked at her co-worker with a sideways glance. Subconsciously she wondered why he had chosen to ask that particular question. Realizing he had no knowledge of the medical aspects of this mission, she answered, "No, she won't be able to speak for quite some time because of the tubes that have been in her throat. Who knows, she may not be able to speak at all depending on her brain function." Olivia glanced back at her screen. "She did, however, appear to understand what I was saying to her."

Viktor's eyes narrowed. "I think I will be working a double shift today. My assistance may be needed with satellite communications."

"Probably not necessary," Olivia said. "But I'm definitely not going anywhere. This is history in the making."

Viktor stared hard at the screen and whispered, "Exactly."

Dr. Utley rushed into the control room less than half an hour after receiving Donald Graham's call. He had obviously spent little or no time on his appearance. Dark strands of hair were standing at odd angles on top of his head and he was wearing blue jeans with a white t-shirt and flip-flops. No one had ever seen him in such a disheveled state. Olivia immediately vacated her chair, knowing the doctor would want to sit down at the control panel.

"Tell me what happened," he demanded, while staring at the screen and checking pertinent data.

Olivia cleared her throat and began telling him about the night's events. Splitting the screen, Dr. Utley began reviewing Kathleen's activities on video. "What time did she wake up?"

"4:10, you're coming up on it now."

Steven Utley froze in front of the screen, intently watching Kathleen's every move. Olivia noticed him cringe when the tubes were yanked from her nose and chest.

"You've obviously flooded the compartment with oxygen, but how is it possible that she is still alive? More importantly, how have we missed this…this…brain function? This shouldn't be happening." He paused for a long moment before taking the video back to 4:10. "At least, not on Earth…but Mars…it's phenomenal."

Dr. Yashkin arrived fifteen minutes later, dressed professionally, carrying his usual air of self-importance. "What is all this—?" The rest of his words jammed in his throat and drifted away in the room's expanse. The small crew of engineers chose to let him watch the phenomenon on the giant screen without explanation.

Dmitry Yashkin's face turned a dark shade of red. "Impossible!" he bellowed. "She had no significant brain activity nine months ago."

Dr. Utley stood and joined his fellow doctor before the big screen. Laying a hand on top of his shoulder he quietly said, "We may be witnessing a miracle, moy tovarishch."

"Miracle, indeed," Dmitry muttered. "Do you think she will awaken again?"

Olivia's heart rate quickened at the sudden thought of Kathleen waking up. She instantly checked the time and spoke to the doctors in haste. "I think we need to try to wake her right now."

Both doctors turned a quizzical gaze. Olivia sat down in the chair Dr. Utley had vacated. "Her muscle stimulation exercises begin in less than twenty minutes. What if she wakes up in a panic? She could do irreparable damage to her suit and capsule."

"Then we have no time to waste," Steven said. "Wake her if you can."

Olivia swallowed hard—her hands shook as she opened the communication system into the spacecraft. "Kathleen?" she said meekly. "Kathleen, wake up." There was no movement, only the rise and fall of her chest with her right hand still grasping the vent tube.

"Kathleen," she said more forcefully. "You need to open your eyes right now."

Astonishingly her eyelids quivered, then slowly opened, albeit at a squint.

"Kathleen, this is Olivia. I talked to you earlier. Do you remember?"

Kathleen closed her eyes for a brief moment, then opened them a little wider than before. Olivia turned around to the doctors, "She understands what I'm saying."

Dr. Utley rested his hand on Olivia's arm. "Don't tell her where she is."

74

Olivia wanted to roll her eyes at the doctor. She wasn't an idiot. "Kathleen, you've been sick for a while…and no one can come in your room right now. I need to prepare you for something that's about to happen. Blink twice if you understand what I'm saying."

Two blinks.

"That's wonderful, Kathleen. I need you to listen very carefully, okay?"

Another two blinks.

"You're wearing a special suit that's been helping exercise your muscles while you've been sick." Olivia checked the time on her panel before continuing. "In twelve minutes you're going to feel your legs and arms moving involuntarily. It's not going to hurt you at all—it's just going to feel a little weird. I need you to stay completely relaxed. Do you think you can do that for me?"

Kathleen's eyes remained open. Olivia perceived a look of fear.

"I'm right here with you, Kathleen. I won't let anything happen to you. Do you trust me?"

Two, slow blinks. Olivia let out a long, grateful breath.

"That a girl. I need you to do something else for me. Can you open your right hand?"

Kathleen's hands were covered by a membrane-like glove with tiny electrodes inside. Her hands would also be stimulated during the exercises and Olivia preferred that she not be holding the tube when those movements began. Everyone wondered if Kathleen had drifted back to sleep, as her eyes remained closed for a very long moment. They watched in amazement as her index finger eventually pointed upward, followed by the release of her other three fingers, and finally the thumb. The tube wafted slowly upward, hovering above her body.

When Kathleen's eyes reopened, Olivia noticed the crinkles at the corners. She was trying to smile. "You did it! I'm so proud of you. There are a couple of other things I need to tell you." Olivia felt Dr. Utley's hand squeeze her shoulder. Wanting to shrug it off, she ignored his cautioning touch, proceeding with her instructions. "You're wearing a soft helmet that covers the top and back of your head and neck. Your head will turn side to side—it should feel pretty good. I just want you to be prepared for everything that's about to happen. You have seven minutes before it starts."

Closing her com Olivia looked back at the doctors behind her. "What about music? Do you think we can get some soothing music piped in?"

Donald Graham instantly jumped into action. "I'm on it."

Turning the com back on, she said, "Kathleen, I'm so thankful to see you awake. I know you must have a lot of questions, but for now, I want you to enjoy your exercises. I'm going to be right here with you while you go through them. I won't let anything happen to you."

>>>

Spa music drifted peacefully into her surroundings and Kathleen felt her heart slow down from its charging pace. Her eyes focused on the long tube floating gracefully above her body. It was dancing a perfect rhythm with the tranquil melody. It almost felt like her whole body was floating in harmony with the euphonic sounds. This must be a dream, she thought. There could be no other earthly explanation. Closing her eyes, she became lost in the sounds of the flute and babbling brook.

"Breathe deeply," she heard. It was Olivia's voice. But who was Olivia?

She opened her eyes again. *Why can't I see you?*

"Okay, Kathleen, here it comes. You should feel it in your feet and legs first. Do you feel the movement?"

She blinked twice, then marveled that her body was in motion without even commanding it to do so. Trying to talk, Kathleen let out another gurgling sound. Immediately she wished she hadn't. Her throat burned with fire. She wanted to cry. *Do you know how much pain I'm in?*

"Don't try to speak, Kathleen. Your throat is very raw right now. Focus on the music."

Please don't leave me!

"I'm going to stay right here with you—all the way. You and I will get through this together. Let your mind rest in the music."

Kathleen took several ragged breaths and imagined her body drifting peacefully on the ocean. She loved the Pacific coast. She longed to be on a paddleboard in the calm of the evening. Water.

I'm so thirsty.

Begging with her eyes, Kathleen stuck her tongue out of her mouth. Just a drop of cold water was all she needed.

"Oh, Kathleen. I'm so sorry. I know how thirsty you must be, but for now your body suit is supplying all the nutrients you need, including hydration. You're going to be okay. I promise."

Kathleen squeezed her eyes shut. She knew she wasn't going to be okay. A person couldn't survive without water.

"It's almost over. Now for your head and neck."

Involuntarily her head turned to the left. Kathleen's throat caught fire again. She wanted to scream for it to stop, but her head kept turning from the left to the right.

Make it stop! Please, make it stop!

"Hang on, Kathleen. It's almost over…one more time to the left. You're done! You made it. I'm so proud of you."

Kathleen closed her eyes. *I just want to die. Let me die now.* She couldn't even conjure any saliva to swallow.

"Kathleen, are you in any pain?"

She squeezed her eyes shut hard, then opened them, and squeezed them tight again.

Olivia Cole felt her gut wrench. The pain in Kathleen's throat and chest must be excruciating. "We need to sedate her until her throat has time to heal."

"I concur," Dr. Utley agreed. Turning to Dr. Yashkin he said, "We can put her to sleep intravenously. We'll do it from the lab." Both doctors immediately left the control room.

"Kathleen, can you hear me? I want you to know that I'm still here. I care about you and want you to get well. I'm going to do everything in my power to help you."

The rims of Kathleen's eyes turned red, but no tears came out. Bless her heart, she couldn't even cry when she wanted to.

"I won't leave you alone. Not ever. I promise."

Gradually, Kathleen's facial features relaxed and she drifted off into the depths of unconsciousness.

>>Chapter 9

It was a puzzling reaction to say the least. Olivia kept a wary eye on Doctors Utley and Yashkin as they argued in a private room next to the lab. Only eight hours had passed since Kathleen's awakening and things were getting nearly as interesting on Earth as they were on Mars. Olivia knew the other workers in the lab must be worried that a physical altercation might break out between the doctors—that's why she had decided to step inside the room.

"We cannot allow this visitation. I forbid it!" Like twisted balloon art, Dmitry Yashkin's neck veins bulged from his jawline to the collar of his shirt.

Olivia had never seen Dr. Utley in any state except controlled, but even his face was turning a deep shade of red, eyes narrowing. With a threatening tone he countered Dr. Yashkin. "Have you bothered to read the contract? The family is allowed to see Kathleen as often as they wish. They are never to be turned away as long as she remains alive."

"But we are not prepared for anyone to know that Kathleen has awakened. This is unacceptable!" he yelled.

Olivia wished she could get involved, maybe help sway the pendulum in Dr. Utley's favor. She had met Kathleen's granddaughter on two occasions—once just before the launch and again on a Saturday when Olivia had come in on a day off. She felt a connection to the girl, even as she felt a bond with Kathleen. But she knew Ally would notice the tubes missing from her grandmother's mouth and nose. It wouldn't take a genius to figure out something had happened…something huge.

"We will tell them we're running sensitive brain scans," Dmitry raged. "They can come back in a week." He spit the words out angrily. "That is okonchatel'nyy!"

"It is *not* final! They're coming in whether you like it or not." Steven turned toward the door, but Dmitry attempted to physically stop him. In one swift motion, Steven Utley pinned his considerably smaller and older colleague to the worktable. Glass beakers scattered across the surface as Steven's forearm came to rest menacingly on Dmitry's throat, his other hand pressing hard on the doctor's shoulder.

"Stop it!" Olivia yelled. "Both of you. This is a disgrace." She felt her cheeks burning as both men turned their gaze in her direction. Almost immediately she perceived a release of tension, like water leaking from a reservoir. Steven Utley loosened his hold while Dmitry Yashkin stood up straightening his tie. Steven ran both hands through his hair and kept them on top of his head. He let out a deep breath and stepped back.

"This doesn't have to be so difficult," she urged. "We can tell them that we're experimenting with her lungs, and the only way it could be done was by removing the tubes." When neither man spoke she sheepishly added, "Or something like that."

Dr. Yashkin spun around, pressing his hands firmly onto the table. He continued breathing short, quick puffs of air. After a long moment he turned back to face the pair, his voice still tight with emotion. "It could work," he conceded. "But we will all give them the same story—no deviation."

"All right," Steven breathed. "Let's get our story straight so they can come in."

Ten minutes later Ally and Marc were ushered into the control center where nearly every station was manned. Kathleen's image was no longer projected on the big screen, and Ally was curious. She noticed Ms. Cole operating the biomedical station—another deviation from their previous visits.

Olivia smiled and rolled a chair back from the station, motioning for Ally to sit beside her. "It's good to see you again, Ally...and Mr. Gale. Is your mother here today?"

Ally's heart took an unexpected dive as she shook her head. Her mother hadn't bothered to visit one time since the Mars landing. "Not today. She had something important to do at work."

"Even on a Saturday? She must be very busy."

With a hint of a smile Ally quipped, "You're working on a Saturday, too."

"Touché," Olivia said, trying to keep the mood light.

"Have there been any...?" Suddenly Ally's next words caught in her throat. She leaned forward, staring intently at the screen. "Where are all Gran's tubes?" she whispered, turning a curious gaze toward Olivia, who didn't miss a beat.

"They've been removed. When tubing is left in a patient too long, the throat tissue begins to close around the tubes. It causes all sorts of complications. We decided to remove them last night, and now your Gran is breathing on her own." Olivia gave Ally a warm smile, hoping her explanation would suffice.

Ally sat quietly for a long moment before asking, "How'd you get them out?"

"That's the interesting part." Olivia told her that they had actually used her Gran to pull the tubes out. "We can control her movements through the special suit she's wearing."

Marc laid his hand on Ally's shoulder and leaned in for a closer look. "You mean to tell us that Kathleen actually pulled her own tubes out?"

"It wasn't easy," Olivia said, "but that's exactly how they were removed. We flooded the compartment with oxygen and Kathleen is now breathing on her own."

"Then...she's getting better...right?" Ally was now probing Olivia with a look of uncertainty. When Ms. Cole didn't respond right away a feeling of elation began working its way up from the pit of her stomach. An inkling of a smile returned. "She's breathing on her own...you weren't really expecting that, were you?"

Olivia cleared her throat and rested her hand lightly on top of Ally's arm. "To be honest, we didn't know if she was going to be able to breathe on her own."

Marc immediately rolled another chair up to the medical station and sat down. "You should've informed us before performing such an important procedure. What if it hadn't worked? We'd be sitting in the waiting room right now listening to some bad news."

"I'm truly sorry, Mr. Gale. I know this was a big decision, but honestly, it wasn't mine to make. I'm kind of low on the totem pole around here. You're welcome to take it up with Dr. Utley or Yashkin."

"Dad," Ally said softly, meeting his eyes, "it's okay. Granny K seems to be a lot more comfortable now." Turning back to Olivia she asked, "May I talk to her?"

Just for an instant Olivia hesitated, then with a grin and determined tilt of her chin, she pushed the communications switch. "Sure. Take as long as you want."

Like beads sliding from a broken necklace, Ally's words spilled out across the cosmos. She had two weeks' worth of living to catch her up on. Summer soccer camp, youth group retreat, early orientation meeting for high school, and an overnighter with her best friend, Reagan. Every now and then, when he could slip a word in, Marc told Kathleen about a few of the dozens of messages they received each day. Today he told her about some of the ones from her former players at Pepperdine.

Bolting straight up in her seat, Ally pointed at the screen. "Did you see that?"

"What?" Olivia and Marc posed at the same time.

"I think Gran just smiled! Granny K? Can you hear me?"

Olivia reacted swiftly and automatically, shutting down the com link. Ally looked at her in dismay. "Why did you do that? I think she can hear us."

"She's not hearing us, Ally. It's simply an autonomic nerve response, that's all. It happens all the time."

"Let me keep talking to her…please," Ally begged.

"That is not such a good idea," Dr. Yashkin interrupted, striding purposefully toward the control station. "She has no brain function and her body has been through a trauma with the removal of her breathing tubes. We will now lower the lights in her chamber."

To Ally's dismay, the screen went dark except for the blinking lights in the space module. "May I at least tell her good-bye?" she pleaded.

Dr. Yashkin pressed the communications button on the control panel while Ally expressed her love to Kathleen. The words had barely left her mouth before he turned it off again. Ally looked at her dad through teary eyes.

"It's all right, Cupcake," he soothed. "I'm sure they know what's best for Gran."

Even more curious, was the fact that Ms. Cole had started crying. Ally watched her get up and move away from the station, obviously trying to hide her emotions. Something was going on here, but Ally couldn't quite figure it out. She felt strangely unsettled as Dr. Yashkin coldly escorted them toward the exit. They had never been treated with anything except genuine hospitality during all of their other visits.

When Ally tried to probe Dr. Yashkin for answers, Marc put his arm around her and gently squeezed her shoulder. She knew it was a cue for her to zip it. She decided to comply…at least for now.

>>>

Outside the complex Marc noticed a drone overhead. It was small and silent, but obviously tracking their movement. When Ally told her dad that the doctors were covering something up, Marc shushed her. "That's not true, Allyson. Your mom and I trust the doctors completely."

His daughter turned wide eyes upward that quickly melted into a dawning reality. Using her full name had done the trick. If his hunch was right, the two of them were not only being watched, but their conversation was also being monitored. Thankfully, she got the hint. "Okay, Father. I guess you're right."

Marc almost burst out laughing. She was a quick study, this daughter of his.

On the hour and a half drive home, Marc voice-activated their course, then reached into a compartment pulling out a pen and notepad. He scrawled, *I think we've got a drone with us. From now on, we won't talk about Gran except on paper. Agreed?*

Ally nodded her head before taking the pad from her dad. *I'm sure I saw Gran smile!!! I think she's waking up.* She added a smiley face and laid the pad on the console between them.

Me too, Marc wrote. *But we need to keep this to ourselves. We don't know anything for sure.*

What about Mom?

Not yet. You know how this could upset her.

Let's come back again tomorrow, Ally scribbled.

Marc sat quietly for a moment, thinking through the options. Finally, he wrote, *We'd better not make waves. They know we come every other Saturday. If we start showing up more often, they might get suspicious of us.*

Ally didn't hesitate. *Suspicious of what?*

He took a long breath, wishing they could talk out loud. Maybe they could, but there was no way of knowing for sure without an audio detection device. Marc had never seen a reason to acquire that type of technology, but he was already thinking about the investment. They could talk more openly inside the townhouse, especially since Karissa wasn't going to be home until dinner. He took the writing pad, attempting to come up with his own hypothesis of the afternoon events.

It's possible Granny K has shown some progress on Mars. Maybe they're not ready to let anyone know their findings until further testing. After all, this is a medical mission. Let's talk about it when we get home.

Ally read the note and settled her head back against the seat. Marc could tell she still had a lot whirring around in that head of hers. He reclined a bit, watching the scenery pass by. It had been a rather odd afternoon, not what he had expected. Something was definitely going on that no one wanted to talk about, of that he was certain.

Inside the townhouse Ally immediately picked up the conversation. "What if we bring Mom back with us in a couple of days? That wouldn't look suspicious, especially since she hasn't even visited yet."

Marc dropped his wallet on the table in the entryway, pondering her idea. "You know, Cupcake, that might not be such a bad idea."

"Only one problem, though."

"What's that?" he asked.

"Trying to convince Mom to go with us."

That evening Marc and Ally combined their cooking skills to create a baked ziti that any Italian Nona would readily applaud. Even Karissa conveyed her compliments to the chefs. "That was amazing," she said, wiping her mouth and dropping the napkin beside her plate. "I don't even mind cleaning up after something that delicious."

"I'll help you clean," Ally chimed in, casting a look toward her dad.

Marc immediately picked up on the cue to give his wife and daughter some space. "I'd be glad to pitch in, but three's a crowd in this kitchen. I think I'll sit outside on the patio and catch a bit of the A's game before I go home." He picked up his tablet and headed for the back door.

Ally thought her mom was in an unusually good mood. Maybe she had landed a big deal at work today. Her mom rarely told her anything about her job, but Ally could always tell when things were going well... and when they weren't.

Before either one left the table, Ally said, "Hey, Mom, do you think you could maybe take some time off from work this week?"

Karissa rested her elbows on the table grinning benignly. "Whatever for?"

"I want you to go see Granny K with me." When her mother's expression made a U-turn Ally pressed on quickly. "The doctors always ask about you—they wonder why you haven't come in to visit. I thought maybe since we don't know how much time Gran has left, you might want to come see her."

Leaning forward Karissa asked softly, "Is she getting worse?"

Ally leaned closer too. "Actually, I think she's getting better. They removed all the tubes from her mouth and nose, and now she's breathing by herself. It's kind of a miracle."

Karissa dropped back in her chair, eyebrows pressing downward. For the first time Ally thought how much her mom looked like Granny K. She kind of wished her mom's personality resembled that of Gran's too. Maybe then she could get over the past. Granny K never held a grudge.

"Sweetheart, I appreciate the offer, but this week is out of the question. I have some very important meetings with clients that no one else can handle." Karissa rose from the table with her plate and glass.

Ally followed her into the kitchen. "Then how about Sunday? Go to church with me and Dad..." Her words came to an abrupt halt as Marc burst in through the back door, fracturing their conversation.

Karissa jumped back, nearly dropping her glass. "Marc, what in the world are you doing?"

"Sorry," he said swiping the lock. "I got a little chilly out there and decided to come in."

"It's seventy-five degrees outside," Karissa carped, turning a critical eye on him.

He pressed an index finger to his lips, sending a chill up the back of Ally's neck. Without a word, she grabbed an open envelope from today's mail and a pen from the kitchen junk drawer. She slid it across the counter toward her dad.

Drone, was all he wrote.

"What does that...?" Ally and Marc both shushed Karissa with a look that said, *put a sock in it.*

We're being watched, Marc wrote, *maybe even hacked. I think the townhouse is clear, but we don't know for sure.*

Karissa grabbed the envelope impatiently, read Marc's words, then reluctantly played their spy game. *WHO and WHY?* she wrote in giant letters.

Ally noticed her dad's hesitation and took the envelope before he could respond.

We saw something we weren't supposed to see today. I think Granny K could hear us talking to her. I saw her smile!

Karissa's eyes grew wide as she read her daughter's message. She quickly grabbed the pen. *Why is that such a secret?*

We don't know...yet! Ally wrote. *Come with us this week and see for yourself.*

Karissa turned her palms upward and shrugged towards Marc. They held each other's gaze for a long moment. Raising his brow and nodding, he finally said out loud, "It's time, Kari."

>>Chapter 10

Jerrod Benton, CEO and head of operations at UISC, obsessed over the possibility of the Gale family bringing a lawsuit. Not to mention what the Russians would do. The implications of Kathleen Raines recovering on Mars were potentially cataclysmic on so many levels. Mr. Benton hadn't left the space center since learning of her *awakening* three days prior. When he wasn't sleeping on the couch in his office or wandering through the control center at all hours of the day and night, he was meeting with lawyers and top level executives in the corporation.

Down in the lab, both doctors agreed that Steven Utley should be the one responsible for keeping an eye on Kathleen's family during today's visitation. Dmitry Yashkin would monitor her sedation level behind the scenes. This was not only an unexpected visit, but an unwelcome one. Immediately after Marc and Ally Gale's last visit, the all-important brain scan had finally been performed. Nothing could have prepared the medical team for their findings—hundreds of thousands of synaptic connections had been regenerated and neurons were now fully firing inside Kathleen's brain. Impossible!

Karissa studied Dr. Utley closely as she walked into the control center with Marc and Ally. His rigid stance beside the biomedical station provided the first insight into his frame of mind. She herself was nervous about this visitation, particularly knowing that they were being monitored. Marc had borrowed a micro scanner confirming their suspicions. The question now was, who was watching them, and why? Karissa had the ability to manipulate people, which she considered a worthy attribute for any lawyer of her caliber. She planned to scrutinize Dr. Utley's every word—perhaps even make him slip up and divulge pertinent information.

The screen at the medical station lay in darkness. Ally immediately asked about her grandmother. "How is she doing? Is she still breathing on her own?"

Dr. Utley gave her an abridged smile, then gestured for the trio to have a seat. "She's still breathing well enough on her own. No complications to speak of."

Karissa adeptly began to exert pressure. "Dr. Utley, how is it possible for my mother to be breathing on her own without any brain activity? Doesn't the brain control every aspect of the body's functions?" She hadn't meant to go for the jugular so soon, but Steven Utley's expression was priceless. If the color draining from his face was any indication of his discomfort, then she knew a king-sized nerve had been struck.

"Uh…Mrs. Gale, we're studying your mother very closely. We believe that her autonomic nervous system has taken control of all bodily functions." He cleared his throat and activated the screen. "In other words, the system that unconsciously regulates bodily tasks such as heart rate and respiration are functioning well enough to keep her alive."

For a moment Karissa disengaged her badger instinct. The sight of her mother only reminded her why she had never wanted to visit in the first place. An unforeseen jolt to the heart temporarily derailed her mission—a cupful of guilt.

Surprisingly, Ally picked up the flag and charged ahead. "Ms. Cole told us about the autonomic nervous system last time we were here. I did a little research on my own. Doesn't the hypothalamus control that system? And more importantly, isn't the hypothalamus located inside the brain?"

Bravo! Karissa inwardly applauded her daughter.

"Well, uh, yes, technically you're right, the hypothalamus is just above the brain stem." The doctor's words trailed away as he kept his eyes trained on the screen.

Karissa knew without a doubt Dr. Utley's current struggle was an ethical one. He had proven himself trustworthy from the moment they first met. Obviously he didn't want to lie to them. She believed it was now or never. "Dr. Utley, is it safe to say that my mother has regained her brain function?"

A four-letter word quietly rolled off his tongue and he hurriedly deactivated a listening device on his wristband. Turning his gaze toward the family Dr. Utley issued an apology for his choice of words. "I can't do this," he uttered. "You need to know something." After hauling in a deep breath he told them, "Kathleen woke up on her own three nights ago."

All three family members reacted with incredulity causing Dr. Utley to raise his hands and beg their silence. Immediately his eyes darted to a point behind them and then back again. "I was not supposed to tell you about this...but I don't agree with—"

Dread propelled its way through Karissa's veins as two security officers and three other men in suits surrounded the biomedical station. One officer immediately slipped his hand beneath Dr. Utley's arm lifting him to his feet. They disappeared into the vast space of the control center and through an unmarked door.

Marc abruptly stood to face the men. "What's going on here?"

"Come with us, please." One of the men stepped back, extending his arm toward the exit. The other three moved in closer to the family making sure they understood there were no other options available.

Marc took Ally's hand and reached for Karissa's, but she pretended not to notice his protective gesture. Karissa had no interest in showing weakness to these men. Her back straightened as she followed the security guard.

Stepping onto a glass elevator, they were given a spectacular view of the indoor workings of the space complex all the way up to the fifth floor. The open design of the building made it possible to see nearly everything going on within its glass walls. Even the walkways were made of a smoky, transparent surface. Karissa was thankful she hadn't worn a skirt as she peered at the people on the floor below. There was, however, one private room without see-through walls on the fifth floor—the office belonging to Jerrod Benton.

Behind the door Karissa thought they had been ushered into a sci-fi museum. Rockets of all generations, including future models, lined the interior of the wood-paneled room. At least four large screens displayed galactic scenes and launches of spacecraft. Karissa quickly identified paraphernalia connected with *Star Wars* and *Star Trek*. Robots of all shapes and sizes roamed freely throughout the space. She could tell Marc and Ally were about as uncomfortable in this fantastical room as she was.

A panel on the back wall slid open and an older gentleman with a salt-and-pepper beard invited their family to enter. Karissa recognized him from their meetings a year ago concerning her mother's flight to Mars.

"Please, come in. It's good to see you again, Mrs. Gale." Mr. Benton took her hand firmly into his own. It was ice cold. "May I call you Karissa? I feel like I know you so well."

Karissa wanted to scream, *absolutely not*, but realized she was in no position to dictate orders to the head of UISC. She merely nodded.

"Please have a seat." He pointed to a gold couch near the wall where Karissa and Marc sat down with Ally in between. Mr. Benton took a leather armchair facing them and dismissed the security detail.

While at first glance Karissa had thought Jerrod Benton appeared arrogant and self-assured, she now realized he was uncomfortable, his mannerisms were twitchy. Inwardly she felt that might give her an advantage if she could figure out his angle quickly enough. But he seemed reluctant to speak.

Just as Marc cleared his throat breaking the silence, the office door slid open again. With a look of relief, Mr. Benton stood and introduced Michael Krennim, his private council. *So that's what this is all about. He doesn't want to start the meeting without back up*—the first hint that perhaps Benton was trying to avoid a lawsuit. Karissa now started loading her chamber with ammunition.

"Well," Mr. Benton began, "we've been presented with an unexpected turn of events. As you were informed a few minutes ago, your mother has made miraculous strides while in deep space. Her brain now appears to be functioning again. We're not positive to what extent, but what we believed was an *impossibility* here on earth, has become a *possibility* on Mars."

Karissa scooted forward on the couch, tilting her chin upwards. "Mr. Benton, we were given full assurance that there was no conceivable way for my mother's brain to recover—the chances were zero. *Zero*," she said again with emphasis. "And now you're telling me that she is awake, all alone on Mars, with no way to get off that godforsaken planet. Does that about sum it up?"

Mr. Benton swallowed hard and turned his attention to Michael Krennim. And his council did not let him down. "Mrs. Gale, let's just slow down a minute. There are a few things I want to show you in the paperwork you signed last September." He quickly scanned through a screen and handed it to Karissa.

"As you can see, there is a small clause at the bottom of page twenty-seven that I've taken the liberty to highlight."

Ally and Marc leaned in for a closer look. Karissa read the clause at least four times, feeling her mouth go dry. Tearing her eyes loose from the screen, she met Mr. Krennim's gaze. "That clause was not there a year ago."

"I beg to differ, Mrs. Gale. Your palm print sealed every word on that page," he smugly pointed out. "It's there at the bottom."

After a prolonged, awkward silence, Marc broke into the conversation, jogging them down a different trail. "Mr. Krennim, we're not here to threaten this corporation with a lawsuit."

Speak for yourself, Karissa thought.

"The only thing we care about is Kathleen. We need to know what's going to happen to her. How do you plan to take care of her if she's conscious and alone on Mars?"

"Mr. Gale, I assure you, we're going to do everything within our power to see that your mother-in-law is comfortable and well-taken care of," Mr. Benton said. "Our medical team has been working around the clock to modify conditions within the space module. But honestly, we don't know the extent of her brain function until we wake her up."

"Why is she still asleep?" Ally asked.

"Right now we're keeping her sedated until her esophagus has a chance to heal. Pulling the tubes out after such an extended amount of time has caused a great deal of damage and pain."

"Then why did you pull them out?" she asked him.

"Surprisingly, your grandmother did that all on her own. There was nothing we could do to stop her. We're all shocked that she's doing so well considering the circumstances."

"When do you plan to awaken her again?" Karissa asked, letting her adversarial role temporarily take a backseat.

"It could be as long as a month. The doctors are putting some meds into her bloodstream to expedite the healing process. When they think it's safe, they'll stop sedating her."

Karissa was dealing with a good dose of reluctance, unsure of her next move. Just the thought of having to tell her mother where she was, turned her stomach inside out. Maybe it would be better to keep her in a state of unconsciousness; waking her up would almost be cruel—unethical. Now was not the time to voice such thoughts with Ally present. She would have to take it up in a private conversation with Jerrod Benton and the doctors. "So what do we do now?" she decided to ask.

Mr. Benton looked to his council for help once more. Mr. Krennim swiped a projection onto the table screen. He had already worked up a confidentiality agreement for each family member to sign. "At this point, we do not want anyone outside of UISC to know of Kathleen's condition. There are many obvious reasons for non-disclosure, the most important being the sensitivity of the nature of her accident. Chances are she will never be able to remember the events that transpired on that day, but the Russian government may try to press certain liberties in the case. We're simply not prepared for that as of yet." Peering at the family through dark rimmed glasses he added, "I'm sure you would agree."

Karissa was determined to read every word of the confidentiality agreement before any of them would sign it. Being caught off guard by some obscure clause on page twenty-seven was not going to happen again! Thankfully, the agreement was short and to the point. Its terms were concise, the limits on information straightforward.

"Well-written, Mr. Krennim. However, we will not sign this without adding a disclosure."

A wry, half-smile touched Michael Krennim's lips. "Such as?"

"You will add a provision stating that in return for agreeing to keep the information confidential, we have the right to receive details about my mother's ongoing health. You will not deny us access to her condition. Today you attempted to deceive us. If it hadn't been for Dr. Utley's honorable conscience, we would not be having this conversation right now."

"And one other provision," Ally interrupted.

Everyone trained a startled gaze on the fourteen-year-old.

"Dr. Utley won't be punished for telling us about my grandmother. He did the right thing." A soft pink hue spread across her cheeks. She now looked a bit embarrassed.

Marc patted her leg. "Well said, Ally."

Mr. Benton immediately stood motioning for his lawyer to follow suit. "You'll have to excuse us for a moment." Both men walked to the far corner of the office, conversing in hushed tones for several minutes. When they returned, Mr. Krennim unlocked the agreement and audibly worded Karissa and Ally's disclosures.

"Does this meet your conditions?"

All three read the agreement, Karissa more than once. After a few moments she nodded to Marc and Ally, "We can consent to this, but I want to make sure you both agree. Ally, this could be a terrible temptation for you to tell one of your friends. Do you think you can manage it?"

"I can," she said with determination.

"I agree as well," Marc stated firmly.

After signing their names, all three placed their right palms on the screen sealing the confidentiality agreement.

"Now that you have our pledge of silence," Marc added, "I have a request of my own—I insist that you stop spying on our family. We've been watched and listened to for the past three days. It ends today... please."

Both men bore a confused expression, Jerrod Benton shaking his head adamantly. "Mr. Gale, there's something you need to know. We have no reason to watch you or listen to your conversations. UISC is not monitoring your family. You have to believe me...whoever is watching you...it's not us."

>>Chapter 11

(ONE MONTH LATER)

Karissa felt a twinge of irritation and inwardly berated herself. How could she put a damper on Ally's exuberance? Watching her beautiful daughter dance around the kitchen, she hoped to unearth at least a smidgen of delight, but all she could conjure up at the moment was a pathetic smile.

"Mom, this is the best day of my life!" Ally grabbed her mother's hands and attempted to draw her into the light-hearted frolic.

"Stop it, Ally…"

Ally's countenance immediately dropped. "What's wrong? Aren't you excited about Granny K waking up?"

"Sweetheart, there's something you're forgetting about. I don't mean to throw a wet blanket over your celebration, but we have to tell Gran where she is today." She dropped Ally's hands and leaned back against the counter. "This may be the best day of your life, but it's undoubtedly the hardest day of mine."

"Oh," Ally breathed softly. "I wasn't even thinking about that. Sorry, Mom."

Adding to her vexation, Marc walked through the front door unannounced. It irritated Karissa that he treated the townhouse like his own home. *It won't be that way much longer,* she thought.

Marc gave his daughter a tight hug and enthusiastic smile. "You ready to talk to Granny K?"

When Ally didn't immediately respond, Marc's gaze settled on Karissa. "I know this is going to be difficult, Kari. I'll support you any way I can," he said.

Why did he always have to be so attentive?

"Have you thought about how to break the news to her?" he asked.

Letting out a faint groan Karissa left the kitchen. "I don't want to hash through all of this twice," she said from the living room. "It's going to be hard enough as it is." Grabbing her bag she headed for the door. "Let's just go," she called—*and get this over with.*

On the way to the space center Karissa sat silently, immersed in her own thoughts—none of them about her mother—all of them about Randall Thomas. Tonight she would be attending a dinner with Mr. Thomas and the firm's most prestigious client. She had shopped for just the right dress, showing off her near-perfect figure, yet not too revealing. She wanted to impress Randall and let him know she was ready to enter his game. The mere thought of it sent a trimmer of excitement throughout her body. She wouldn't give Randall everything he wanted tonight, but the carrot would definitely be dangling a little closer to his grasp. A partnership was sure to follow.

This evening's anticipation quickly melted into the background. Dread held Karissa in a chokehold as she sat down in front of the screen at the biomedical station in mission control. Olivia Cole was present. She had been the only person to talk to Kathleen thus far. All her mother knew at this point was that she was in quarantine due to a severe illness. It was now up to Karissa to break the terrible news that she was on Mars...alone. Every fiber of her being rebelled against the task; after all, it was she, and she alone, who had consented to this absurd restitution. She consoled herself by evoking the fact that it was her mother's own fault. Kathleen Raines herself had set this nightmare in motion.

"Are you ready?" Olivia asked quietly.

Dr. Utley hovered beside Marc and Ally. He appeared to be as uncomfortable as Karissa. He spoke a few last-minute instructions.

"Your mother will only be able to hear your voice. We can see *her*, but she can't see *us*. There's no video monitor inside her capsule, unfortunately."

"Poor planning," Karissa muttered.

Clearing his throat, Dr. Utley continued. "Try to break the news as gently as possible. Dr. Yashkin is in the lab in case we need to sedate her again."

Karissa wondered if her mother was awake. Her eyelids lay closed; she appeared to be unconscious. "How do I wake her up?"

"I'll take care of that for you, Mrs. Gale. She's used to hearing my voice and trusts me." Olivia put her hand on the communication button. "Just tell me when."

Swallowing hard, Karissa took an exceptionally deep breath, then let it out slowly. "Ok, I'm ready."

> > >

An important volleyball match was about to begin. The net sagged nearly to the floor and the men's basketball team was holding practice on the court. "You've got to get out of the gym," Kathleen told the basketball coach. "We're playing UCLA in five minutes."

"Sorry, we have the gym reserved," he countered, turning back to his team.

Kathleen stared at the crowd—the gym was full. Now two of her players were taking the net completely down and the fans started booing.

"What are you doing? Put that net back up."

"We can't, Coach. The game's been moved to the swimming pool."

As the crowd wandered out of the gym, Kathleen's entire volleyball team paraded across the floor…in their bathing suits. She started screaming for everyone to stay, but no one would listen. Her voice was completely lost in the confusion.

Throwing her shoulders back, Kathleen marched over to the basketball coach, ready to kick him and his team off the court. He completely disregarded her mandate, shaking her hand loose from his arm. Exasperated, she turned her attention back to the stands. Only one person remained.

"Karissa? Is that you?"

"Yes, Mom, it's me."

Kathleen wanted to go to her, but her feet felt like chunks of lead. Suddenly, Karissa turned away and followed the crowd out of the gym.

"No, wait..."

"Mom, can you open your eyes?"

Rousing from sleep, fuzzy surroundings and lightheadedness welcomed Kathleen back to the real world. "A dream," she whispered in a low, raspy voice. Throughout all of her years of coaching she had never been able to ditch the reoccurring dreams. At least a half dozen times a year her sleep was disturbed by either a major screw up before an important match or, even worse, her players showing disrespect during practice or a game. Now that she cognitively took in her strange environment again, she wasn't sure which was worse, the nightmare or reality.

"How do you feel?"

Kathleen started to speak but was pretty sure she'd swallowed a package of aquarium gravel. Come to think of it, she felt like her body was *inside* an aquarium. Every laborious breath reminded her that something was wrong and no matter how hard she tried, she couldn't shake that floating sensation. Swallowing near nothing, she tried to answer. "I'm not sure. Where...am I?"

After a long pause she heard her daughter's unsteady voice. "Um, Mom, do you remember Olivia telling you that you've been very sick?"

Her head bobbed slowly.

"You actually had a car accident...it was a pretty bad one. I don't know how to tell you this, but no one thought you were going to live."

A prolonged silence ensued. Kathleen didn't know how to respond. She simply lacked the memory needed to do so. Instead, she focused on the strange room in which she found herself. A panel of blinking lights drew her attention first, then the strangely shaped bed where she lay, and finally, the lack of a window or a door that she could detect.

"Your body was not too banged up, but your brain was non-functional. We were told that you would never wake up again."

"Well...I guess...they missed that one."

Kathleen heard her daughter laugh, albeit nervously.

"Anyway, the doctors wanted to use your body to run some experiments. They thought we were going to have to make a decision to take you off of life support...so..."

When Karissa's sentence trailed away, Kathleen began to release the words inside her head, bit by bit. "So you gave...my body...to science...a little too early?"

Another edgy laugh. "Something like that."

"Ok...the jig's up," she coughed out. "Can I just go home... please?"

"I can't do this," she heard her daughter say. There were more hushed voices in the background, but Kathleen couldn't make out what they were saying or who they belonged to.

"Granny K?"

"Oh, my sweet...angel girl." Kathleen's heart quickened to her granddaughter's voice. "Come in and...let me hold you."

"That's not going to be possible, Gran. You need to brace yourself...you're not on Earth anymore—you're on Mars."

The key to Kathleen's intellect rushed to unlock a myriad of doors. Behind one she found a plausible explanation. She was still dreaming. Breathing out a sigh of relief she verbalized her thoughts. "For a minute...I thought...I was awake."

"Granny K, you are *wide* awake," Ally said gently. "The doctors really did tell us that your brain would never recover, so they wanted to see what effects deep space would have on your body. You truly are on another planet...you're on Mars."

Kathleen's mind whirred out of control. Her body convulsed as she tried to sit up.

"No, Gran, don't do that. You need to be still and listen to my voice. Please, Granny K, just relax."

"Kathleen, this is Marc. I'm here with Ally and Karissa. Don't try to move, okay?" She talked her body into going still as the previous darkness slid closer. Marc pressed on. "Ally is telling you the truth. I know it seems impossible..."

"Lu...di...crous!"

"Yes, ludicrous. But the fact is, you're in a space capsule on Mars— the first person to make it there alive, as a matter of fact."

Kathleen struggled to follow along with this preposterous train of thought. The-first- person-on-Mars? "Gonna be...pretty hard...to pin a medal on me, huh?"

Marc chuckled. "Yeah, I don't think a medal is coming any time soon."

"But, *you're*...coming for me...right?"

She heard a muffled choking sound, then another familiar voice. "Kathleen, this is Olivia. Do you remember me?"

Kathleen blinked her eyes twice before she realized she didn't need to respond to Olivia that way anymore. Quietly she uttered, "Yes."

"It took a little over eight months to get you all the way to Mars and this is day fifty-one on the planet."

"A new...record?" Kathleen quipped solemnly.

"Yeah, your record will be hard to beat."

Kathleen could detect the smile in Olivia's voice and already felt a connection with her—the kind of connection she would have with a player on one of her teams. There was something endearing about this young woman whom she couldn't see. But all of a sudden her heart plunged to a depth she hadn't thought possible. "What are you...trying to tell me?" she choked out. "Is someone...on the way here...or is this it for me?"

Ally burst into tears and Karissa felt trapped. She didn't want to be here anymore; she just wanted to forget about all of it. This impossible situation was dragging her to the ocean floor, lungs collapsing with the horrible weight of it all. Thankfully, Olivia tried to pick up the pieces of their execrable conversation.

"Kathleen, my dear, I'm sorry to tell you this, but for now, we don't have a way to get you back home." Kathleen's chest heaved and Olivia tracked her heart rate as it steadily climbed higher. "I know this is a lot to take in right now, it must seem like a terrible nightmare..." Olivia's eyes misted as she searched for a spark of hope to give the woman she now cared deeply for. "I promise you this, I will do everything in my power to take care of you. I'll stay with you night and day if I have to. You are not going to be on Mars alone...do you hear me? You are *not alone*."

The heart monitor ticked down a couple of notches while Kathleen lay unresponsive. Her eyes were open, but there was no way of knowing what was going through her mind—a perfectly good mind at that.

"Granny K?" Ally pleaded as tears continued to roll down her cheeks.

"Yes…angel?"

"I'm not leaving you either."

Oh, for heaven's sake, Karissa chafed. Now she would have to deal with getting her daughter out of here today. When she started to counter Ally's declaration, she felt a firm hand on her shoulder—it was Marc's. His touch did nothing to quiet her nerves; just the opposite, in fact.

Turning in the chair to wrest his hand free, she hissed, "Do something." She stood up and whispered to him, "We can't stay here much longer. I have to go."

Disappointment thinning his mouth he took up the chair his wife had vacated. "Kathleen, I'm not leaving you either." He could literally feel Karissa's indignation at his back. "And this is how it's going to work. We're all going to be talking to our Father unceasingly…about everything, but especially about your situation. You can rest assured that He's going to be our go-between…you, me, Ally…and Kari. He'll hear everything we're saying, so when we can't physically be here to talk to you, He's going to send you peace and comfort through the Spirit. We'll all be talking to Him at the same time."

Her lids closed for several heartbeats, then opened revealing a steely determination. "God is my refuge…and strength."

"Yes!" Marc and Ally cried.

"In fact, we'll start talking to Him now, while we're all together," he declared.

Immediately Marc inaugurated their prayer bond with a deeply moving plea for God's intervention. Ally carried on with a sweetness and innocence that must have gone straight to the Father's heart. Even Karissa spoke a prayer, stilted as it was. And finally, Kathleen herself breathed a poignant supplication to the One who had already walked this path—He had been here on Mars all along. No, she would not be alone, even though millions of miles lay between her and those she loved on Earth. The One who made both planets would be by her side; *He* would sustain her; *He* would hold her hand and light her way; *He* would be enough.

>>Chapter 12

Just after midnight Ally lay in bed quietly sobbing. She'd been waiting for her mom to come home from the fancy dinner with one of her law partners. Too excited to sleep after talking with Granny K that morning, she touched her bedside table screen to check the front porch monitor. Her timing had been perfect. The screen revealed a sleek silver car pulling up to the curb in front of the townhouse. It sat there for quite some time until a nice-looking, older gentleman stepped out. Her mom's hand reached for his and he drew her from the backseat straight into his arms. Ally watched in utter shock as her mother's arms encircled his neck, drawing their lips together. His hands roamed up and down her sleek dress and Ally literally thought she was going to be sick. Even as the scene slashed through her heart, she couldn't make herself stop watching—not until Karissa untangled herself and came inside.

Ally made sure the silver car had driven away before clearing her screen. A few minutes later, she pretended to be asleep when her bedroom door softly opened, then closed. All she could think about was her dad. He had always treated her mother honorably, yet she chose to push him away day after day. And now, she was cheating on him. Ally squeezed her eyes shut as a sea of tears drenched her pillow. Sleep would be as far away tonight as Granny K. There would be no escape from the ache her mother had caused.

>>>

At two o'clock in the morning, the grandfatherly Mason Hill leaned on his mop handle, peering over Olivia's shoulder. "She's a pretty woman, even with that space suit on, isn't she?"

Olivia agreed. "Yes, she is."

"How long has she been asleep?"

"About five hours now. That gave me some time to catch a nap of my own. I've been here since early yesterday morning."

Victor Belkin stepped around the night janitor and rolled up a chair. "I believe I will sit and watch for a while, okay?"

Olivia gave the satellite engineer a surprised look. He mostly kept to himself but was showing unusual interest in Kathleen's condition since her second awakening.

"I'm afraid there's not much to see, but you're welcome to join us."

Casting a wary look in Belkin's direction, Mr. Hill said, "Well, I need to get back to work."

Olivia smiled and said she'd let him know if Kathleen should wake up again.

"Please do." He gathered his cleaning supplies and headed for the lab.

Victor began a methodical exploration of the biomedical station, asking Olivia to explain its workings. When he lifted the clear cap to a red switch, she grabbed his arm and yanked it back. "Don't touch that!" She immediately closed the switch cover.

With a startled glance, he asked, "What is it?"

"Victor, you can't just come over here and start messing with things. Why the sudden interest? Don't you have a satellite you're supposed to be monitoring or something?"

"Okay, okay," he said, the heavy Russian accent sliding over his thick lips. "I will go if you tell me why that switch is so important."

"I will, because I don't want you to ever mess with it again. That's the cremation switch. Kathleen's life would be over in a matter of seconds at the flick of that switch. Now, shoo."

Victor looked down at his feet. "Shoe?"

An exasperated breath passed through her clenched teeth.

"S-h-o-o. It means time for you to go." Olivia had nearly panicked thinking about Victor flicking that switch. She would need to talk to the doctors about installing a lock on the cover.

Slowly he rose from his chair and rolled it back to the robotics station where he had gotten it. "You will let me know if she wakes up, hmm?"

"Yes, Victor, I'll let you know," she declared, knowing full well she would not.

Thirty minutes later Kathleen began to rouse. Olivia peaked over her monitor to see if Victor was still at his station. She grinned slyly. He was leaning back in his chair with headphones on. He wouldn't be able to hear a thing.

When Kathleen's eyelids fluttered apart, Olivia opened the com system and immediately spoke. "Kathleen? I'm here with you, my dear."

Kathleen's lips turned upward ever so slightly. She tried to speak, but her throat was clogged and a fit of coughing ensued.

"Take your time, let me do the talking for a while." For the next few minutes Olivia told Kathleen a few details about her own life—the small apartment she shared with her schnauzer named Max, her collection of poetry books dating back to the nineteenth century, and her addiction to coffee.

"What...about...family?" Kathleen finally choked out.

"My family? Well, not much to tell. My parents split up when I was four. I've pretty much lost track of my dad and the other life he chose to live. I visit my mother a couple of times a year in Seattle, and I have an older brother living halfway across the world in Australia. I keep threatening to go visit him—I've never met my little niece—but something always seems to come up."

"Tell me...where I am, again?"

"Kathleen, dear, you're on Mars. Remember?"

Her lids closed and Olivia thought she saw moisture seeping from the corners. How she wished Kathleen were only in the next room. She felt an incredible urge to hold her.

"Kathleen?"

"Call me...Kat."

Olivia smiled, "Okay, Kat. Would you like some music or would you like me to read to you?"

Pondering for a long moment, Kathleen finally responded. "Can you help me…sit up?"

Taken aback, Olivia said, "I don't know if that's such a good idea."

"Please," she rasped.

Olivia worried her lower lip between her teeth. This could be tricky considering all of the attachments Kathleen's suit shared with the bio-bed. But many were wireless and the most important conduits were actually attached near her hips, which made her muscle stimulation exercises possible.

"All right, Kat, if you think you're up to it. Let's do this slowly—we don't want to lose any vital connections to your capsule. Can you put your hands up on the sides of the bed?"

Kathleen's arms slowly bent and her hands reached up for the edge of her cradle-like structure.

"That's good, Kat. Now don't move yet. I want to make sure your hands aren't covering up anything important." Olivia zoomed her camera all around Kathleen's hands, determining them to be in a safe location.

"Okay, that's perfect. See what you can do."

Kathleen let out a grunt as she consciously exerted her own energy for the first time in months. Her head and shoulders lifted a few inches off of the bed before dropping back with a thud.

Olivia shuddered. "Did that hurt?"

"Not that I know of. I'm…trying again."

"I don't know if that's such a good idea. Why don't we let you get stronger before trying to sit up again."

"One more…" Grunting louder Kathleen drew herself up to a forty-five-degree angle for a good three seconds, then let herself back down more gently. Her eyes closed and didn't reopen immediately.

"Kat, are you okay?"

"Just a little…queasy." Her lids remained closed.

"Then we need to let you rest. That's enough excitement for one day. Do you feel like sleeping again?"

She responded by opening her eyes. "What time is it?"

Olivia grinned. What good would time do her on Mars? "It's three o'clock in the morning in California—that's where I am." She explained a little about the Universal Intergalactic Space Corporation and her job as assistant biomedical engineer. "I'm on the night shift."

Kathleen seemed to contemplate everything she had just been told. "Then...let's make sure I'm on...the night shift, too," she said slowly. "I want to...sleep during the day and be...with you at night."

"Oh, Kat, dearest, I would like nothing better."

"Then...we have a deal." Kathleen's smile only lasted a second. "Why can't...I see you?"

A deep sigh escaped Olivia's lips. "We weren't expecting you to wake up on this mission, so unfortunately, we don't have a monitor for you. But our electronic engineers are working on something that might make it possible. This whole month, while you were sleeping, they've been developing some new technology. It will probably require you to help out on your end a little—"

"So I'd better...keep exercising."

"Precisely. We'll do a little every night. As a matter of fact, why don't we work on some hand dexterity? That won't require you to sit up."

Kathleen agreed wholeheartedly, and for the next several minutes allowed Olivia to lead her through what she tagged *finger gymnastics*. Olivia could see the determination on her patient's face—her work ethic didn't disappoint. It was probably one of the many qualities that made Kathleen Raines such a successful coach.

When the hand exercises were complete, Mason Hill reentered the command center with a cartload of cleaning products. Olivia motioned across the room for him to join her while simultaneously glancing to make sure Victor was still in his own world beneath the headphones. Even Donald Graham happened to be working in another part of the building tonight. Olivia didn't mind having Mason with her, but her other coworkers could sometimes distract her from what she really wanted to do. She knew the two engineers were probably bored, but they could be annoying at times.

"Kat, I have someone I'd like you to meet," Olivia said, as Mason joined her at the biomedical station. "This is Mason Hill. Mason, meet Kathleen Raines."

Mason leaned in a little closer. "Hello, I'm pleased to meet you," he said in an overly loud voice. "I'm glad to see you awake."

Olivia put an index finger to her lips and pointed with the other toward Victor's station. Mason's dark brow shot up as he realized he needed to keep his voice down.

"Nice to meet…you too," Kathleen responded. "Do you…work with Olivia?"

Lowering his voice he said, "Nearly every night. But I don't do anything as important as Olivia. I'm the night janitor."

"Well, Mr. Hill…that's still…an important job."

He smiled at the unexpected compliment, then looked to Olivia to take the lead.

"Mason, why don't you tell Kat a little about yourself?"

Clearing his throat, Mason took the chair Olivia offered and began talking to Kathleen like an old friend. He was no enemy to small talk, so before long, he had related details of his childhood in the projects of LA and his basketball scholarship to California State University in Long Beach. "I was the 49ers point guard back in '94 and '95. I could shoot like a pro until a career-ending knee injury. It happened my sophomore year. Never could get it back to rights after that, so I had to drop out of school. Mostly been doing maintenance and janitorial work ever since." He seemed to take on an air of importance. "Of course, I'm glad to be working here at UISC now. It's been an honor to keep up with your progress."

A smile touched Kathleen's lips, "Thank you…Mr. Hill."

"Oh, you don't have to call me that. Please call me Mason."

"And…are you married…Mason?"

A sad expression touched his features. "Yes, ma'am, for over forty years now to my sweetheart, Jolene. We have two beautiful daughters, both married, and three little grandbabies."

"You're…a blessed man."

Olivia could tell Mason was holding back details of his wife's cancer. She knew he wouldn't want to burden Kathleen.

"Well," he finally said, "I expect I'm not getting paid to sit around and talk with you two fine ladies. I'm so happy to finally meet you, Coach Raines."

"The pleasure…is all mine, Mason," Kathleen softly rasped.

"I'll stop by and check on you later."

Mason met Olivia's gaze and she couldn't help but notice the moisture in his coffee-colored eyes. Laying a light hand on his forearm, she thanked him for taking time out to talk. "I know it helped Kat to pass the time."

Giving her a wink, he rose and headed to the front of the room with his cleaning supplies.

The rest of the night passed with Olivia and Kathleen talking like old friends. Truthfully, Olivia did most of the talking, but Kathleen seemed to push the conversation along with stunted quips and questions.

At four-thirty Olivia's phone hummed and she was surprised to see it was Ally. She had given the girl her personal contact and told her to call any time. She just wasn't expecting it to be so soon—nor at this time of morning.

"Hello, Ally," she said, after activating the call. Ally's face appeared on screen. Olivia could see in the dim lighting that she was lying on her stomach with a pillow scrunched beneath her chest, her chin rested in her hands. "Don't tell me you get up this early in the morning?"

Ally's eyes belied something akin to grief. Olivia's heart went out to her. Poor girl, she must be missing her grandmother like crazy.

"No," Ally said quietly, "not usually. I was just thinking about Granny K and wanted to see how she's doing."

Olivia glanced at the monitor and noticed what a spark her granddaughter's voice had ignited on Kathleen's face. "Is that…my angel?"

Moving her phone a little closer to the com link, she answered, "It sure is. She called to check on you."

Kathleen's tear ducts must've discovered an opening. A steady stream of liquid slid down her temples and disappeared beneath the hood of her suit. "Tell her…I love her."

"She heard you, Kat. You two can talk freely."

For the next hour Olivia felt honored to be privy to the extraordinary bond of love between Kathleen and her granddaughter. They shared an easy laugh, a positive outlook, and a common spirit that almost made

Olivia feel like she had been missing out on something significant all of her life.

As Kathleen's eyelids grew heavy, remarkably Ally's did the same. Eventually, Olivia swiped off her phone and dimmed the lights in the chamber on Mars. Both grandmother and granddaughter had talked themselves to sleep.

>>Chapter 13

Within two days Dr. Carter Dunleavy, the Pioneer program director, allowed for a personal communication link to be established between UISC and the Gale family. No more long trips to the space center. Requests for contact with Kathleen had to be submitted to Dr. Dunleavy each day. Without his approval, the link would not be established. Ally immediately set up a time of ten-thirty to midnight. She reasoned Olivia would have thirty minutes to get settled in at her station each night before she linked in. Marc had chosen five o'clock in the morning to spend a few minutes with Kathleen. Olivia found herself looking forward to both Ally and Kathleen's light-hearted banter at the beginning of her shift and Marc's poignant prayers at the end. She thought it odd that Karissa Gale had made no such requests.

A little after one o'clock in the morning on Kathleen's fourth day awake, her mood began to plummet. "I don't know how much longer I can keep this up." It was the first disparaging comment Olivia had heard her make, and it tore through her heart.

"What can I do for you, Kat, dearest?"

Red coloration formed around Kathleen's eyes; she was close to tears. "Every moment I'm awake, I thirst. It's becoming harder to bear. And the metallic smell is almost nauseating."

"That's the smell of space, Kat. I wish we could do something about both of those things for you, but we simply can't. The only thing I can do for you is keep encouraging you not to give up. We need to keep your mind elsewhere."

A grim laugh escaped Kathleen's throat. "I used to be able to motivate my players through anything—pain, fatigue, doubt—but I can't seem to motivate myself through even one of those now." She blinked and a thin stream escaped both eyes.

"That's what I'm here for, Kat. I'm your coach now. I'll be the one to get you through—"

"But for how long?" Kathleen blurted out. "I could be here for months, years even!" Her face crumpled and shoulders began to tremble. Soon they convulsed as one sob after another wracked her body.

Olivia found it gut-wrenching to watch, knowing she was utterly helpless to relieve such emotional distress. "Kat, I'm putting my arms around you right now. Do you feel them? I'm pulling you close, holding you tight. You can cry on my shoulder…it's okay."

The sobs grew louder, her heaving more violent. Olivia began to fear for Kathleen's wellbeing. She was close to calling Dr. Utley for permission to sedate her until one final swell of anguish was released and the whaling subsided. For the next few minutes she wept quietly while trying to convince Olivia that she would be all right. Rubbing her thinly-covered hands across her eyes, she sniffled loudly. "Sometimes…I just need…a good cry."

Olivia laughed, while drying her own tears. "That makes two of us."

After several minutes, the two women talked themselves down from the ledge Kathleen had crawled onto, but the conversation and mood remained somber. Eventually, Victor made his way over and pulled up a chair. Olivia had introduced him to Kathleen two nights ago. It was no surprise that he would be barging in at least once a night—with or without an invitation.

For a while Victor tagged along with the women's conversation, feigning vague interest. But to Olivia's dismay, he suddenly sat forward, spitting out a question Kathleen was not ready to hear. "Do you remember anything about your accident?"

Olivia jammed her hand down on the com button, stabbing Victor with her gaze. "What are you doing? She's not ready for that!" she hissed. "This is not your station to man, Victor. It's time for you to leave."

He threw his hands up in surrender. "Okay, okay. I am sorry. Please remove your scorn." He stood up. "I am leaving."

Olivia glanced at her screen to make sure Kathleen was still okay, then watched Victor's slow retreat. The doctors had all agreed that their patient was not to be pushed or coerced in any way where the accident was concerned. Dr. Yashkin was adamant on that point. If Kathleen were to find out what she had done—whom she had accidently killed—it could cause a devastating emotional cascade. She was to be spared that grief at all cost.

Drawing in a deep breath, Olivia vowed to have Victor banned from the biomedical station. He was a hazard to the mission. She contemplated Kathleen's deeply furrowed brow and hoped she could easily change the subject. Opening the com Olivia said, "Kat, I was thinking I might read to you from your favorite book during our nights together. How would you like that?"

Kathleen took a precious long moment before responding. Unfortunately, she had not been following along with Olivia's change of tack. "I was in my car, right?"

Heart pounding wildly, Olivia felt like pummeling Victor with her shoes—even better, her fists. "Kat, dearest, we don't need to talk about that. Let's just move on. Tell me what your favorite book is and—"

"I was...supposed to meet..." she slowly recalled. "Oh...I don't remember. It's all so fuzzy."

"That's because it's not important now."

Kathleen's brow suddenly smoothed. "In that case...the Bible... and *To Kill a Mockingbird*."

Olivia breathed a deep sigh of relief knowing a potential disaster had been averted, at least for the time being.

Karissa opened the back door to call her daughter in for dinner. She had stopped by their favorite Mexican restaurant for take-out on the way home from the office.

"Oh, hey, Mom." Ally kicked one more shot against the fence before picking up her soccer ball and trotting across the tiny lawn into the kitchen. "I guess you had a good day," she quipped, eyeing her mother's meal choice.

Karissa practically glowed. "I guess I did," she said, a smile tickling her lips. Nothing she cared to share with her daughter, particularly since she had spent the entire day working closely with Randall Thomas. His every brush against her, his subtle innuendos, even the arch of his brow she found intoxicating. Karissa had never taken mood-altering drugs in her entire life, but she was addicted to Randall Thomas just the same.

Ally said the blessing, as she did at every dinner with her mom, and they began preparing their plates with chicken burritos, Spanish rice, and guacamole. Taking advantage of her mother's good mood, Ally said, "Mom, I want to ask you something, but I don't want you to get mad about it. I was just wondering why you haven't decided to talk to Gran in the last few days?"

A tiny groan escaped Karissa's lips. She tried to come up with a plausible excuse. "Sweetheart, in case you haven't noticed, I've had a lot on my plate lately. This is the first night I've actually gotten home before eight."

"But it doesn't have to be a long conversation. You could maybe talk to her for a couple of minutes before you go to bed. We could talk to her together tonight if you want to."

Karissa drew a long breath knowing she would have trouble escaping her daughter's net. Just enough guilt had seeped in to do the trick. "Oh, all right, you got me. What time should I join you?"

Barely able to contain her enthusiasm, Ally told her they would be making contact at ten-thirty. "I usually talk to Gran until midnight, but you can stay as long as you like."

Quietly accepting her daughter's call to duty, Karissa changed the subject to keep from losing her appetite altogether. However, Ally didn't seem to follow her lead. She obviously had more on her mind than Granny K.

"Mom, can I ask you something else?"

Dreading her daughter's hypervigilance, she asked, "What is it, baby child?"

Ally looked down at her plate for a long moment, visibly struggling to choose her next words. When they finally came out, Karissa bristled. "Are you going to divorce Daddy?"

Color rose slowly to Karissa's cheeks. She hadn't intended to have this conversation so soon. But it had definitely been planned for the near future. It might as well be now. "I've been meaning to talk to you about that."

Ally's fork dropped to her plate, her face stricken.

"Sweet girl, listen. I know this is hard for you, and I truly am sorry, but…"

"No, don't tell me." Ally's eyes welled with tears. "I shouldn't have asked."

When Karissa reached across the table, Ally's chair slid backwards. She pulled her hands away. "Seriously, I don't want to know."

An awkward silence ensued before her daughter took one final bite, then headed upstairs. Karissa rested her elbows on the table, staring at the remains of their Mexican feast. Ally's reluctance to hear the truth had left her in a sullen mood. Finishing dinner held little appeal. Not wanting it to go to waste, she covered what was left and placed it in the refrigerator. She would put this conversation on hold for now, but within the next week she not only planned to discuss a divorce with her daughter, but with Marc, as well. It was finally time.

Olivia received an urgent message from Dr. Dunleavy to join a full staff meeting at nine o'clock that evening. She quickly walked Max in the park across the street and settled him inside for the night. Her neighbor had a key to the apartment in case she couldn't get home to feed him and let him out in the morning.

She prayed all the way to the space center, fearing something had happened to Kathleen. Religion had never held any significance in her life, but she had found comfort in the Gale family's prayer bond. Whether there really was a God listening and acting she wasn't sure, but she liked the peace that prayer somehow afforded.

After checking through security, Olivia greeted several colleagues as they made their way to a large room on the first floor usually reserved for press conferences. She found a seat on the second row to the left of the podium. The room was full to capacity with engineers, technicians, lab workers, and doctors. Some of the world's top minds were crammed inside this room.

Striding to the podium with a tablet in hand, Dr. Dunleavy welcomed his team. Olivia was among a host of people who had a great deal of respect for this forty-eight-year-old former astronaut. He led with brilliance and confidence that few could rival. He was tall and athletic with short brown hair and hazel eyes. He had spent six months aboard the international space station at the age of thirty-two. Shortly after returning home he pursued a doctorate in Aerospace Engineering before joining the Universal Intergalactic Space Corporation.

"Good evening, team," he began. "Thank you all for your promptness. I want to start by saying that Kathleen Gale's condition is still quite good, thanks to the zealous care of doctors Utley, Yashkin, and Cole. Ms. Gale has made amazing strides both physically and mentally this week." Olivia felt a slight blush at the unexpected mention of her name. "However, Dr. Myles Ramsey and his deep space orbit and analysis crew have discovered disturbing evidence of an impending solar storm approaching Mars. Unfortunately, due to the storm's trajectory and the current orbital path and rotation of the planet, the Pioneer spacecraft will be affected. I've asked Dr. Ramsey to convey the details to all of you." Dr. Dunleavy stepped back from the podium and nodded his head. "Myles."

"Thank you, Dr. Dunleavy." Dr. Ramsey projected an image on screen of the solar storm in question. "As you can see, this is an image of a massive solar flare." He pointed out the vast, arcing plumes venting high above the sun's surface. "These flares are caused by sunspots, which are larger in size than Earth itself, creating a violent phenomenon that projects magnetized plasma and radiation from the Sun's surface at millions of miles per hour. We've been watching these flares for decades and they appear to be on an eleven-year cycle. Unfortunately, for us, this is an eleventh year, and because of the location of this particular flare, this solar storm is headed directly toward Mars."

Olivia, willing her heart to stay in her chest, felt like racing to the control center to be with Kathleen. Worry seeped into every pore. Surely this would not be how it all ends.

"From our calculations, the storm should affect Mars at approximately 19:55 hours on July 30. That gives us roughly three days to prepare the Pioneer capsule as best we can. There is no way of knowing the severity of the geomagnetic storm, however, we are certain that we will lose all communications with the Pioneer spacecraft during the course of ninety-six hours—in other words, there will be four days in which Kathleen Gale will have no contact with Earth."

Dr. Dunleavy immediately stepped back to the podium. "Thank you, Dr. Ramsey. We'll spare all of you from further details of the solar storm itself. There are obviously several decisions to be made before July 30th." He pointed to the screen at the front of the room, which listed every member of the Pioneer team and their crew assignments. "As you can see, everyone has been appointed a specific duty along with your immediate supervisor for this task. Our top priority is to save Kathleen Gale's life. Whatever you can do to ensure her safety must be done. Your overtime work will be honored. I will be staying at the space center throughout this week in order to avail myself to all of you. And as always, may I remind you of your sworn oath to this mission concerning Ms. Gale's state of consciousness."

Taking hold of the podium with both hands, he leveled an earnest gaze toward the audience. "It is of utmost importance that we not let Kathleen down. You are dismissed."

Olivia hurriedly found her name on the medical personnel list. She would be reporting directly to Dr. Yashkin concerning Kathleen's mental and emotional wellbeing. Dr. Utley headed a team that would take care of all of her physical functions and medical needs.

Running along the corridor to the biomedical station, Olivia's wristband vibrated with a message. She slowed her pace and skimmed the text—it was from Dr. Yashkin. *We must meet in my office before she wakes, to determine the best way to break the news.*

Of course, they couldn't just blurt out that there was a storm heading toward Mars, *and by the way, Kat, you'll be all alone for four days.* Olivia blinked, realizing she was about to rush headlong into something she hadn't thoroughly thought through. She tapped her band and spoke, "On my way," then switched course.

At ten-thirty, as a link between Kathleen and Ally was being established, Olivia felt more fittingly prepared to face the immediate course of action for the night. She and Dmitry Yashkin had prepared a timeline, which included Ally and Kathleen's chat session, another session immediately afterwards with both Olivia and Dmitry breaking the news about the solar storm, and finally a session with the Gale family tomorrow that Dr. Dunleavy had decided to conduct. Olivia noticed Ally's melancholy demeanor right away—not her usual perky self. Eventually, the reason for it became apparent.

"Gran, I need to talk to you about something, but I don't want it to upset you."

"Angel, you know…you can talk to me about anything. I can… handle it."

For a long moment Ally stared at Granny K, who was sitting up in her bed for tonight's discussion. So far, this was the longest period of time that Kathleen had stayed in an upright position. She held to the side of her capsule bed for support.

Quietly, Ally said, "I think Mom is about to ask for a divorce."

Olivia noticed Kathleen's legs start to quiver just before she lowered herself back to a prone position.

"Are you okay, Granny K? I'm sorry, I shouldn't have…"

"No, Angel girl, you should have. I don't want…to be left out of what's going on in the family. I'm only sorry I can't be there for you."

"But you *are* here for me, Gran, maybe not in the way we'd like, but I'm so glad I still have you."

"Me too," Kathleen breathed. "How's your dad taking it?"

"I don't think he knows anything so far. I kind of pushed Mom a little bit tonight at dinner, but I decided I wasn't ready yet, so…we really haven't discussed it or anything."

"Is your mom home right now?"

"She is."

"Do you think she'd talk to me?"

"She told me she would, but I think she's changed her mind. Do you want me to see if she'll come?"

Kathleen folded her arms against her body and captured a deep breath. "No, not yet. I want her to…come to me on her own. Does that make sense?"

"Yeah, I think it does," Ally said. "I'm sorry about everything, Gran."

"Oh, no, my girl, none of this is your fault. I want you to remember that. You have…*nothing* to feel sorry for."

Just before midnight Ally and Kathleen shared a prayer together, then expressed their heartfelt love for one another. Once more Olivia felt deeply honored to witness such a sweet and pure relationship. It somehow made her want to be a better person.

With session one complete, Olivia now turned her attention to the next task. Taking a much-needed swallow of coffee she observed Dmitry Yashkin and Victor Belkin entering the control room together. As Victor walked by, an unexpected chill ran all the way up her spine and she spent the next several minutes tacitly endeavoring to rid herself of a terrible premonition—the death of Kathleen Raines.

>>Chapter 14

W here's your fishing pole, Cupcake?"

"It's in the garage, I'll go get it. That's all I have left."

Marc stood at the back of his jeep, packing everything Ally had just brought out of the townhouse. His two-man tent took up quite a bit of space, as did their two backpacks. He and Ally had learned to live on MRE's (Meals Ready to Eat) a few years ago when they first started camping. It meant a lot less food had to be carried to the campsite. They could eat a hot spaghetti dinner right out of a pouch without any hassle. Of course, a good mess of fish was usually the highlight of their trip as far as dinner was concerned.

Surprisingly, Karissa wandered outside onto the driveway. "Ally's been a whirlwind trying to get ready, I haven't had a chance to ask her how things went with Gran this morning."

Marc rested one hand on the vehicle and slid his sunglasses on top of his head with the other. "It went fine. Kathleen seems well prepared to handle whatever is coming her way." He glanced toward the garage where their daughter was still putting her fishing gear together. "Ally got a little emotional, but Kathleen seemed determined to hold it together for her."

Karissa's gaze rested for a moment on Marc's. "I think you're doing the right thing by getting her away during these four days. She'd just be moping around here worrying about Gran in that storm."

He grinned at her. "Sure you don't want to go with us? It's not too late." Marc knew what Kari's answer would be, but he couldn't seem to give up hope. The sun sparkling in her eyes made him want to kiss her.

"No, thanks. You two can have the wilderness all to yourselves."

Ally came out of the garage with her fishing gear in tow. Noticing her mom, she asked, "What time are you going to the space center?"

"Not until evening. I still have a case to work on at home this afternoon, then I'll head up after dinner. Come 'ere, sweet girl." Karissa opened her arms and pulled her daughter in. They hugged for a long moment before she kissed her forehead. "Try not to worry about Gran while you're gone. When you get home, she'll be waiting for you."

Ally stepped back with a slightly worried look. "You'll be the last one in the family to see her. I hope…"

When Ally's words trailed away, Karissa asked, "You hope, what?"

"I just hope you have a good talk, that's all."

The corner of Karissa's lips turned upward ever so slightly. "Don't worry, sweetheart. I have no intention of upsetting your grandmother. We'll have a great talk. Now, you two get going and don't fret about a thing."

She gave her daughter one more hug and nudged her toward the door. "I love you, sweet girl."

Ally flashed her mom a capricious grin. "You'd better. And for the record," she said while climbing into the jeep, "I love you, too."

"You'd better."

Karissa stood in the driveway watching until the jeep disappeared down the street. As she turned back toward the house, she was surprised by the sudden heaviness of heart. There had been a tiny spark from somewhere deep within that had wanted to go with them. Acknowledging that fact scared her just a little. Karissa hoped she wasn't getting cold feet where the divorce was concerned.

By the time she settled back down to work in her office she was laughing at herself for even entertaining the thought of going camping. In fact, as soon as her thoughts wandered onto Randall Thomas, Karissa's soon-to-be ex-husband was the farthest thing from her mind.

Close to eight o'clock that evening, Karissa arrived at UISC. After making it through three security checkpoints and a half-hour meeting with Jerrod Benton and Carter Dunleavy, she sat down beside Dr. Yashkin at the biomedical station inside mission control. She planned to make this conversation brief and even vowed to tell her mother she loved her, just in case...

The storm was a mere twelve hours from reaching Mars. Kathleen's schedule for the past three days had been much different than before. She was awake during the day learning as much about the space capsule as possible. If the storm knocked out her power, she had learned how to turn on the auxiliary systems while encased in total darkness. Dr. Utley had walked her through every possible scenario should her bio-suit malfunction after a power outage. There was a lot to take in, but she had proven to be adept at memorizing all of the necessary controls.

"Hello, Mom."

"Karissa, is that you?"

"Yes, it's me. How are you holding up?"

A deep breath escaped in the form of a sigh. "Better than I thought I would. I just hope I can remember...everything I'm supposed to."

"Dr. Dunleavy told me you've been a good pupil."

She smiled tightly. "I'm not as worried about remembering everything as..." Her voice broke and Kathleen lay silent for a long moment.

"As what, Mom?"

"As being alone. I'm battling the *what ifs*. What if contact is never established after the storm? What if—"

"Just stop right there," Karissa interrupted. "You do what you have to do minute by minute. Try not to look ahead."

Kathleen blinked nervously. "That's what I keep telling myself." After a long pause, Kathleen seemed to come to a decision. "Listen, Kari...I have something I want to tell you before it's too late. Ally told me the other day...that you were probably going to ask Marc for a divorce, and..."

"You can stop right there, too, Mom." Karissa felt her ire rising.

Dr. Yashkin quietly excused himself and walked to the Onboard Data and Interface station to give them privacy.

"Honey, I don't want to...have an argument with you," Kathleen continued with a wry grin. "Especially since we're eight months apart."

There was such an extended silence she added, "Um, that was kind of a joke."

Karissa cleared her throat and forced a laugh. "Yeah, I know, I know."

"Kari," she sighed, "you've been mad at me all your life."

That statement caught Karissa completely off guard. A tear trickled from her eye running all the way down her cheek. The salty stream reached her neckline before she rubbed it away with the back of her hand. "That's not true," she countered in a shaky yet defensive tone.

"It is, and I know why." Kathleen licked her parched lips determined to press on. "I need to tell you the truth…in case I don't make it. Honestly, I should've told you years ago, but I didn't want to burst your bubble, so to speak. I've realized now, that by…withholding the truth from you, I've caused more harm than good."

Karissa contemplated walking away right then. But her mother continued—unmercifully.

"I'm going to tell you…about your father—things you didn't know about him because you were too young. Kari…this is really hard for me to say, but he had other women in his life. He was unfaithful to me."

Karissa's gaze flickered toward the exit. She didn't want to hear this.

"When you were only three years old I caught him with my young assistant coach. I had come home unexpectedly from a coaching clinic… and there they were…in my bed—"

"Stop it!" Karissa cried out. "I don't want to hear any more of this."

"Kari, honey, I'm sorry. Please…hear me out." Kathleen paused for the course of several heartbeats. "Are you still there?"

As much as Karissa wanted to run, something held her in the chair. Grudgingly, she answered, "I'm here."

"He promised it would never happen again. We actually…went through marital counseling and I gradually learned to trust him again. But the night before his accident, when you were twelve, I got a phone call from one of my best friends. She happened to be…on the same flight with a woman who was met at the airport by a man who welcomed her with a hug and a very passionate kiss. She was shocked to recognize the man…it was your dad. He didn't come home until sometime in the early morning hours, then got up…and went to church with us like nothing ever happened."

Karissa's mouth dropped open. She now realized where all of this was going. She put her hand on her forehead and closed her eyes.

"I know…you heard us arguing after church. I thought my only course of action was to kick him out. He wasn't…even sorry this time. And then—"

Something in Karissa snapped. "You know, Mother, I guess you felt like you had to tell me all of this, but right now, I don't see the point. I'm not sure what you thought this would accomplish, but whatever it was, I hope you feel better now, because I sure don't." She let out an inappropriate word, then stood up. "I have to go. I hope…"

"Kari, please," Kathleen pleaded. "Please don't—"

"Mom, I'm sorry our conversation had to end like this. I know that's probably hard to believe, but I *am* sorry." She shook her head searching for something to hold onto other than anger, but it roared so loudly in her ears there was nothing else. "I wish you the best," she practically snarled and turned to leave. Even Kathleen's tearful pleading couldn't entice her to stay. Would there ever be an end to the pain her mother could inflict?

Thankful to let her car's onboard computer do the driving, Karissa tried to sift through the wreckage of her mother's words. How dare she ruin the image she carried of her father? He had loved her unconditionally—always playing with her, making her laugh, treating her like a princess. Maybe if her mother had tried harder she could've held his attention. Instead, she was always after the next win—another championship. What a farce.

By eleven o'clock Karissa was back in Los Angeles at the law office certain Randall would be there till midnight. She had finally come to a clear decision that he wouldn't be going home tonight at all. Her only aspiration was to escape into his arms. It wouldn't be wrong—she and Marc already had a legal separation, and while he was camping, she would file for divorce.

With every step toward Randall's office her heart quickened. Unbuttoning her blouse a little further, she hoped he would still be at his desk. He wasn't, but there was a faint light underneath the door to his private room—a room with a bed where he sometimes slept after long days. She thought about knocking, but with a seductive smile opened the door instead.

The dim lamp cast its glow on Randall, who was sitting up in bed. He and Karissa locked gazes for a prolonged moment. His eyes spoke to her as plainly as if the words were coming directly from his mouth, penetrating her very core. She detected no remorse—only arrogance. *You're a big girl, Karissa. You knew what I was like*, they seemed to convey.

The woman in his arms was asleep, but Karissa had no trouble recognizing her. How long had she been at the firm? Six months? Seven? Randall had been proud of the new hire. Karissa had often heard him say that with a little more experience, she could be one of the top corporate lawyers in the city. The young woman obviously had no qualms about how to accomplish that feat.

Without a word, Karissa pulled the door closed, half expecting Randall to follow her. He didn't. Dumbstruck, she made her way to her own office, shutting the door behind her. For a long time she stood in the shadows with her palms pressed to the huge glass window overlooking the city. Rain had begun to fall, blurring the city lights. Feeling hollow inside, she leaned her forehead into the cool glass and closed her eyes. How could she have been so foolish? She had come within a breath of giving everything away.

Slowly opening her lids, Karissa glimpsed her open blouse. Heat rushed to her cheeks as her fingers fumbled with the buttons. Pressing her hand tightly to her chest she sat down in the desk chair. "What have I done?" she whispered.

All of a sudden she saw Randall Thomas for who he really was, an egotistical womanizer—someone who couldn't be trusted. And in that same instant, she recognized her father. Karissa had been too young to understand the kind of man he was, but now, it all made sense. Even her school friends had been drawn to her father's flirtatious behavior.

Karissa's next thought struck her like a knockout punch to the chin. It lifted her feet off the mat and left her lying flat on her back. *I'm no different.* She had shoved her husband aside, all for the sake of a prestigious title. She was destroying her family the very same way her father had. Mercifully, she hadn't gone as far, but she might as well have. She had been unfaithful to Marc in her heart for a long time—a man as steady as the rain falling outside her office window.

And what about her mother? She had accused her of unrestrained ambition, but Karissa was no different on that count either. In spite of their similarity, Kathleen Raines had never sacrificed her integrity for a championship. But Karissa had, or at least she had come within an eyelash of doing so. She had been ready to throw away everything in her life that was truly meaningful, for what? Power? Status? A name on the wall? It most certainly wasn't in the name of love.

Karissa's mind jolted painfully back to the scene in Randall's private room. There was only one word she could think of to describe the woman in his bed. Burying her face in her hands she felt a deep sense of shame. That could've been her. By some random fluke she had caught them together. Humiliating tears scorched her eyes. Over the last year she had allowed her self-worth to become entangled within Randall Thomas's opinion of her. It had taken less than five seconds for him to blow it all to pieces. The look in his eyes had totally annihilated her significance as coworker, and even more so, her value as a woman.

Disgrace pulled a tight knot inside Karissa's chest. She had to get out of here, but when she walked into the townhouse sometime after midnight a morose spirit left her completely despondent. There was nowhere to turn—no one to confide in.

At 3 a.m. she drifted into a fitful sleep on Ally's bed, still fully clothed. Her daughter's room had brought some small measure of peace Karissa couldn't seem to find anywhere else. Waking four hours later, she rolled onto her back, draping an arm across her eyes to ward off the bright rays of sun streaking through the window. She should already be on her way to work. Recoiling from the very thought of seeing Randall Thomas, she slowly sat up. Her eyes wandered to a photograph on the mirror. Ally had taken a selfie with her dad on one of their excursions. She studied Marc's rugged good looks and found herself wondering if it was too late. Maybe he had grown tired of waiting—what if he had already found someone else?

Rising to go take a shower, Karissa found herself locked within a deeply personal struggle. By the time warm water pulsed through her hair and over her weary body, she was able to name it for what it was—she was unworthy. For the first time in her life, Karissa felt undeserving of her family's love and trust. Last night's debacle had left her rowing upstream through uncharted waters. Now she wondered if she was capable of turning her painful humiliation into a spirit of humility. And most importantly, did she have the courage to try?

>>Chapter 15

Olivia's voice began fading amidst the communications static, then suddenly vanished.

"Olivia?" Kathleen tentatively spoke. There was no answer. "Olivia!" she shouted.

Except for the whir of electronics all around her, the capsule was encased in silence. She could feel her heart begin climbing a mountain of fear—a mountain she had moments earlier determined not to scale. But her reaction to the lack of human contact was something she hadn't been able to predict. Preparing to face the crisis was one thing, but knowing she was now utterly alone felt devastating—almost crippling.

"Funny what another voice can do," she whispered to herself.

With some effort, Kathleen pulled herself into an upright position. "Lord, I know this isn't your usual habit these days, but if you could start talking to me right now, I'd feel a lot better."

Though the swishing sounds continued, none of them provided the significance of merely one spoken word. This would be the ruination of her spirit—she sensed it in her core. The storm had yet to hit and within seconds, Kathleen felt herself being reduced to hopeless abandonment.

Closing her eyes, she began to take slow, deep breaths. *You can do this,* she told herself. *You can do anything you set your mind to.*

"I can do all things through Christ, who gives me strength." Saying it out loud momentarily shoved away the tendrils of the closest demons. She may have to say it a million times to make it through ninety-six hours, of which only a scant minute had passed.

Tap, tap, ping—tap, tap, ping. A new reverberation outside the Pioneer spacecraft began to compete with the electronic symphony on the inside. Evoking memories of the spring rain on her grandparents' tin roof on their wheat farm in Kansas, Kathleen nearly smiled, until remembering what it felt like to cower in the root cellar to escape a tornado's destructive path. What she wouldn't give for a hole in the ground and her grandmother's consoling arms, as the force of the storm began to drown out her fleeting recollections.

Kathleen had felt thoroughly prepared to face glitches in Pioneer's systems. She knew that as each control panel blinked and choked out, she would immediately proceed into action, bringing backup networks online, tapping into years' worth of auxiliary power. Her fingers lay poised on the sides of her capsule, ready to methodically restore the energy that would sustain her very existence. But in one fell swoop, without the slightest hint of a problem, every single electronic component within the Pioneer spacecraft failed, hurling Kathleen into utter darkness and crushing stillness. An overwhelming sense of dread compressed her lungs so tightly she had to consciously remind herself how to take the next breath.

When oxygen finally inflated Kathleen's lungs, it did so in quick, short bursts of panicked gulps. The sound of millions of particles slamming against her small container on a giant planet muffled the tiny whimpers and groans that came with every labored exhale. For what seemed like precious long minutes her mind raced down a trail of terror—every single life-saving bit of information emptying itself into a bottomless pit. No matter how hard she tried, nothing she had so meticulously memorized and practiced for the last three days remained. Numbness encased her brain…all was lost.

Slowly, Kathleen lowered herself back into a prone position. The darkness was so thick she wasn't sure if her eyes were even open. It was better this way, really. Going home to be with Jesus was far more enticing than living by herself on Mars. A genuine smile eased across her lips, prevailing over the chaotic loss of memory and brain function. The struggle would soon be over. Her eyelids gently descended and a feeling of resolution brought inner peace and warmth within her rapidly cooling chamber.

"Lord, come quickly," she breathed. "I am yours."

> > >

Marc relaxed on a flat rock with his legs immersed in the cool river. The towel across his shoulders and neck warded off the day's scorching sun. He was enjoying watching Ally turn backflips in the deepest part of the inlet pool of water they had chosen for swimming this afternoon. Five feet at its deepest, their swimming hole was protected by several large boulders that had years ago tumbled from the mountain into the swift river. He ran the towel across his wet hair, then laid back, pulling a baseball cap over his face. The warmth began to lull him into sleep until he felt the vibration on his wrist.

Shoving the cap from his eyes, he checked his wristband. It was a text from Karissa. Twice he read it before sitting up wondering if it was a joke. But after a third reading, it finally started to sink in.

"Cupcake," he called. "I just got a message from your mom."

Ally glided through the water and pulled herself up onto the rock beside her dad. Reaching for her t-shirt, she pulled it over her head. "What's going on?"

When Marc noticed his daughter's worried gaze he instantly put her mind at ease. "Believe it or not, she wants to join us."

Ally's brow shot up. "Nuh, uh. Are you kidding?"

"Nope, read it for yourself."

She grabbed his wrist and read it out loud. "I was wondering how to find you all. I've decided to join you for the rest of the camping trip. That is, if it's okay with you and Ally."

"Dad, call her," Ally said excitedly, "before she changes her mind!"

With a gleam in his eye, Marc tapped his wrist phone. Soon Karissa's voice tentatively answered. She remained cloaked, making him wonder if she might already be regretting her text. But, within seconds she was confirming its authenticity.

"I'm already packed, just let me know how to find you."

"Mom, this is awesome!" Ally interrupted. "What made you decide to come?"

There was a slight hesitation before Karissa answered her daughter. "I don't know. I finished up a project at work, and...well, I felt a little lonely around here. You don't mind, do you?"

"Are you kidding? This is like a dream come true!"

"We'll meet you at the park entrance. I'll text you the address," Marc said. "Before you leave, get the one-man tent out of the garage—the orange one. I'll let you and Ally have the tent for two. And by the way, be prepared for a little hike. We're nearly four miles in from the parking area."

Karissa laughed. "Maybe I can get a little help with my pack."

"We gotcha covered," Marc quipped. "We'll see you in about an hour."

When the connection was terminated, Ally stared into Marc's eyes, her grin ever widening. "Tell me that was really Mom."

With a quick smile of his own, he teased his daughter. "I'm not sure who that was, but we better get up to that parking lot to find out."

You're a fighter.

The words were *felt* more than heard. Kathleen lay motionless, fine-tuning her emotional acuity to whatever was awakening from within. Precious seconds passed as she waited for some sort of validation. Suddenly, she was keenly aware of the frigid temperature within the capsule. Her fingers grew painfully numb—it was increasingly more difficult to draw a breath. Still, she lay paralyzed until the voice screamed, "FIGHT!"

She had never risen from her bed so quickly, but now Kathleen found herself sitting straight up, realizing that the screaming voice had been audible. Hers! Like floodgates bursting open, all of the life-saving information she had amassed came gushing back. Her fingers danced automatically along the outside of her bio-bed, pushing critical buttons, making crucial maneuvers to restore the power that would feed her, hydrate her, exercise her...keep her alive.

During her first volleyball National Championship match, Kathleen called a timeout in the fifth set. Her girls had been warriors all season long—battling against bigger, stronger opponents, yet always finding a way to win. There was something deep within each one of their hearts that wouldn't give up. But now, their backs were to the wall. Down 13-9 in a 15-point set, the Pepperdine Waves were two points away from accepting the runner-up trophy.

Holding hands tightly in their huddle, Kathleen gazed into the eyes of her daughters-of-the-court. "I love you," she said with deep emotion, drawing the hands of the players to her right and left up to her heart. The entire team drew their hands upward and close to their chests as well. Their huddle compacted further. "Whatever the outcome five-minutes from now, I could never love you more. We have always had each other's backs—we have given everything we have for each other and not for ourselves—we have kept the faith and relied on our Father who gave each one of you your talents and abilities. It has never been about us." Coach Raines could literally feel the energy from her players as she continued. "Right here, we make our stand— we will fight to the end." Hands now reached inside the circle, high above their heads. "Do what we do," she said quietly. "Do what we do!" her team roared and sprinted out to the court.

Moments later Kathleen stood on the sidelines with a stream of tears flowing freely down her cheeks as she watched her team collapse in a pile of exuberance. She knew better than to join in the fray. They had done the unthinkable, taking the next six points in a row to win the National Championship.

"Do what you do," Kathleen told herself as the lights on her bio-bed rejuvenated. Instantly, she could feel the warmth of liquids pumping through her suit and into her body. "Keep fighting."

In the dim light now cast from her bed, she was able to work on the other systems inside the capsule. Within the minute, an avalanche of pure oxygen saturated the spacecraft and the heating system came online. It took a while for the white vapor trails escaping her mouth to finally disappear, but when they did, Kathleen relaxed her rigid position and breathed a deep sigh of relief. Warmth was soon restored to her fingers and toes. She had won yet again.

> > >

Marc had never heard such a glorious sound. Lying on top of his sleeping bag inside the orange, one-man tent with arms folded behind his head, he couldn't help but chuckle. Ally and Karissa were nearly shrieking with laughter over Karissa's first experience with an MRE.

"Mom, you were supposed to use the spoon!" Ally bellowed from the tent a couple of yards away.

Karissa dissolved into another fit of laughter. "I think I have a heat blister on the back of my throat," she cried, and more giggles ensued.

"Tomorrow, I'll teach you how to eat breakfast."

"Oh, no. I'm not touching another one of those MREs in the morning. Besides, I cheated and brought your Pop-Tarts."

"What!" Ally squealed. "Well, at least we don't have a toaster, so you can't burn yourself."

More laughter drifted upward into the night while Marc basked in the pure pleasure of it all. What did he do to deserve this delightful gift? Only God could've orchestrated such a surprising turn of events. As much as he wanted to join in their laughter, he kept the joy to himself—he didn't want to take a chance on ruining the moment.

Soon, their mirth faded into a quiet conversation. Marc couldn't make out the words, but just the lilt of their voices carried a groundswell of hope to the depths of his soul. Maybe Kari's presence would confer little aid to their marriage, but he could already detect the boon it had brought to her relationship with Ally. Silently he prayed that it would last—so few things ever did where Karissa was concerned.

>>Chapter 16

In cool water up to his waist, Marc glanced warily in Kari's direction. She had been a good sport to swim with them this afternoon, but now she sat wrapped in a towel, hugging her knees to her chest. Her mind was definitely elsewhere. He couldn't help but think she was regretting her decision to join them.

"Come back in," Ally called. "It's too hot to sit out there on the rock."

Karissa's eyes drifted back toward Ally, but her chin lingered on the top of her knees. With barely an acknowledgment, she answered, "No thanks." Then rising to her feet, she added, "I'm heading back to change."

Marc watched her walk up the hill toward their campsite, all the hopefulness he'd felt last night quickly bleeding out. He knew her all too well. *Nothing gold can stay.* Kari had helped him memorize the Robert Frost poem in their senior English class. It had been easy—only eight short lines. Yet he had called that verse to mind many times over the years—it had been a tag line of sorts to Kari's changing moods and whims. He didn't doubt that she would ask them to hike her back to the car this afternoon.

Ally dove beneath the surface, almost certainly hiding her disappointment. Her mother's complexities often wreaked havoc with their daughter's budding emotions. Marc wished Kari could see what she was doing to her impressionable daughter.

Karissa ducked inside the tent and changed into a pair of cargo shorts and white cotton, V-neck shirt. She brushed out her damp, shoulder-length hair before sliding her feet into flip-flops and heading back outside. Marc had strung a hammock between two large pine trees behind their tents. Swaying side-to-side in the shade, it practically called her name. She hadn't slept much last night, unaccustomed to the lack of air conditioning and a soft bed, not to mention the unusual sounds of night activity in the San Gabriel Mountains. More than once she thought she'd heard the distinct cry of a mountain lion. How Ally could sleep through all the noise, she had no idea, but she took some comfort in believing that Marc would be able to protect them.

Grabbing a small camp pillow, Karissa wiggled her way down into the hammock, finally finding a comfortable position, but her thoughts were far from comforting. Every moment she was in this setting with Marc and Ally made her realize how far apart they had grown. The chasm felt overwhelming at times. Over the past ten years she had been physically present at home with both of them, at least up until the separation, but now she realized how little she had invested in a relationship with either one. She had been completely consumed with her job and her life's goal of making partner. Everything else had taken a backseat.

Karissa drew a long breath deciding it would be better to go home. She felt unprepared to face her shame. There seemed to be no way to breach the enormous rift she alone had created.

Unworthy. Every few minutes that one word darted through her head, causing apprehension to spread its wings. She not only bore anxiety over how to repair her relationship with Marc in particular, but what about her job? Should she walk away from something so lucrative? Marc lived on a teacher's salary—albeit a good one, considering the fact that he taught in Malibu, but nothing compared to what *she* brought home.

When a vision of her mother melted into her mind's eye, the angst was almost more than she could withstand. She didn't even want to go there right now. Not one thing was right in her life—not one single, solitary thing. Never had she felt so mired. *Unworthy.*

As her eyelids grew heavy, Karissa's troubling thoughts began tumbling to the back of her mind. The warm, gentle breeze had rocked her into a state of relaxation, momentarily assuaging her misery. A much-needed sleep soon smoothed the worry lines along her brow and sabotaged her intentions of packing for home.

When she awoke, Karissa knew several hours had passed. She was still lying in the same comfortable position she had worked so hard to attain. She guessed it really was possible to sleep in a hammock after all. Hoping not to tip over, she grabbed a handful of fabric and turned on her side, taking in the scene before her. Marc and Ally worked side-by-side preparing dinner around their campfire. Conversation flowed easily between the two and Karissa envied their easy relationship.

Setting her feet on the ground she knew it was too late to leave. Even if she hiked out on her own, it would be dark before she could reach the car. Besides, she didn't relish the thought of coming face to face with a snake or a mountain lion. Only one choice remained: if reconciliation was ever going to take hold, she would need to stay and make the first move. While Karissa's impatient nature told her to jump in with both feet, her heart compelled her to start with baby steps.

"I'm sorry," she offered, approaching the fire. "I left you all to filet the fish I caught this morning."

Ally's smile brought such a delight to her soul, Karissa felt a deep wave of emotion. "It's okay, Mom, we didn't mind."

"Well, I guess you'll have to show me how to clean up after a fish fry since you two did all the hard work."

Marc gave her an easy grin bringing a canvas chair over for her to join them. "You can help us finish cooking, then we'll all clean up together."

While he turned the filets over on the grill, Karissa studied her husband's handsome profile. She could already feel her heart being tugged back to him. What could she say or do to give him a hint that she wanted to start over? This was going to be harder than she thought. At some point he would have to know the awful truth of her behavior with Randall Thomas, but that would come later.

"Can we go tonight?" Ally asked her dad, interrupting Karissa's introspection.

Marc shook his head. "Not yet, Cupcake. The moon will be completely gone tomorrow. Let's wait."

Both Ally and Marc were obviously in cahoots. "Wait for what?" Karissa asked.

"It's a surprise. There's someplace we want to take you."

Karissa rested her elbows on her knees. "Tell me about it."

"Oh, no, Mom. We don't want to ruin it for you. This is something you're going to have to see for yourself."

Casting her gaze back to Marc, Karissa realized he'd been staring at her. His eyes however, didn't falter, but held hers unapologetically. She knew this was her chance. "I'll be here tomorrow night, too," she said softly.

Marc's eyes narrowed ever so slightly—she knew his mind must be overrun with questions about their present situation. He returned a half-smile that gave almost no hint as to what he was thinking. Clearly, she would have to make the first move. Providing they survived another night in the wild, Karissa hoped to find sufficient courage on the morrow to shred her shameful past and start anew.

Kathleen awoke with a start, wondering how long she'd been asleep. As usual, reality set in like a knife to the gut. While she was hoping, by the grace of God, that she had slept for days, deep down she knew it had only been a few hours, if that.

"Is anyone there?" she called tentatively. After a long silence, she sighed deeply. "Well, I'm still here, you know, in case anyone's listening."

It's a wonder you're still here after what happened.

Her brow pressed downward as the thought flickered through her conscience. For the first time, a scene from the past began taking shape in her mind, much like an artist's pencil sketch before beginning to paint. Nothing firm, but the blurry lines were slowly coming into focus.

She had just turned into the parking lot at Ocean Terrace restaurant. Liz and Carolyn seldom beat her there, so she always parked at the top of the cliffs, never tiring of the beautiful view. A barricade, however, kept her from driving to her usual spot. *Why was it there?* Before backing out, she heard a startling knock at the window. Kathleen lowered it slightly for a man in a black suit. "You're fine," he said, pointing toward the barrier that another man was removing. The other man was wearing a black suit, too. There was something about the man's voice...

A shadow fell across Kathleen's face. As quickly as the images had come, they faded away. But at least now all the border pieces of the puzzle were in place. Something had happened after that barricade was removed. With time, she hoped to figure out what that was.

Luckily for her, time was all she had.

> > >

Marc readjusted his headlamp after misjudging the height of the passageway.

"Dad, are you okay?"

Reaching up to his forehead he definitely felt moisture at his hairline. "Yeah, I'm fine, but I think I'm bleeding."

"Stop and let us look at it, Marc." Karissa moved past Ally in the cavern they were exploring and shined her light on his face.

"No, I'm sure I'll be fine. We're nearly back to the entrance."

He started out again but almost immediately felt a trickle of blood down the bridge of his nose. Head wounds tended to bleed worse than any other kind. He was kicking himself for not paying closer attention. If he required stitches, it would ruin their star gazing excursion tonight. *Please, Lord, don't let it be serious.*

When all three made it out into the late-morning sun, Karissa gasped. "Marc, sit down right now. I had no idea it was that bad."

He didn't argue. The sheer amount of blood in the palm of his hand was startling. He was even feeling a little light-headed.

Marc leaned back against a boulder and Karissa knelt beside him. She carefully removed the headlamp, then probed his hairline to find the actual wound. "We need something to stop the bleeding."

"I can run back to camp and get the first-aid kit," Ally offered. "I'll be back in less than fifteen minutes."

Marc didn't like the idea of Ally going off alone but was surprised when Karissa gave her approval. The wound must be worse than he thought.

"Be careful, sweetheart," Karissa told her, "and call me when you get there."

Ally said she would, then took off down the trail at a jog.

"Marc, we need to use your t-shirt to stop the bleeding. I'll help you get it off."

He leaned forward while Karissa gently pulled his shirt over the top of his head. Folding it into a tight square, she pressed it into his forehead. He was fully aware of her other hand resting on his bare chest. For a long moment he probed her face, desperately trying to read her thoughts. This was the closest they had been in over two years—he couldn't remember the last time her hands had touched him so intimately.

Karissa settled in close, keeping good pressure on his head, while he poured water from his bottle onto his bloodstained hand. "Your wound is actually not as bad as the blood is making it out to be," she said.

"Then why did we let Ally run back to camp?"

"Because we need to have a few minutes alone," she answered quietly. Karissa dropped her hand from his chest to his thigh. "I have a confession to make…"

Marc watched her take several deep breaths and noticed the color rising to her cheeks. Dread for what he was about to hear circumvented the pain of his injury. He dried his hand on his shorts and gave her his full attention.

"I've never been the kind of wife you deserved, Marc. I've been headstrong and self-centered. Nearly everything I've done for the past several years has been all about me. But *you* on the other hand…you've been kind and thoughtful, going around cleaning up all of the messes I've made in our family." Tears formed in her eyes and she momentarily looked away.

Marc felt his pulse quicken. Was Kari trying to make amends for the past? If so, what had caused such a sudden turnaround? He forced himself to remain silent, fearful of ruining the moment.

When she shifted her gaze back to his, the egocentric veil had fallen away. Her eyes revealed a deep sense of regret, and something more—passion. He hadn't recognized that emotion in her for the last few years of their marriage.

"Marc," she said softly, "I want you to come home."

He released a deep breath in the form of a groan, liberating years' worth of frustration and pain. Choking back tears of his own, he held her eyes unswervingly. "Kari, I don't know what's happened to bring you to this point, and we need some time alone to sort it all out. But there is nothing on earth that could keep me from coming back home if you truly want me."

"I want you," she breathed in a trembling voice. "I'm sorry I pushed you away. Please forgive me."

Marc cupped the side of her face in his hand feeling the heat pulse through his veins. The moment seemed surreal. He fixed his eyes on her mouth, surrendering to the strong urge to kiss her. When their lips met, she melted into his body and his arms engulfed her.

That's when Karissa's phone chimed. Marc groaned again, releasing his hold on her. She sat up answering breathlessly.

"Mom, are you okay?"

Karissa gave Marc a wide-eyed expression causing him to chuckle. She cleared her throat. "Yeah, I'm fine. Are you at camp?"

"I'm actually on my way back to you guys. I forgot to call when I got there. I'll see you in a few minutes."

"Okay, sweet girl. See you in a few."

Karissa lifted the t-shirt from Marc's head to check the injury. The bleeding had nearly stopped. Still studying the wound, she said, "Set your watch for two minutes."

"Why?" he asked, puzzling over the request.

"Because I need you to finish that kiss before Ally gets back."

Marc gladly obliged, hastily setting his watch. Then, with an eager smile, he wasted no time hauling Kari back in.

>>Chapter 17

Olivia pinched herself to stay awake as Sharon Conner, UISC's Director of Public Relations, laid out a carefully scripted plan during a staff meeting. It was time to inform the public about the solar storm on Mars and the loss of contact with the Pioneer space capsule.

Olivia's stomach had been in knots for the past two days, dark circles ringed her eyes from the lack of sleep. All she could seem to do was worry about what Kat was going through. What was her current state of mind? What if she had been unable to restore power to the Pioneer capsule? They might never know what really happened to her. And even worse, what if Kathleen continued to survive on the planet without any form of communication being reestablished?

Stop it! Periodically screaming those words inside her head kept Olivia's nerves from careening completely out of control. If she allowed it, her emotions could easily overrun her ability to think straight. She couldn't afford to show any kind of weakness if she was going to achieve her goal in the space agency. But right now, Olivia's biggest enemy was time. She had too much of it on her hands. There was so little for her to do until the storm passed over.

When the staff meeting with Ms. Conner ended, Olivia decided to head home. She had stayed an hour past her night shift in order to find out how much information was going to be shared with the media. As much as she would've liked to be around for the press conference at noon, her body was beginning to shut down. She already had the next hour planned out in her fuddled brain—a short walk with Max, an even shorter hot shower, then fall into bed for a very long nap. She grabbed a warm bagel from the lounge and headed for her car.

Even through her grogginess, Olivia knew something was wrong the moment she opened her apartment door. Max always came to greet her at top speed. Many times she had to brace herself to catch him in mid-air. There was no such greeting today. Frantically, she made her way through the living room and both bedrooms. He was nowhere to be found. Dropping her bag on the kitchen table, she ran next door to the apartment of Warren and Jill Byerly, but no one answered her frenzied knock. If Max were inside, he'd be barking his head off.

She ran back to her apartment and grabbed her phone to call Jill, a retired nurse. She knew Warren would be at work.

Jill barely said *hello* before Olivia blurted out, "Have you seen Max?"

"Hi, Olivia, yes, I've got him in the park. Are you home?"

Olivia sank into a kitchen chair, willing her pulse to slow down. "Yes, I was worried something was wrong when Max didn't come to the door."

There was a slight hesitation before Jill said, "Well, I think something *was* wrong in your apartment. Are you inside?"

Olivia felt a chill run the course of her spine. Her eyes slowly roamed about the room as her heart galloped away. "I am," she said quietly.

"Um, if I were you, I'd come over to the park. I'll explain everything when you get here."

Easing out of her chair, Olivia walked cautiously toward the door, opened it slowly, then closed it noiselessly. Once out in the hall, she sprinted toward the building exit and across the street. It only took a moment to spot Jill's short, silver hair, and there was Max on his leash. They were walking toward the park entrance to meet her.

"What happened?" she asked breathlessly, squatting down to take Max in her arms. He seemed fine, kissing her on the mouth, coaxing a nervous giggle out of her.

"Honestly, I'm not sure. Just a few minutes ago I heard Max barking uncontrollably, you know, the way he barks at a deliveryman or a stranger. At first, I thought it was you coming home, but this was different. He was really agitated."

Olivia pointed toward a park bench, and both women sat down. She still cradled Max possessively in her arms. "Was someone at my door?" she asked.

"No, I peeked outside, but the hallway was clear. Warren's going to kill me, because I should've called you first, but I got the key and went inside. It took me a few minutes to coax Max out of the apartment, that's when I sensed something was wrong."

"Oh no, Jill, do you think someone was in there?"

Jill let out a deep breath, worry lines creasing her forehead. "I don't know for sure, but I got the distinct feeling that Max was defending his turf. I was just about to call you when *you* called me."

Glancing across the street, Olivia's intuition told her not to go back to her apartment. Swallowing hard, she said, "As much as I hate saying this, I think we need to call the police. I need to know that it's safe before we go back inside."

Without hesitation, Jill agreed. "I don't care if it's a false alarm. I'm not letting you step foot in that apartment until we know for sure."

Less than ten minutes later Olivia and Jill met two police officers outside the apartment building. After Jill explained Max's odd behavior, the officers told the women to remain outside until the apartment was cleared. Several minutes later, they came back out to escort them inside.

"Ms. Cole, we've checked every inch of the apartment and there's no one here. Does anyone else have a key?"

"Only Warren and Jill, my next door neighbors. They sometimes feed my dog and take him out when I can't get home from work. But she was in her own apartment when Max started barking."

The officer nodded. "Your door lock appears to be fine and all of your windows are secure. But we did find something of interest in your bathroom."

Olivia followed the officers down the hall to her bedroom. The light was on in her bathroom. That was the one place she hadn't searched for Max when she first came home. She asked the policeman, "Did you turn the bathroom light on when you came in?"

"That's what I wanted to ask you. It was on when we came inside."

Olivia's skin crawled. Slowly shaking her head, she said, "It wasn't on when I first came home."

The officer nodded, then asked her to step inside the bathroom. "Does it look like anything is out of place?"

Immediately, she noticed the shower curtain was pushed completely across the rod and bunched at the end of the tub. She never left it like that. She told the officer that she always spread it out to dry after her showers.

"Then that explains this," he said, pointing into the tub.

Olivia didn't want to look inside, but when she finally gathered the nerve, her heart skipped a beat. In the back of the tub was the unmistakable imprint of a man's shoe. Her hand flew to her chest. "He was in here when I came home," she whispered.

The officer confirmed it with another nod. "We'd like you to check your apartment and let us know if anything is missing."

Olivia's hands trembled as she went through all of her closets and drawers. Not one thing seemed to be out of place or missing. "It's all here," she said. "I can't see where anything has been tampered with."

The officers spent another fifteen minutes with Olivia and Jill while finishing their electronic report. "If I were you, Ms. Cole, I'd stay with family or friends for the next couple of days. We'll send a squad car around and check things out for the rest of the week. You also need to talk to your apartment manager about getting your locks changed."

"I will," she said quietly. "And thank you for your help."

"Our pleasure." Both officers picked up their caps off the table, and that's when Olivia noticed her bag was in a different location than where she'd put it when first getting home. It was even open slightly.

"Wait a minute before you leave," she told them. "I think my bag has been moved."

It was a good-sized shoulder bag that could hold all of her personal items as well as her computer and any other tech devices she used at home or work. If her computer had been stolen, she would be most distressed. Although it was heavily password protected, all of her research was on that particular computer. But thankfully, it was still there. Nothing seemed to be missing from her bag.

"False alarm," she said in relief. "Everything seems to be here, too."

The officers grinned, then reiterated the fact that she needed to get her locks changed *today*.

Jill spoke up as soon as the policemen were gone. "Grab your things and head over to our place. You look like you haven't seen a bed in days."

"But what about the lock? I need to—"

"No back-talk, young lady. I'll take care of everything with the manager. You go get a shower and crawl into our guest bed." Jill gave her a warm smile and a gentle nudge. "Warren and I will take care of you and Max for the next few days."

Olivia didn't argue. There was no way she was going to stay in this apartment until she knew it was safe. Packing an overnight case and grabbing Max's bed and bowls, she and Jill headed next door. Soon she was snuggled in bed beside Max, feeling safe and secure.

Just before drifting off, Olivia had one final conscious thought: *What about the micro drive? I don't remember seeing it in my bag.* She told herself it was probably there, and if not, it was safely locked in her desk drawer at work. She was more cautious with that particular item than even her computer. That's where all of her conversations with Kathleen were being secretly recorded.

Time was becoming a problem for Kathleen. Her entire life had been ordered around the hands of the clock. Not knowing the time of day or night made her feel utterly helpless. She needed to be able to cope in this sardine can, but the only way she knew to bring order out of chaos was to manage her time. For a while, she held two fingers below her jaw counting the pulse in her carotid artery. Sixty-five to seventy beats would probably be one minute. Finally settling on seventy, she counted her pulse for the next ten minutes. It kept her lucid until she grew tired of counting—and for what purpose? There was still no way of knowing what time it was.

Kathleen's world began to darken. Positive mental thoughts were hard to come by. Several minutes of dread over her family's situation on Earth nearly incapacitated her—nagging at her nerves—gnawing away bits and pieces of her sanity. Cold chills covered her body and sweat broke out on her forehead leaving her with an icky feeling.

You're stronger than this, Kat. Your body may be on Mars, but your mind can be anywhere. Focus on what you can control, not on what you can't.

The thought was profound, carrying a remnant of grit and courage. "That's right," she said out loud, raising herself up from the bed. "Does the mind rule the body, or the body rule the mind?" She had asked her teams that question more times than she could count. *The mind rules the body*, they always answered heartily.

"Yes!" Kathleen had learned in her first few years of coaching that fatigue was her team's greatest opponent. If she could convince them that they weren't tired, that the match had just begun, that they were still fresh, then they could fight their way through anything.

She spent a long period of wakefulness coaching her girls again. Choosing the team of 2021, Kathleen recreated the season from recruiting the nation's number one middle hitter, to preseason workouts, team-building activities, the opening match, losing to Illinois in the regular season, then rebounding to defeat them in the NCAA tournament. She reproduced as many details as possible, giving her team pep talks and working through post-game stats. Her visualization was thorough, involving the use of most of her senses. Just before taking her team into the national championship match, Coach Raines fell into a deep, and necessary sleep. Her body relaxed, her nerves unwound, and her closest enemy, *time*, finally provided a long respite from the fight.

>>Chapter 18

As dusk fell, Karissa's breath came in quick spurts. She only felt a shade more secure sitting on the ledge between her husband and daughter than she had moments earlier trying to climb down to their perilous perch. Marc had coaxed her off the top of the cliff by promising not to let go of her. "This better be worth it," she told them in a shaky voice after getting settled in.

Ally leaned against her. "Oh, Mom, this will be something you'll never forget."

"It already is!"

"Just try to relax," Marc offered. "Don't think about the height, think about how secure you are on this solid rock. It'll be fine, I promise."

Karissa finally took in a deep breath, letting the cool air fill her lungs. This had not been at all the *surprise* she was expecting. She tried to make small talk, but neither husband nor daughter would respond with more than one or two words. Frustrated, she glanced at Ally, whose head was resting against the rock surface behind them, eyes fixed on the horizon. Marc's posture was nearly identical.

"Is this the part where I'm supposed to be quiet?" she asked sarcastically.

"Uh, huh," they both muttered.

A little perturbed, Karissa wished they had told her straight up what their plan had been. Maybe she could've prepared herself a little better. On the other hand, had they told her they would be sitting on the very edge of death, she probably would've refused to leave camp. She had to hand it to them, they knew exactly who they were dealing with.

As they waited for *whatever it was* they were waiting for, Karissa's thoughts turned to Marc. While he had demonstrated his physical attraction for her earlier in the day, she sensed he still had a long way to go in trusting her. She didn't blame him. The last two years had been rough on him—*she* had been rough on him especially. As much as she hated to admit it, they were probably going to need counseling. But for the first time ever, she was more than willing to fight for her marriage.

The last remnant of light slid away and Karissa began to fear the trek back to camp. What if she was unable to crawl back up to safety in the dark? What if they couldn't get her off this dreadful ledge? What if…

"Oh, my," she whispered, suddenly in awe of the beauty all around them. Her mind couldn't seem to grasp the depth of her view. An ocean of stars engulfed them. All she could do was partake with wide-eyed wonder. She felt like she was floating in the heavens.

Several awe-filled minutes passed before Ally broke into their thoughts. "It's hard to believe Gran is up there somewhere." Those quiet words caused Karissa's heart to shudder so violently her ribs ached. Awe and anxiety immediately switched places. She now felt trapped on all sides. There was nowhere to run from the terrible guilt that swallowed her whole. She drew her knees up tight to her chest as the pain wound a deep path through her.

"You know," Marc said, "we may be able to pick out Mars if we search hard enough."

Karissa let out a moan from deep within, rupturing the solitude of the moment. Both Marc and Ally turned to stare at her.

"Mom, I'm sorry, I shouldn't have brought it up."

Karissa leaned her head back against the rock, tears stinging her eyes. "No, sweet girl, you don't understand."

Ally's arm intertwined with hers. "Then help me understand," she said softly.

Weary of carrying such a heavy burden, Karissa knew it was time to come clean with her family. But when she tried to tell them about her visit with Granny K, her emotions got the best of her. Dropping her forehead to her knees, she began to weep softly. Marc laid a gentle hand on her back, then finally drew her into his arms. Ally released her hold but leaned in close to her side. Marc included their daughter in his embrace, as well. In no way did she deserve such an affectionate gift. *Unworthy.*

After a while, Karissa regained control and sat up ready to confess her dreadful mistakes. She started by recounting the truth about her father that Kathleen had shared with her. "I know why Mom never told me about his affairs—she wanted to preserve my untainted memories of him. But she did so at her own expense. It caused me to distrust her. There were times I hated her for being the one parent I had left." Karissa sighed deeply. "I was so misguided."

She now looked intently at her daughter. "I'm so sorry, sweetheart, for the things I said about your gran. You didn't deserve to hear any of that. And I'm sorry for the way I left things with her before the storm." Karissa's voice quivered. "I only hope I'll have the chance to ask for her forgiveness."

>>>

Ally couldn't imagine the anguish Granny K was suffering from the conversation she had had with her mom before losing all contact. She had been so certain that her mother would be able to keep things civil, considering the circumstances. But learning about her father's devastating affairs must've dealt her a hard blow. She knew all too well how her mother dealt with issues that made her angry.

All of a sudden, the irony of it hit Ally like a slap in the face. She pulled away from her mother, feeling the sting of betrayal.

"What is it, sweet girl?"

Ally wasn't sure how to say what she was thinking, or even if she should. After all, her dad was sitting here with them. An internal battle ensued between confronting and overlooking what she already knew. Ally finally decided to deal with it in the open. She needed to clear the air if she was going to be able to fully trust her mother again. Letting out a faltering breath, she whispered, "What about *your* affair?"

Ally watched her mother's breathing change dramatically. Her chest rose and fell rapidly. Even in the dark, Ally detected a slightly angry look in her eyes. She didn't dare glance over at her dad.

Karissa's voice stiffened. "I planned to have this conversation with your dad *alone*. You're talking about something you know nothing about."

Chin tilting upward, Ally didn't back down. "I saw you with him."

Karissa stared out into the night. After a long moment Marc broke into the awkward silence. "We don't have to do this right now."

"Apparently we do," Karissa said quietly. Recapturing Ally's gaze, she said, "I don't know what you saw, but whatever it was, I'm sorry... truly I am. What happened between me and the man from my firm was a mistake. But there is something I need you to know, Ally. And Marc, I want you to hear this, too. I never had an affair with him, or anyone else for that matter. Yes, I was wrong to do the things I did, and I was wrong to entertain the possibility of an affair. But I promise you with all my heart, I have never slept with any man except your father. Never."

Relief washed over Ally like a spring rain. It would take a long time to erase the image of her mother kissing another man, but down deep, she believed her. In her heart, she knew her mom was telling the truth. Tears spilled over her eyelashes and her mother reached to wipe them away. "Please forgive me," she breathed. "I never meant to hurt you."

Ally bobbed her head, releasing more tears. "I forgive you, Mom."

Karissa tenderly kissed the tears from Ally's cheeks, then cradled her daughter for a very long time. She was very much aware of Marc's presence, but he didn't touch her. She wondered what was running through his mind after hearing her confession. Relief? Maybe. Anger? Possibly. Forgiveness? Hopefully. There was still so much more she needed to say to him, but not in front of Ally. She wanted her husband back, but this time around, things would be different. *She* would be different.

"Mom?"

"Yes, baby?"

Ally moved out of her arms, as Karissa continued stroking her hair. "I want Dad to tell you what his grandpa told *him* up here."

Taking a sip of the night air, Karissa cast a wary glance toward Marc. He was leaning back against the rock, staring at the panorama. Without turning toward her he said, "My grandpa first brought me up here when I was ten. As much as he wanted me to experience God's creation, he wanted me to understand God's grace even more."

For the next several minutes, Marc explained the vastness of God's amazing grace and mercy. Karissa was mesmerized by her husband's smooth voice and straightforward message. He wove a beautiful picture of the essence of God's love for all of creation—particularly the ones made in His image.

When he fell silent, Karissa didn't know what to say. She felt so corrupt deep within her soul. All her selfishness and impure thoughts had led her down a path so far away from God, she didn't know if it was possible to find her way back. Truthfully, she had never really given God a chance in her life at all. The door to her heart had slammed tightly shut when her father died, and she had never ventured close to it again. Now she felt compelled to draw near—her hand was poised to knock.

Karissa took a nervous breath. "I feel so…stained. What if I'm beyond redemption?"

"You're not," Marc responded fervently. "No one is ever beyond God's grasp."

Resting her head against the rock, Karissa contemplated her next words. "I was so close to giving my life to Christ when I was young. So very close. But when my father died, I allowed anger to control my life—I never really gave love a chance." Her eyes stung with tears, once more. "I want to start over," she said, her voice breaking. "I need to feel clean, but I don't know how."

"It starts with believing. Let me read you something." Marc unzipped a pouch on his jacket and pulled out his phone and pressed the Bible application. He scrolled to a place in the book of John and read the words of Jesus and his disciples. "Then they asked him, 'What must we do to do the work God requires?' Jesus answered, 'The work of God is this: to believe in the One he has sent.'"

"Kari, the first thing you need to do is simply *believe* in the One God sent. Jesus goes on to say, 'For my Father's will is that everyone who looks to the Son and believes in him shall have eternal life, and I will raise them up at the last day.'"

> > >

It was well past midnight when Kari waded out into the river with Marc and Ally. He told her that every stain from the past was about to be washed clean by the blood of the Lamb—she would soon be a new creation. Kari couldn't think of anything more fulfilling than that and proclaimed her belief in Jesus, the One and Only.

"We're going to hold you under a little longer than necessary," he said. "We want you to remember this night forever, and your commitment to walk a new life with Jesus."

A smile turned her lips. "I'm ready to die to my old self. Hold me under as long as you see fit."

Beneath the dark water, Kari felt the hands of her husband and daughter pressing her shoulders. *Oh God, wash me clean.* Seconds before they lifted her back to life, a new word replaced the old. It was only a whisper, but she heard it as sure as she was alive—*worthy.*

When they brought her up out of the river, tears of joy intermingled with the water trailing down her cheeks. She found herself enfolded within Marc's arms as she pulled the night air into her lungs. "I'll be here for you every step of the way," he promised. "You don't have to do this alone." Then he kissed her forehead and released her.

Their daughter stood in the cold water, hugging her arms to her body. When Kari turned, Ally threw herself into her embrace, sobbing. "I...love you...so much, Mom," she managed to utter.

Kari drew her tighter to her chest. "You'd better. And for the record," she said, kissing her cheek, "I love you more."

Several minutes later, Kari and Ally emerged from their tent sporting jeans and sweatshirts. Marc already had a fire roaring in the pit. "This is nice," Kari remarked, taking the canvas chair beside his.

Ally moved her chair a little closer to the fire, rubbing warmth back into her hands. Kari noticed how tired she looked. "Hey, sweet girl, why don't you go on to bed? I need to let my hair dry out by the fire for a while." Ally remained by the fire a little longer until her eyelids refused to cooperate. Nearly sleepwalking, she got up and kissed both parents, then headed for bed.

Kari, on the other hand, felt like her night was just getting started. There were so many things she needed to get off her chest—things that only Marc would be privy to. They talked quietly long into the night, crying at times, laughing at others. The longer they talked, the lighter her burdened past became. And though Marc admitted his struggle in accepting Kari's sudden change, she assured him over and over that time would prove the sincerity of her heart. His forgiveness had come swiftly and without condemnation, but she knew the barrier between them would take weeks, perhaps months, to completely fall away.

At three o'clock in the morning, they finally decided it was time for bed. As they stood, Marc took her into his arms. "Keep believing, Kari. Commit for the long haul and His grace will do the rest."

"Thank you, Marc," she breathed into his chest, then let go and walked toward the tent.

Marc knelt beside the fire pit and stirred the embers, making sure it was safe for the rest of the night. When he turned back around, Kari was standing at the entrance to *his* tent, drawing back the flap. He didn't move, holding her gaze for the space of several heartbeats. Finally, he closed the distance between them and gently cupped the side of her face. "Are you sure about this? If you need more time—"

Kari drew his head down to hers and kissed him long and slow. Then without a word, she took his hand and pulled him inside the tent.

The next morning Marc found Ally sitting in the sunlight on the riverbank, hugging her legs to her chest. He ambled over and sat down beside her. He could feel her gaze, but kept his eyes on the river. Finally, she shoulder bumped him and he glanced sideways at her. "What?" he asked.

The grin on her face was precious.

He cleared his throat. "Oh, breakfast? No, I haven't eaten yet. What about you?"

She rolled her eyes and he looked away trying not to laugh.

Another shoulder bump—this one a little harder.

"What?" he asked again.

"You tell *me*, Pops, and this is not about breakfast."

"First of all," Marc responded, "*Pops* was my grandfather. Let's just keep it at *Dad*."

When he fell silent, she bumped him one more time.

This time he looked her full in the face, brow raised. "What?"

"Dad, I'm not a little girl anymore, you know." She giggled. "Mom didn't come home last night."

Marc laughed, his brown eyes shimmering in the sun. "Okay, okay. You caught us."

Ally turned to face him, sitting cross-legged. She rested her elbows on her knees. "Does this mean you're coming home?"

He gazed at his beautiful daughter for a long moment. The joy in his heart was nearly overwhelming. He had waited so long to say these words to her, but had feared the opportunity would never come. *With God, all things are possible.* "Yeah, Cupcake," he said, years of heartache gushing into the river. "I'm coming home."

They talked for quite a while until both of their stomachs started growling. Marc leaned over and kissed the top of her head before standing up. "I'm gonna head back to camp and see what we can scrounge up food-wise. It's a good thing we're going home this afternoon. We don't have much left."

"I'll be up in a minute," Ally said. "You know, give Mom a chance to get up."

Marc winked. "Good idea, Cupcake."

Ally never dreamed of such bliss in her family. For as long as she could remember there had been an underlying tension. As a kid, she hadn't understood the cause of it, but at nearly fifteen she was beginning to understand the complexities of relationships. She realized how much her dad and Granny K had sheltered her from what was really going on.

Scanning the opposite bank for wildlife, her eyes caught a tiny movement beside a large pine. Yesterday she had spotted three deer in that location and was hoping for another siting. At first, she stared intently, then quickly moved her gaze elsewhere, her heart pounding wildly in her chest. She knew she needed to sit here for a few more minutes, but panic was starting to seize control. *Breathe, Ally, breathe.* Picking up a rock by her side, she lazily threw it into the river, two more followed. Pretending to be bored, she stared up into the cloudless azure sky. *Oh,*

God, help us. Moving her gaze slowly downward she trained her eyes to the right of the pine tree, searching the shadows with her peripheral. No mistake. The man in black with dark glasses was still there, a very large gun strapped to his side.

>>Chapter 19

One last rock splashed into the river before Ally rose to her feet. She made her way back to camp at an unhurried pace. It took every ounce of self-control to hold her legs back from an all-out sprint.

As she walked into camp, her mom was taking their dry clothes off the line and folding them to be packed. She turned with a smile that instantly faded. "Ally, you look like you've seen a ghost. What's wrong?"

"We have to get out of here right now," Ally whispered vehemently.

Marc immediately dropped the corner of his tent and rushed to her side. "Sit down, you don't look well."

"Dad, I'm not sick, there's a man out there watching us."

Marc felt his pulse quicken. "What do you mean? Where?"

Quickly, Ally described the man standing in the shadows, including the gun at his side. "He was watching me—he had been watching *us*, Dad!"

"Show me," Marc demanded, feeling his blood boil.

"Marc, no!" Kari cried. She grabbed his arm. "He's obviously dangerous." Letting go of Marc she took Ally by the shoulders. "Does he know you saw him?"

"No, I pretended nothing was wrong. I stayed at the river longer than I wanted to just to make sure he wouldn't think I spotted him."

"Good girl. We should just go, Marc."

Although he wanted to see this man for himself, he knew Kari was right. If his family was in danger, he wanted to get them out of these mountains as quickly as possible. Plagued by questions of who this man was and why he was there, Marc helped his family get packed and they hit the trail within half an hour.

"Ally, you take the lead and I'll take up the rear. Both of you keep your eyes peeled and your phone in your hands." Marc followed behind Kari with a knife in one hand and a hatchet in the other.

Kari kept glancing at him with a worried look. "How do you think he found us?" she asked softly.

Wondering the same thing, Marc tried to ease *her* mind, if not his own. "They probably tracked our vehicles to the parking lot, then spent the rest of the time searching for us. We can't worry about that now. I'm sure it's the FBI or some other government agency. Who knows, maybe they were sent to protect us."

Neither of the women fell for that one. "Highly unlikely, Dad."

They remained silent for most of the four-mile hike, stopping only once to lay down their packs and take a drink. Each one pounded down an energy bar, then grabbed up their load again. Marc didn't exactly feel comfortable carrying such a large pack that obstructed his rear view, but if they could keep up this pace, they should be back to the parking area a little after the noon hour.

By the time they got Kari's car and Marc's jeep packed, all three were exhausted. "Why don't you two ride together," Marc suggested. "I'll follow behind."

Once settled in the car, Kari left the driving to her onboard computer. She wanted to keep a sharp eye on their surroundings. She knew Marc would be doing the same thing. Ally pulled out her tablet for the first time to see if there was any news about the storm on Mars. She and her dad had made a pact that there would be no electronics on this camping trip. Except for the texts with Kari, they had been totally unplugged from society for four days.

Kari leaned toward her daughter, anxious to see what news they could find. For a long moment both of them sat in utter shock. One of the top hits on Ally's news feed read, "Pioneer Woman Lost in Space."

Every minute felt like an hour, every hour a day. Kathleen knew beyond a shadow of a doubt that four days had long passed. Everything around her seemed fuzzy, the lights blurred, the sounds dulled. She now spent the majority of her time in a reclining position with no desire to give her arms and hands a workout or exercise her mental toughness. Doubts about keeping herself alive constantly invaded her mind. Why had she fought so hard to live like this? It hadn't been worth it.

Sitting up grudgingly, she focused on the connection at her hip to the bio bed. One tug and her misery would be over. The hunger pangs would eventually vanish and her thirst would be quenched. No more loneliness. Who would ever know what she'd done?

I would know.

Even in her bio suit, Kathleen felt the hairs on the back of her neck rise. She took in a shuddered breath, feeling her chest tighten. "Oh, Father," she breathed. "Help me break free of this existence." Tears escaped her eyes, moistening her cheeks. She rested her hand lightly on the tube connection.

Seek the kingdom, first.

Her hand began to tremble. "I'm so tired. I need to rest."

Immediately, Kathleen's thoughts plunged toward the night her husband was killed. *That dreadful visit from the police at ten o'clock—waking Kari from sleep to tell her the awful news about her father—trying to juggle a funeral, a full coaching schedule, and a mother's responsibilities all within the same week. Family and friends coming and going—it had all been overwhelming. Her life spun wildly out of control until she was nearly paralyzed by fear. She remembered sobbing alone in her bedroom one night and opening her Bible. It wasn't an instance of letting the pages fall where they may, but she had subconsciously turned to Matthew chapter six and started reading. Jesus' words at the end of the chapter filled every void that very night. "Therefore I tell you, do not worry about your life..."*

Kathleen breathed deeply through her nose, then released the air through her mouth. Her hand eased away from the tube at her hip.

Matthew 6:33 had changed everything for her during that time. She had read that scripture all her life, even sung songs about it, but had never had the opportunity to fully trust Jesus on his promise until that horrific week. "But seek first his kingdom and his righteousness, and all these things will be given to you as well." That was all she had left back then; there had been no other choice but to seek his kingdom and his righteousness. Every time she saw 6:33 on a clock or on her watch, she'd stop and pledge, "I'm seeking your kingdom first, Lord." All of her other troubles seemed to fall to the wayside. She trusted Him fully.

Looking back on it now, she could see how God had worked everything to her favor and had led her every step of the way. Sad to think she had never taken Jesus up on his promise until all else had failed. She wished she had a clock in her chamber on Mars. At least twice a day at 6:33 she could be reminded to seek His kingdom first.

"Do not worry about tomorrow," Kathleen pronounced out loud, "for tomorrow will worry about itself. Each day has enough trouble of its own. *Verse 34*," she said with emphasis.

Without warning, Kathleen's bio suit began her exercise routine— she felt the activity commencing with her feet. Immediately lying back down, she allowed her body to be led through each movement. It struck her for the first time that the same regimen occurred every twelve hours. *Every* twelve hours! *Oh, Lord, why didn't I think of this before?* Now she had something to hold onto in the storm.

"I deem this exercise time to be 6:33 in the morning," she declared. "My next one will be 6:33 in the evening. Now I can count my days!" She smiled brightly, new life coursing through her veins. Kathleen finally had a driving purpose—something she could hang onto with both hands, the tube connection at her hip all but forgotten.

To say that Olivia was surprised was putting it mildly. Shocked was more like it. Thinking she was answering her phone to Ally Gale, she was taken aback to be connected with Ally's mother, Karissa.

"Mrs. Gale, I wasn't expecting to hear from you."

The screen widened, including the whole family in Olivia's view. She waved. "It's good to see all of you."

Ally and Marc both said a brief hello.

Mrs. Gale cleared her throat, her words amazingly nonabrasive. "Ms. Cole, thank you for taking our call. We've been camping in the wilderness for the past four days without being able to receive news until now. Have you been in contact with my mother?"

Olivia shook her head, letting out a sigh. "Unfortunately, we haven't been able to reestablish communications with her. The storm passed a few hours ago, but so far, there's no link. I came in early so I could be here for her."

"We want to be able to talk to her as soon as you regain contact. I plan on calling Dr. Dunleavy today, as well. We noticed the space agency released information about the solar storm. We came home to another batch of reporters on our lawn."

"Oh, yeah," Olivia said. "I forgot they'd be hounding your family again for a statement. I'm really sorry about that."

"We'll manage the reporters for now. I mainly wanted to check in with you about communications. Ally tells me she trusts you implicitly where her grandmother is concerned."

Olivia thought she detected a shimmer of tears in Mrs. Gale's eyes. "Ally is very special to me. I'm glad that I can be here for her. It's been such a privilege to be a part of her conversations with Kat."

After a brief pause, Olivia continued. "Actually, Mrs. Gale, I think it would be helpful if you and I could have a private conversation soon. Would that be possible?"

She noticed Karissa glance at her family for a moment then look back. "I'll move to my office. We can speak privately there."

Olivia waited until she was assured of privacy. She dreaded the subject she needed to discuss, mainly because of the reaction she might receive.

"We're alone now," Mrs. Gale finally said.

"Um, Mrs. Gale…"

"Please call me Kari," she quickly asserted.

"Okay…Kari. One of my duties with the space agency is to take care of your mother's emotional wellbeing. The reason why I take that job so seriously is because I care a great deal for her—Kat and I have grown extremely close since she awakened."

"Thank you for that, Ms. Cole. I'm sure you've been a great strength to my mother in this situation."

For a moment, Olivia thought she might be talking to an imposter—a twin sister, maybe. "You're welcome to call me Olivia," she offered, before proceeding with such a hard conversation. "Mrs. Gale…I mean, Kari…your mother was in a very agitated state before the storm hit Mars. I was called in to help calm her nerves and offer her as much reassurance as possible. It really wasn't an ideal situation when we lost contact with her." Olivia drew a nervous breath, remembering how worried she had been about Kat. She feared her distress would cause her not to be able to act if she lost power. Honestly, she still feared the worst. "There have been some discussions over the past four days, and I'm not sure how to tell you this...it would've probably been better in person. But we feel it would be prudent for you not to speak with your mother when we reestablish contact with her."

Kari felt her heart crushing like a piece of tin foil. Olivia's words left an ache so deep she felt like sobbing. Just another reminder of how thoughtless and self-absorbed she had been.

"Ms. Cole, I know my mother and I had an argument before all of this happened, and believe me, I'm not proud of that fact. But I simply need the opportunity to talk with her again."

"I'm really sorry, Mrs. Gale, that's just not going to be possible. It's not even my decision—it comes from the top."

Kari swallowed hard, she felt her natural anger rising to the surface. But that was her old way of life—that was who Karissa had been. Calmly she said, "I understand the decision that was made—I deserve that. Would you at least do me a favor?"

"Sure, if it's possible."

"When...and if...you reestablish contact, please leave the decision up to my mother as to whether she wants to talk to me or not. Trust me, I want to make things right with her. Could you please ask her what *she* wants?"

"And if she doesn't want to speak to you?" Olivia asked.

"Then I'll respect her decision. But Ms. Cole, I think I know what my mother will say."

Olivia gave her a thin smile. "Honestly, I think I know what she'll say too."

After her phone conversation, Kari went back to the front room to find it empty. Following the clanking in the kitchen she saw Marc putting together a mid-afternoon snack of fruit and granola. She watched him for a long time without his notice. She had married a man who lived to serve—he had always been the giver, she had mostly been the taker. Now that the eyes of her heart had been opened, it was almost like understanding him for the first time. Her heart beat faster just looking at him. Karissa had rejected so much of Marc's way of life for the past seventeen years. Now she wanted to embrace everything about it. Standing there in the kitchen doorway she gladly confessed that she was in love with the man…deeply in love.

Marc must have felt her presence as he turned to face her, a smile touching his lips. "Is everything all right with Olivia?"

Kari nodded. "It will be. But that's not what I want to talk about now."

"Oh, really?" Marc's smile broadened as she pressed up against him.

"Really," she whispered close to his mouth.

Teasingly he asked, "Then what did you want to talk—"

Kari gave no chance for him to finish his sentence, as she made it very clear talking was not on the menu.

Ally stopped on the lower stairs, catching a glimpse of her parents' passionate embrace in the kitchen. Instead of feeling uncomfortable, she watched for a moment, then turned and quietly headed back to her room with a spring in her step and a grin on her face.

>>Chapter 20

By Kathleen's estimation, three full days had passed since she began counting exercise sessions. It had helped her focus on her true priority, seeking the kingdom first. A greater trust in God left her feeling more at peace and able to make it through the arduous days. It even helped her sleep better at night...or at least what she believed to be night.

Family had been on her mind constantly throughout this ordeal. She had tried so hard not to dwell on the unfortunate episode with Kari, but it continued to harass her at every turn. Kari and Marc would most likely be going through a divorce by now. Oh, how she longed to be there for her angel, Ally. What must *she* be going through?

Kathleen's mind wandered down a senseless path. What would life with her daughter have been like if she had told her the truth about Kyle soon after his death? She could imagine Kari being terribly upset, but Kathleen could've helped alleviate her adolescent fears and emotions. Within a few months they probably would've had a close and loving relationship. Why had she allowed her daughter's anger to fester and grow?

Just then a loud cracking noise shattered her reverie. A hissing sound and a tiny trail of smoke emitted from a small panel to her left—a panel far beyond her reach inside the capsule. She watched the instrument lights flicker on and off. A loud pop caused her to scream—her body jerked wildly. All of a sudden, she was driving her car into an unfamiliar parking area. It was around a curve, farther away from her normal spot. Something about it didn't look right, but the man in the suit told her it was where everyone would have to park today. She pulled off her sunglasses to see the spot more clearly. It appeared to be protruding out over the cliff, like an optical illusion. But as she pulled closer, she could see the parking barrier that would stop her wheels, so she continued inching forward. At the last second Kathleen slammed down hard on her brakes—it felt like her front wheels had run out of solid ground. Grabbing the steering wheel tightly, both feet jamming against the brakes and floorboard, she glanced at the man for help. He stood back away from the car, nodding his head menacingly, urging her into nothingness.

Kathleen emerged from the trance gasping for air. Perspiration broke out on her brow. Fear ruled her heart. Whatever happened that fateful day, she had been coerced into it. Her accident had been no accident at all—she had been manipulated into that parking spot, of that she was certain.

>>>

Seven days had come and gone since the solar storm struck Mars. Olivia continued working her shift, night after agonizing night, with not even a blip on her monitor. If *she* was falling into despair, what must Kat be feeling?

"Do you think she's still alive up there?"

Olivia's doleful eyes rested on Mason. If she didn't look away from him, she was going to lose composure, but something compelled her to hold his gaze.

"You know," he said, in a sympathetic tone, "you got your hand restin' on all the answers, don't you?"

She looked down where her fingers had been drumming on top of the two books at her station. "*To Kill a Mockingbird?*"

Mason chuckled softly. "No, ma'am, I mean the Word."

Olivia's fingers smoothed the leather cover tenderly. She loved books—the feel of the pages, the crackle of the spine. She much preferred holding a book in her hand than reading on a tech screen. She sighed deeply, "I was reading passages to Kat before…"

"Her faith is strong," he declared, pulling up a chair. "You can read to me a little, if it would help you pass the time."

"Mason…I don't know…"

"Oh, come on," he urged. "Just read me something from the Psalms. It'll do us both good."

A grin turned her lips as she contemplated his plea. "All right," she said, turning on a small light over her station. Opening the Bible to Genesis, she began a painstaking search for the Psalms.

"It's in the middle," Mason told her with no censure.

She cleared her throat when she found the book. "Here it is. Do you have a preference?"

He leaned over a bit. "What've you got there?"

"Psalm 139."

"Perfect, go ahead."

Running her hand across the page, she took a long breath. "You have searched me, Lord, and you know me…" After a few verses, she glanced up at Mason. His eyes were closed—such a peaceful expression on his dark face. She went on.

"Where can I go from your Spirit? Where can I flee from your presence? If I go up to the heavens, you are there; if I make my bed in the depths, you are there. If I rise on the wings of the dawn—" Olivia's voice broke as she felt the warmth of tears. She tried to continue reading, but her voice quavered and she had to stop.

Mason lightly patted her hand and slid the Bible onto his lap. "Let's see…If I rise on the wings of the dawn, if I settle on the far side of the sea, even there your hand will guide me, your right hand will hold me fast."

Olivia cried softly as he read the remaining verses. When the passage was complete, a long silence fell between the unlikely companions. Mason finally closed the Bible and laid it in her hands. "We may never know what happened to our dear friend," he quietly remarked, standing up beside her. "But she's never once been out of God's grip—not even in the heavens." Gathering up his cleaning supplies, Mason slowly made his way to the exit while Olivia reopened the Bible and made her way back to the Psalms.

Just before her shift ended Olivia was roused from deep introspection by a commotion at the communications control center. She left her station and ran across the room toward the animated cluster of technicians. Dr. Dunleavy stood to the side, hands on his hips, intently observing the communications team at work. The sleeves to his dress shirt were rolled up, usual tie missing, and hair a bit disheveled. They must have woken him for whatever was going on.

"Ms. Cole," he said, inviting her to stand beside him. "We may have made a breakthrough."

Her heart accelerated into another gear while watching the team in action. As several white-knuckle minutes passed she began to fear what they would find. She suddenly felt weak in the knees at the thought of seeing Kathleen again, especially if she were no longer alive.

Dr. Dunleavy must've read her thoughts. "Here, let me get you a chair."

She waved him off. "Oh, no. That's not necessary, but thanks."

The glitchy screen suddenly cleared and the communications team began congratulating each other. The camera lens was focused on the capsule's ceiling and Travis, one of the team technicians, took control. As the lens made its descent, an eerie hush came over the small gathering. No one dared move. Olivia held her breath.

The camera swept downward finding Kathleen's feet, then upward to her knees, her hips, her midsection. Everyone leaned forward in anticipation as the camera moved to her chest and face. "She's definitely breathing," Travis announced. Cheers and congratulations broke out.

Olivia was beside herself with relief. "Can she hear us?"

"Let's hope," Travis answered. He turned to face her. "Would you like to do the honors?"

Tears instantly filled her eyes. "Yes," she breathed, stepping up to the panel.

Travis opened the communications link and moved aside.

"Kathleen?" Olivia called in a shaky voice. "Kat, dearest, can you hear me?"

Kathleen's eyes promptly flew wide open. Her arms and legs flailed as she tried to sit up.

"No, Kat, just relax. It's me, Olivia. We finally got the communications back online. Stay calm. I'm here with you now."

Kathleen took several deep breaths as if trying to find her voice. "Oh, thank God," she finally rasped.

A great hoopla commenced as agency workers came together from all over the complex to surround the communications center. So many vied for a prime position. Dr. Dunleavy finally projected Kathleen's image onto the big screen up front. As the day shift arrived, dozens more flooded into the giant control room. The hubbub of the surrounding crowd was of little consequence to either Olivia or Kathleen. The two women chatted and laughed and shared stories as if they were the only two in the room…long lost friends, finally and gratefully reunited.

When Kathleen drifted off to sleep a few hours later, Olivia took the opportunity to rest as well. After calling Jill to make sure Max would be taken care of, she grabbed a blanket and pillow stashed away in her file cabinet and headed for the couch in Dr. Yashkin's office. He and Dr. Utley would be busy all day running tests and making sure Kat's bio-bed and suit were functioning properly. They promised to let her know if Kathleen should awaken.

At four o'clock in the afternoon, Olivia's phone alarm roused her from a deep sleep. Five uninterrupted hours left her feeling refreshed for a change. After checking in on Kathleen, who remained fast asleep, she freshened up in the restroom, then headed to the cafeteria. Dr. Yashkin joined her for dinner.

"She is much stronger than I ever imagined," he commented from across the table.

Olivia agreed. "I'm looking forward to spending private time with her tonight. I'd like to know what her true state of mind is, and how she kept from going completely bonkers up there all alone for seven days."

Dr. Yashkin's expression stiffened. "Did you get a sense from her this morning that her memory from the accident had returned?"

Finishing her bite of baked potato, Olivia shook her head. "I didn't see any indication of that. Did you?"

Visibly relaxing, he concurred with her opinion. "I still believe it would be in her best interest emotionally, to stay away from that particular subject. The fragility of her psyche must be preserved at all cost."

"My thoughts exactly. I'll probe carefully tonight."

For a while the two ate in silence before Dr. Yashkin spoke again. "Olivia, Dr. Utley and I are most grateful for the work you've done with Kathleen. She has needed a trustworthy companion, and you have provided just that. There is no one else here who could have taken on such an important role."

Flushed with gratification, Olivia beamed. Maybe this would be the opportunity she had been seeking to move into a more important position. But his next words came like a bolt out of the blue, leaving her fearful and confused.

"When the experiments are concluded, I'm sure you will miss your friend dearly."

That night Olivia sat quietly at the biomedical station contemplating Dr. Yashkin's statement at dinner. She had been so taken aback she hadn't found the words to respond before he excused himself from the table. When she looked for him later for clarification, he had already gone home for the night. What could he have meant? Was she being moved into another job or perhaps losing her job altogether? And what about Kathleen? Did the doctors know something about her condition that they weren't telling her? It was all so mysterious.

Willing her mind not to jump to conclusions, Olivia decided something had been lost in translation with Dr. Yashkin's English. She drew in a deep breath, letting it out slowly. She needed to be relaxed and cheerful when Kat woke up. Grabbing her bag from the floor she plopped it in her lap and gazed about the room. There were some extra team members at the communications center still working on a two-way video feed for the Pioneer capsule. She noticed Donald Graham moving back and forth between their station and his. As usual, Victor Belkin was in a semi-conscious state beneath his headphones. She was certain he would make an appearance at her station later in the night. Now was the time to get the micro drive in place.

Olivia searched each pocket of her bag more than once. Finally, she removed every single item and turned it inside out. No micro drive.

It had completely slipped her mind to look for it after the apartment break-in. She hadn't needed it for the past seven days.

Convinced that Kat was still sleeping soundly, Olivia rushed from the control center. Just outside the main lab, inside her cubicle, she pressed her thumb print to the scanner that unlocked her desk. There was a small compartment at the back of her top drawer that only she knew about, but the space was alarmingly empty. Frantically, she pulled the drawer completely off of its runner and searched again. Squeezing her eyes shut, she felt her heart plummet over a dangerous precipice. Whoever had been in her apartment a week ago had come for only one thing—the micro drive.

Fortunately, Kathleen had yet to recall any significant details of her accident—the micro drive was essentially worthless. But Olivia knew, should Kathleen ever remember what happened that fateful day, both of their lives would be forfeit.

>>Chapter 21

Kari's hands still gripped the steering wheel long after her car's engine shut off. She didn't even notice Marc coming out of the townhouse into the garage. When he tapped lightly on the window, she turned her head to meet his gaze. Reality settled in like an unexpected tragedy and she lost her composure.

He had the door open in seconds, pulling her into his arms. "Babe, it's all right. We'll get through this together." Marc held her tenderly, kissing her hair. If it had been anyone else, Kari wouldn't have allowed such vulnerability. But she had learned over the past few days what it meant to trust this man, and more importantly, what it meant to trust her heavenly Father. Trust required giving up power—something she had ferociously held onto in the past, but at a terrible cost.

Feeling a little embarrassed by her lack of control, Kari tried to step back, but Marc held her firmly against him. "Don't move yet, just let me hold you." She had to admit, her husband's arms were much preferred over the turmoil she had just endured at the law firm. Randall Thomas had not made her resignation an easy one.

Marc eventually loosened his hold and led her toward the door. "Let's go sit down and talk about it…if you want to."

"I do," she admitted quietly. "Where's Ally?"

"She headed to the beach with Reagan and her family. She's actually spending the night. They wanted to have a last summer hurrah before school starts next week."

Kari was thankful for Ally to have a semblance of normalcy back in her life. Their family had been living under so much stress for the past year, mainly due to Kathleen's accident and Kari's own disastrous decisions. At least by repairing her relationship with Marc, Ally no longer had to worry about her parents splitting up. That situation had weighed heavily on their daughter.

"You want some coffee or tea?" Marc asked.

"Mm, tea sounds good." Kari kicked off her heels, threw her jacket in the chair, and nestled down on the couch pulling her feet up beside her. She had dressed in her best professional skirt and jacket to face the partners of Thomas, Tanner & McGill.

Marc handed her a hot cup of tea, sweetened just the way she liked it. He sat down beside her with his hand resting on her legs. "I'm really proud of you, Kari. That had to have been hard."

"You have no idea." She went on to tell him how she stood her ground, despite the fact that they offered to nearly double her salary. "They really put on the hard sell."

"Tempted?" he asked.

"A little. I'd be lying if I said the numbers didn't turn my head, but…" Kari's mind instantly snapped to the difficult situation she had found herself in when the other two partners left Randall's office. His remarks and behavior had turned completely inappropriate. If money couldn't woo her back to the firm, Randall planned to use other means, even pressing her to join him in his private room.

"But what?"

Kari felt the warmth rise to her cheeks and prayed Marc wouldn't notice. "There is no amount of money that could get me to stay at that firm. I'm sure another door will open soon." She took a sip of tea and set it on the table. "Marc, I feel the need to apologize to you again for my behavior. I want you to know," her voice broke as tears swelled. "I *need* you to know how sorry—"

"Kari," he interrupted. "I've already forgiven you. There's no need for you to keep apologizing." His hand slid up her arm until it rested on the side of her face. "What you had to do this morning was tough, but you did it. That part of your life is over and done. Don't ever go back

176

down that path again." He kissed her affectionately, then turned her away from him and pulled her up against his chest, enfolding her in his arms.

They stayed in that position for quite some time before Marc broke the silence. "Do you mind if I get up for a second?"

She released his arms and sat up. He had a devious look on his face. "What's going on?"

Marc didn't answer as he took the stairs two at a time. An instant later he was back standing in front of her. She started to get up but he pressed his hand on her shoulder. "No, stay right where you are."

Unexpectedly, he went down on one knee and held out the engagement ring he had given her seventeen years ago. He must've gone through her jewelry box while she was away this morning.

His handsome smile caused her heart to palpitate. "Kari, would you do me the honor of marrying me...again?"

Joy bubbled up inside as if this were Marc's first proposal. Teasingly, she answered, "Only if the ring fits."

He slid it easily onto her finger, then captured her gaze with a roguish expression. "Well? What say you now?"

"Oh, Marc, I say yes! There is nothing on earth that could keep me from marrying you...again. I love you so much."

"I love you, too," he said, before kissing her more thoroughly this time around.

Over lunch on the patio, Marc and Kari made plans for a small ceremony and a second honeymoon during his fall break. He told her he would stay at his apartment until then if she preferred. "Are you kidding? Not a chance. Let's get that thing cleaned out tomorrow. I don't want you ever leaving my bed again."

Marc chuckled. "I was hoping you'd say that."

Kari's phone chimed. Immediately her playful demeanor slid away. "It's Dr. Dunleavy. There must be news about Mom." She swiped *reveal*.

"Dr. Dunleavy."

"Hello, Mrs. Gale. I called to let you know some good news. We've been able to reestablished communication with the Pioneer capsule, and more importantly, with your mother."

"Oh, thank God. How is she?" Kari pressed.

"Surprisingly well. Olivia spent a few hours with her yesterday, but she's been sleeping soundly ever since. I think it's safe to say she didn't get much sleep over the past week."

"Dr. Dunleavy, I really need to talk with my mother when she wakes up."

"That's one of the reasons why I called. She asked for you before she went to sleep. We had a meeting this morning about your situation." When he paused, Kari bit her lip trying not to encroach on his hesitation. "We've decided to rescind our earlier decision."

"You mean I can talk with her?"

"Yes. We plan to wake her late this afternoon, unless of course she wakes on her own before then. I wanted your family to know that we will not be able to reestablish a personal com link for you at home. There are still complications from the storm's aftermath. Unfortunately, that means you'll need to make a trip to the space center to talk with her."

Kari took in a frustrating breath. "That *is* unfortunate, but I understand. May we come in this afternoon?"

"Yes, if you come around four o'clock she should be awake."

Thanking him for the call, Kari hung up and leaned back in her chair. While she looked forward to clearing the air with her mother, she didn't relish the thought of humbling herself in front of the staff at the space center. If only her conversation could be held in complete privacy she might be able to save face.

At four o'clock Marc and Kari made it through the last security check. They'd decided not to contact Ally about her grandmother since it would be a huge temptation to share the news with Reagan. To be honest, Kari was surprised her daughter had held out this long. Ally and Reagan were practically joined at the hip. They'd been sharing their deepest secrets since third grade.

Drs. Dunleavy and Yashkin met the Gales inside the control center. Kathleen's image was projected on the screen at the biomedical station, but thankfully not on the huge screen up front. She appeared to already be awake.

Before the communications system was activated, Dr. Yashkin brought them up to speed on her physical and emotional condition. "First, I will talk to her for a few moments, then allow you to have time with her." He leveled a chary gaze toward Kari. "Mrs. Gale, please be careful with your words. We are doing everything we can to keep her calm."

Dr. Yashkin's condescending attitude was enough to make Kari want to scream. She swallowed an inappropriate phrase, reminding herself she no longer used such words. Even so, the old habit was rearing its ugly head. She merely nodded her assent to the doctor, biting back her irritation.

Kari watched with interest as her mother and Dr. Yashkin spoke. It was a very impersonal conversation, nothing like the ones with Olivia Cole. Something about this man made her uneasy. Maybe it was the fact that he was a Russian and relations still remained strained between their countries. Not to mention the fact that it was the Russians who had demanded restitution for her mother's accident. Whatever the reason, Kari would rather be sitting here with anyone other than Dr. Yashkin.

"Kathleen, we have two visitors here to speak with you today. Your daughter and son-in-law are here. Do you still want to speak to your daughter?"

Kathleen remained in a prone position, color flooding her face. "Oh, yes, I need to speak to her. Kari, are you there?"

Kari leaned in close, her voice tight with emotion. "Yes, Mom, I'm right here."

"I never thought...I'd ever get a chance to talk to you again." She took in a shuddered breath. "I almost died."

A tear slid from Kari's eye. "I'm so sorry, Mom, but you're still here. That's all that matters. I have something I need to say to you."

"No, honey, I want to go first. They told me I was alone for seven days, so I've had a long time to think about this. I want you to know how sorry I am for telling you about your father. You've gone all your life without knowing what happened, it was foolish of me to tell you now. I desperately need you to forgive me."

"Mom..." Kari didn't have a clue where to start. The words she'd practiced all seemed so empty, like a well with no water. Emotional tears spilled onto her cheeks. "There are so many things I need to share with you, but right now, there's only one thing I want you to know...I love you."

Kathleen's anxious expression immediately changed to one of astonishment. Clasping the side of her bed, she pulled herself into an upright position. She took several shallow breaths, obviously trying to keep her composure. "Oh, honey, I love you too. I love you more than you can possibly imagine."

Both women laughed quietly with a joy neither had experienced in each other's company in over twenty years. It somehow slid back the bar to the locked prison cell Kari had been living in. She finally felt free to share her life with the one woman who deserved it the most.

"Mom, I actually want to *thank* you for telling me about Daddy. If it hadn't been for that revelation, I'd still be living in my own little messed up world. But hearing the truth helped me take a hard look at what I was doing."

Kathleen sat in stunned silence while Kari went on.

"I've made some pretty drastic changes in the last few days. I quit my job this morning."

"Oh, Kari…"

"No, it's fine, Mom. I know I can find another one. It's just a matter of putting myself out there again at the right kind of firm this time. I've also accepted another proposal of marriage from Marc." Kari turned a dazzling smile toward her husband. "He's sitting here with me now."

Kathleen clasped her hands to her chest. "That is the most wonderful news I could ever receive! Congratulations, you two. And Marc?"

"Yes, ma'am, I'm right here."

"Thank you for not giving up on our Kari. You are the finest man I have ever known."

Kari felt a twinge of guilt squeeze her heart. She had wronged Marc in so many ways over the years. She knew there would be subtle reminders occasionally thrown in her face, but that still didn't keep the sting away.

"Thank you, Kathleen, but Kari hasn't told you the best part yet." He glanced at his wife beneath a raised brow. "Do you want to tell her?" he whispered.

Laying a gentle hand on his arm, she shook her head. "I want you to tell her."

"Tell me what?" Kathleen asked breathlessly.

Marc leaned forward with a stouthearted grin and proceeded to tell his mother-in-law all about Kari's new life in Christ. They talked for the better part of an hour, all three sharing in God's great mercy and hope for their lives. As the afternoon turned into evening, Kari finally heard the prison door slam shut—and this time, by God's perfect grace, she was standing on the other side.

>>Chapter 22

The control center was surprisingly empty at one o'clock in the morning. Donald Graham had stopped by the biomedical station for a brief chat but was now working in another part of the complex. Olivia contemplated Victor Belkin's whereabouts. She hadn't seen him since her shift began. Even the communications team was at work in their lab on the second floor tonight.

Sitting down with a fresh cup of coffee, Olivia poured over Dr. Yashkin's report for the second time. Kathleen's session with her daughter and son-in-law earlier that day had gone much better than anyone ever expected. Olivia leaned back in her chair observing Kathleen as she slept in semi-darkness. She was itching to wake her up, especially since the two had yet to speak since their initial conversation after the storm. That had been two days ago on Wednesday. She longed to ask Kat about the reconciliation with her daughter. Even more so, she wished she could've been here to witness it for herself.

At one-thirty, Olivia's yearning got the best of her. Kat had been sleeping for the better part of six hours and an empty control room was too good to pass up.

"Kat, dearest, time to wake up," she spoke softly.

Kathleen's lids fluttered open slowly.

"It's me…Olivia. Do you mind if I turn the lights up a bit?"

"No," she rasped, covering her eyes with her hand. "It's so good… to hear your voice again."

Olivia only bumped the light up enough to see her more clearly. "I heard you had a great visit this afternoon with your daughter. Do you want to talk about it?"

Kathleen seized the chance to fill her in on all the details. Olivia was amazed by Kari's sudden transformation. She only hoped it was genuine for Kat's sake. But genuine or not, it had done a world of good for her friend's emotional stability.

After a while, Kathleen grew pensive. There was something she wasn't telling her. "What is it?" Olivia asked.

She didn't respond right away but slowly came to an upright position. After a short bout of coughing, Kathleen said in a dry voice, "I remember what happened before my accident."

Olivia's eyes snapped to the secret micro drive nestled in its place, then quickly scanned the control room. They were still alone. Heart pounding wildly she spoke in an ominously low voice. "What do you remember?"

Kathleen described the moments leading up to her accident with surprising clarity. There was no doubt that her comprehension of that day was accurate. She had been steered toward that particular parking spot with intent—intent to kill the Deputy Prime Minister of Russia. This was the moment Olivia had been trained for. She knew what she had to do and she went about her mission swiftly and efficiently while continuing their conversation.

"Kat, dearest, I need you to listen to me very carefully." Olivia was already wiping the video hard drive clean and replacing it with a video feed of Kathleen sleeping peacefully. As she reset the time stamp on the feed she instructed, "You mustn't talk about this with anyone else."

"But what about—?"

"Hush," Olivia hissed, her nerves getting the best of her. She grabbed a deep breath. "I'm sorry, Kat, I didn't mean to talk to you like that. But I'm very serious. This information needs to stay between you and me for now. I'll take care of everything, I promise."

Kathleen's brow wrinkled deeply. "Olivia, what happened...*after* my accident?"

Olivia closed her eyes briefly and shook her head. She couldn't concentrate on what she was doing and talk to Kathleen at the same time. It was imperative that she get this right. There could be no trace left of this conversation.

"Hang on, Kat. There's something I need to take care of. Just give me a moment."

"Okay," Kathleen breathed unsteadily. She lowered herself back into the bed, folding her arms against her body.

At that very moment Victor Belkin entered the control room. *No, no, no.* Olivia silently willed him to walk a separate path to his station, but he was headed directly her way. Her hands finished one last stroke on the control panel then fell to her lap.

"Ah, she wakes."

"Yes, Victor. Is there something you need?"

"Why so angry with me? I only want to see how our Pioneer Woman is doing."

"Fine, Victor. She's doing very well. I'll let you know if anything changes."

When he reached for an empty chair, Olivia held up her hand. "Oh, no you don't. I seem to remember Dr. Yashkin telling you not to spend time at the biomedical station. Move along. You've checked in, now you can leave."

Victor's churlish smile was maddening. He looked at his watch, then ambled away causing Olivia's heart to turn over in her chest. What if he remembered seeing Kathleen awake at this very time?

Olivia knew she was being followed home as sure as she knew Max would be waiting for her. She congratulated herself on hiding the micro drive in the secret compartment at work instead of carrying it in her bag. She couldn't take a chance on it getting into the wrong hands. Having proof that Pavel Vasiliev was essentially assassinated was a heavy weight to carry by herself, but it was imperative that she shoulder the burden alone until the time was right. What she did from now on could have momentous consequences.

Instead of entering her own apartment, Olivia knocked on Jill's door.

"Well, good morning, neighbor. Would you like to come in for a cup of coffee?"

"No thanks, I'm afraid I don't have time for that now. I was wondering if you could do me a huge favor?"

Jill opened the door wider. "Anything. What is it?"

"Would you mind taking care of Max over the weekend? I have something related to work that I need to focus on so I won't be staying at the apartment."

"Sure thing. Max can come over and keep me company." She followed Olivia down the hall and into her apartment.

Olivia took a few moments with Max before handing him off to her neighbor. "You have no idea how much I appreciate this. I should be back by Tuesday."

Jill helped gather up all of Max's things, then wished Olivia the best in her work endeavor. "We'll be waiting for you when you get home."

Minutes later Olivia had a bag packed and a taxi on the way. She instructed the cab driver to pull up behind the parking garage on the backside of the apartment building. She would sneak out the basement door under the cover of the garage and into the waiting cab. Changing clothes and putting her blonde hair beneath a wide-brimmed hat transformed her appearance sufficiently to lose whoever was following her. A hotel room not far from UISC would be her home for the next three days. She didn't like leaving Kathleen in such a vulnerable position during the day, but she also couldn't hang around after her shift for no apparent reason. Everything would need to continue as normal—even though nothing would ever be normal again after Monday.

Kari lay on her side in bed watching Marc sleep. Though it was barely six o'clock in the morning she wanted to talk. "Marc, are you awake?" she probed.

"I am *now*," he answered, turning over on his back.

"Good. I was wondering something."

She noticed the hint of a smile as he opened his arm to her. Scooting over to his side of the bed she laid her head on his shoulder.

"What could you possibly be wondering at this time of morning?" he asked, hugging her close.

She draped her leg over his, resting her hand on his chest. "Is this right?"

Marc's eyes opened a little wider. "What are you talking about? Are you having second thoughts?"

"Oh, no, not at all. I mean…we're still legally separated. We haven't had the lawyer go through the reversal process yet."

"And?"

Marc's sleepy response made her giggle. "*And*, I was wondering if us being together, you know, like this, is right in God's eyes?"

When Marc didn't respond, Kari raised up on one elbow. She needed to see his eyes.

He gently smoothed the hair away from her face taking his own sweet time before answering. "Kari, technically we're still married. We never went through with a divorce, so I think it's safe to say that us being together *like this*, is not wrong." He gave her a lopsided grin and started to pull her back down, but she obviously had other plans.

"Good," she said, dropping a kiss onto his shoulder. "That makes me feel better." She instantly threw the covers back and got out of bed.

"What are you doing? Like I said, it's okay for us to be together."

"Oh, I know. But we have so much to do today. Let's get over to your apartment and start cleaning it out, then I'll call the lawyer and have him start the reversal process."

Marc folded his arms behind his head chuckling as Kari continued her *to do* list from the shower.

> > >

Mired by suspicion, Kathleen was unable to sleep. For the first time in her relationship with Olivia, she wasn't sure if she could fully trust her. They had conversed quietly for a very long time after her disclosure about the day of the accident, but frankly, Olivia had done most of the talking. She had made it absolutely clear that Kathleen was not to discuss this topic ever again—not even with her. Her instructions were to feign memory loss. And if she found herself struggling with

187

such a heavy burden of secrecy, she would need to use the phrase, "My throat is hurting," to which Olivia would respond with understanding and encouragement. It would be their little code. Unsure of how that was supposed to help the situation, Kathleen now felt utterly vulnerable. Something was dreadfully wrong and she knew it had to do with whatever had happened after her car went over that cliff.

Dr. Utley talked with Kathleen for a short time after coming into the lab that morning. He had been curious to find her still awake. Kathleen told him she'd slept most of the night, then felt a spasm of guilt about telling a lie. Worry and guilt and suspicion were uncomfortable companions.

Oh, how she longed to talk openly with her family. They were coming to visit again on Sunday after church, this time with Ally—what if she told them everything? But would that put them in a dangerous position? For a long time she prayed and contemplated her options until her thoughts turned into strange images and her body rolled on the waves of slumber.

> > >

When Olivia came back to work at ten o'clock, Victor Belkin was the first person she met in the control room. "What are you doing here on a Saturday night?" she asked curtly.

A humorless smile turned his lips. "I could ask you the same question."

She was quick with a lie. "I have to take a couple of days off next week, so I'm working Saturday and Sunday night."

For once, Victor had no retort. He simply walked away to his station and applied his headphones.

Drawing in a nervous breath, Olivia checked her monitor for the first time. Kathleen was sitting up in bed. Her hands were at work on a nearby panel. Immediately she activated the com system. "Kat, dearest, what on earth are you doing?"

"You mean Mars?"

It took a moment for her response to register, but when it did Olivia chortled. "Let me rephrase that question. What on Mars are you doing?"

"Apparently no one's told you."

"Told me what?"

"I'm working with the communications team. We're trying to get a video connection in this crate."

Olivia picked up Travis' voice. It seemed strange hearing him inside the Pioneer capsule when she knew he was in the building on the second floor. Immediately she rolled her chair back. "Tell Travis I'm on my way up to his lab."

"He just heard you," Kat replied.

Moments later Olivia watched a small crew of tech guys lead Kathleen through several intricate procedures. Travis tried to explain the details of the operation to Olivia, but she couldn't understand their complicated lingo. Although she had been trained in computer science while on the job, her college degrees were actually in biological engineering and medical technologies. Electronics at this level were mind-boggling.

Travis clapped his hands together. "Coach, you did it! Now, turn the lens toward the white panel at the foot of your bed."

Kathleen adjusted the lens until a fuzzy image was projected onto the surface. "That's me," he told her. "I'm Travis Bolton."

The look on Kat's face was priceless. "Oh…" She took in several quick breaths. "Travis, it's so nice to meet you."

"I think there's someone else you'd probably like to see for the first time." Taking Olivia by the arm he pulled her into view. "Coach Raines, I'd like you to meet Olivia Cole."

Kat blinked back tears. "Olivia," she breathed, "what a beautiful sight you are to me."

"Oh, Kat, dearest, this is wonderful."

Travis only allowed a short conversation before butting in. "Sorry, ladies, I'm going to have to cut in on your chat. We have several things we need to do on our end to clear up the image a bit." His eyes met Olivia's. "We'll be down within the hour to hook up the camera at your station."

True to his word, Travis and two of his team members showed up at the biomedical station with a cartload of equipment. It took the better part of three hours to bring the camera online. Kathleen dozed on and off during that time, the work on her end mainly complete. Olivia took the opportunity to check on the micro drive inside the compartment of her desk. To her relief, it was still safely hidden. At eight o'clock Monday morning she would be able to hand it off, her work concluded. But she was determined to keep her assignment at UISC as long as possible. She loved Kathleen dearly and wouldn't dream of leaving her now—the very thought of it made her shudder.

By four-thirty in the morning Olivia and Kat had been talking to each other *face to face* for over an hour. Thankfully, Victor had vanished to another part of the building. One thing they didn't need was that man prying into their business.

"Would you like me to read to you?"

Kathleen lay back in her bed, eyelids tilting downward. "I'd like that," she sighed. "I need to rest in the Word for a while."

Olivia opened to the Psalms, eager to hear the words for herself. There was such peace among the verses, yet surprisingly sprinkled with violence. She determined to read more about the life of King David on her own.

After several minutes Olivia felt a hand settle on her shoulder. She jumped, having heard no one approach. When she saw who it was, she relaxed, "I'm sorry. You startled me, I didn't hear you come in."

Kathleen's eyes immediately opened and her gaze flickered toward the video panel. For an instant she lay frozen in place, then in one great gasp, she cried, "My throat is hurting!"

>>Chapter 23

Kathleen's reaction left no doubt in his mind that she had just recognized him from the parking lot on the day of the assassination. Why had he not been informed about the two-way video feed coming online? This was a most unfortunate situation. He immediately reached for the communications switch and the screen went black.

Olivia turned stiffly to face him, confusion scrawled across her features. He had always liked her, even respected her for the way she carried out her duties at UISC. But her usefulness had now come to an end—just like Kathleen's. Restitution had been executed for Russia in the most unlikely way possible. No one could've written a more bizarre scenario. *Random individual manipulated into assassinating the Deputy Prime Minister of Russia—said individual survives with permanent brain damage—enter Universal Intergalactic Space Corporation proffering a solution to prevent war—Russia stakes its claim to Mars.* It was a perfect sequence of events…until the *Pioneer Woman* awakened.

His mind now calculated every possible course of action. Only he and Olivia were in the control room. Its vast darkness and the perfect location of the biomedical station meant he could do what was necessary and be long gone before anyone ever discovered Olivia's body. He would be in Russia by midnight with a fresh identity and a new assignment.

Olivia seemed to find her voice. "What are you doing? I need to help calm Kathleen down." When she reached for the com switch he grabbed her wrists in a tight vice and pulled her up out of the chair. Her eyes grew wide with fright. With a surge of adrenaline, he took both wrists in one hand and covered her mouth with the other. One strike of his knee to her abdomen and she collapsed to the floor, air driven from her lungs. He easily dragged her petite frame behind a large control panel near the wall to finish the job.

Moments later, he returned to the biomedical station inserting a key into the cover of the cremation switch. Flipping it open, his forefinger lingered below the red switch while he contemplated watching the demise of Kathleen Raines. A charge of self-preservation exploded through his veins and he decided to forego the spectacle. Instead, he quickly destroyed the communications link. Then, with a smirk of pride, he flicked the switch upward.

>>>

Mason Hill entered the control room from a door at the back. His gaze was immediately drawn to something crumpled on the floor along the wall. Moving closer he realized it was Olivia lying in a strangely awkward position. Heart stampeding through his chest, he ran to her side dropping to his knees. Placing two fingers beneath her jaw, he desperately searched for a sign of life. There was a tremor of a pulse, ever so faint. He inwardly cursed the clause in his contract that forbid him to carry an electronic device at work. He needed to call for help without delay.

Panic-stricken, he pulled himself up and searched the control room. Victor Belkin stood hunched over the biomedical station. Something was wrong—the screen was blank and Victor seemed agitated. Mason started to ask for help, but instantly choked back the words. *Someone* was responsible for Olivia's condition—what if it was Victor? He made a hasty decision to run for the door at the back. Olivia's life was now in his hands.

At that very instant, Victor turned around, stabbing him with his gaze. Mason froze—his feet had become blocks of cement.

"Where is Olivia?" Victor questioned, moving intently toward him.

Mason stepped in front of the large panel. "Stay right where you are," he called. Though Victor was younger and of stockier build, Mason was determined to protect Olivia at any cost.

Surprisingly, Victor halted. His eyes narrowed shrewdly. "Something terrible has happened. I need to know where Olivia is."

Before he could catch himself, Mason glanced back at the young woman on the floor. That was Victor's opening. He closed the space between them in three giant steps and stared behind the panel at Olivia's motionless body.

Victor immediately knelt beside her, speaking in frenzied Russian. He grabbed Olivia's wrist, then switched to English. "Go for help, *now*."

Mason didn't move. He was afraid to leave Olivia alone with Victor Belkin. This could all be a ploy to finish what he'd started. Then again, if he waited too long, she might die anyway.

Thankfully, Carter Dunleavy entered the control room on the opposite side and Mason felt a flood of relief. He wouldn't have to make such a critical decision after all. "Over here!" he yelled, waving his arms wildly. "I need your help."

Dr. Dunleavy zigzagged through the maze of control stations until he stood before them. His eyes grew wide at the site of Olivia's body on the floor. "What happened?"

Victor stood to face him. "Someone has tried to kill Olivia, and what is worse, Kathleen Raines has been cremated."

Horrified by the news, Mason turned and ran from the room, determined to call for help.

Eating Sunday lunch at their favorite Chinese restaurant, Ally chattered excitedly about seeing Granny K for the first time since the storm. Kari had to admit she was looking forward to this visit, as well. She felt compelled to prove that the confession to her mother had been sincere, and the only way to do that was by continuing to visit with her on a regular basis. They had so much of life to catch up on. Even so, Kari shouldered a tremendous load of guilt concerning Kathleen's current location. Not even her newfound faith could alleviate the feeling that her mother's bleak future on Mars was entirely her fault. There seemed no escape from the ache.

"Mom, what did you think about this morning?"

Kari yanked herself away from such torturous thoughts, giving her daughter a stilted smile. Her first time back to church in years had thrown a little more fuel on the fire of anxiety. "It was good. I'm glad I went."

"Everyone was so pleased to see you," Marc interjected.

Honestly, Kari hadn't expected such warm hospitality after being away for so long. But she had found herself in the embrace of numerous church members welcoming her back into the fold. Unaccustomed to feeling so self-conscious, she doggedly stayed by Marc's side throughout the morning, hesitant to fully engage. She realized, like everything else in her new life, this too would take time.

Two hours later Marc dropped his window for the security guard at UISC, alarmed by the extraordinary number of cars in the parking area and the mass of FBI vehicles and personnel roaming the grounds. "What's going on?"

The guard bent closer. "There's a press conference in an hour. I've been instructed to lead your family to a separate entrance."

Kari leaned around Marc. "Why the press conference? What happened?"

If the look on the security officer's face was any indication, something terrible must have taken place. Instead of answering her questions, he simply replied, "Follow my vehicle."

A thick silence fell among the three as Marc trailed the officer. No one wanted to be the first to speculate what could've happened. It had never been first nature for Kari to pray, but she was praying now, pleading for her mother's welfare.

Public Relations Director, Sharon Conner, met the Gales at their car. She and two more security officers rushed the family inside through a private entrance. Within minutes, they were seated inside Jerrod Benton's paneled office. This time, instead of a lawyer at his side, the corporation's CEO was flanked by Carter Dunleavy and Dmitry Yashkin. Ms. Conner also remained with the small gathering.

"Mr. and Mrs. Gale, and Ally," Jerrod Benton began, "we have some difficult news to share."

Kari felt Ally tense beside her and immediately reached for her hand. Deep down she feared the worst but held on tightly to a single strand of hope.

"Early this morning, an incident occurred at the biomedical station. Olivia Cole was assaulted and is barely clinging to life in an intensive care unit. I'm so very sorry to inform you that the perpetrator also activated the cremation system in the Pioneer capsule." Mr. Benton lowered his voice sympathetically. "We all share in the sorrow for the loss of your mother."

Ally burst into tears, while Kari and Marc sat in stunned silence. This had to be a bad dream. Surely this was not how her mother's life was supposed to end.

"We want to assure you, that the process was quick and painless. Your mother did not suffer," Dr. Yashkin expressed.

Kari let go of Ally's hand and rubbed her temples. It seemed that one minute she was reconciling with her mother and the next she was mourning her loss. Anger welled up within. "How could this have happened? Who is responsible?"

Mr. Benton swallowed hard but was not the one to answer. Instead, Carter Dunleavy's even tone drew their attention. "For the time being, we can only speculate who committed this heinous act and for what purpose. The FBI is conducting a full investigation." He let out a weary breath, shaking his head. "I simply can't tell you how sorry I am for your loss. We all loved Kathleen dearly."

Hearing the news from Dr. Dunleavy somehow made it absolute. Tears shimmered in Kari's eyes. She glanced at Marc over their distraught daughter. "I'm so sorry," he breathed, then took Ally into his arms.

Whirring with a million questions, Kari turned her attention back to Dr. Dunleavy. "How is it the press is crawling all over this?"

Carter Dunleavy leaned forward in his chair. "I'm afraid it's all my fault. When I saw Olivia's condition this morning, I didn't take matters into my own hands quickly enough. Unfortunately, the head of our cleaning staff called 9-1-1. From that moment on everything snowballed out of control."

Ms. Conner spoke up for the first time during the meeting. "We've decided to finally let the public know that Kathleen came out of her coma on Mars. It's a bit of a sticky situation," she lamented, "but considering the FBI's criminal investigation, we no longer feel the need to keep that information private. I hope you understand."

Before the family could respond, Kari noticed everyone but Dr. Yashkin check their wristbands simultaneously. Each one seemed to be receiving the same message. Carter Dunleavy momentarily turned his head toward Jarrod Benton. "He won't stop ranting. Someone needs to hear him out," he whispered.

Mr. Benton thrust his chin in the direction of the door. "Go."

"I'm sorry," Dr. Dunleavy told the family. "I'm needed elsewhere at the moment." He rose and offered his hand to each member of the family expressing his condolences, then quickly exited the room.

Mason continued pacing the cubicle area and begging to speak to someone other than a security guard. The FBI had given strict orders to keep the night janitor secure until they could debrief him. He kept telling the guards he not only needed to call his wife, but he had vital information about Kathleen Raines. "My wife will be worried that I haven't come home. She has cancer, you know. She needs me!"

"I'm sorry, Mr. Hill. We're under strict orders," the security officer uttered in exasperation. "Please, sit down and try to relax. I'm sure they'll be here any minute." The young officer glanced at his colleague who was somehow able to ignore Mr. Hill's desperate tirade. As a matter of fact, he looked downright bored, but when Carter Dunleavy entered the room, all three men gave him an effusive welcome.

"Someone has to call my wife immediately and let her know I'm all right."

Dr. Dunleavy moved inside the cubicle and cupped Mason's shoulder. "Let's do that right now. Don't tell her anything that's happened, but you can tell her you had to work a little later today."

"Mr. Dunleavy, Sir, there is no way on this planet she's going to believe that. Did you know my shift ended seven hours ago?"

A little taken aback, Dr. Dunleavy was shocked by Mason's proclamation. "I'm so sorry, Mason. We should've taken care of this situation hours ago. The press conference starts in half an hour. Why don't you simply tell her that you're okay, and ask her to watch the news for further details? Would that work?"

Mason visibly relaxed and Dr. Dunleavy motioned for the guard to give him access to a phone. "You'll need to be interviewed by the FBI before you can go home. Have they brought you any food?"

"Yes, Sir, I've had a big lunch, but that's not what's really important."

"I know," Carter said as he stepped outside the cubicle. "Your wife needs to know you're safe."

"Uh, that's not what I'm talking about."

"Listen, Mason, I've got a lot to do before this press conference, so why don't I come back—"

"Coach Raines is still alive!" Mason interrupted.

Carter halted in his tracks and immediately trained his gaze back on Mason. "What are you talking about?"

"Has anyone bothered to check on her?" Mason asked.

"Unfortunately, the perpetrator sabotaged our communication system. We're working on getting it back up and—"

"I don't mean to be rude," Mason butted in, "but you might want to check her vitals in the main medical lab. Olivia told me she completely disabled the cremation switch not long after Coach Raines came out of her coma. Even with that locked cover being installed, she was afraid someone would accidently do her harm. It was kind of a secret between me and Olivia, I guess."

Carter Dunleavy had to stop himself from hugging the janitor. Mason's news was like an invigorating breeze sweeping off the ocean. He immediately tapped his wristband, calling for Dr. Yashkin to meet him in the medical lab. Foregoing the hug, he took Mason's hand in an iron grip and thanked him for sharing such vital information. "You're my hero," he said emotionally. "I'll be back in a few minutes. If what you say is true, I'll want you by my side at the press conference."

Not waiting for a response, Carter Dunleavy dashed out of the cubicle and sprinted toward the medical lab.

>>Chapter 24

The medical lab was on lockdown, Agent Ryan McGuire stationed at the door. Carter Dunleavy was not about to be denied entry. "You have to let me in the lab immediately," he demanded.

"I'm sorry, Sir. As soon as we've finished our investigation, you'll have full access, but not until then."

Carter raked his hands through his hair in exasperation. "You don't understand, Kathleen Raines may still be alive and—"

"Hy bot!" Dmitry Yashkin broke in as he rounded the corner of the hallway, bewildered by the program director's declaration. "What do you mean?"

Hurriedly, Carter explained the details of his conversation with Mason Hill while color drained from Dr. Yashkin's face. "We must be admitted at once," Dmitry pronounced.

Carter Dunleavy leveled his gaze at the FBI agent. "The press conference is scheduled in twenty minutes. If Kathleen Raines is alive, this changes everything."

"I see your point," Agent McGuire conceded. Without delay he tapped his earpiece and explained the situation to his immediate superior. Within moments, the door to the lab clicked open and all three men swiftly entered.

Dr. Yashkin's hands trembled as he logged into the computer system's medical program. Perspiration blanketed his brow while he waited for the facial recognition software to authorize access. Carter

Dunleavy stood behind him, heart racing like a frightened rabbit. "Come on, come on," he muttered impatiently.

Dr. Yashkin leaned closer to the screen, intently scrutinizing the data. "Bozhe moy, ona zhiva!"

"In English, Doc," Carter pressed.

"She lives!"

Carter Dunleavy blew out a gigantic breath, excitedly clamping his hands onto Dr. Yashkin's shoulders. "You're absolutely sure about this?"

"No doubt. See for yourself." He pointed out Kathleen's current heart rate and body temperature. "Her respiration rate indicates she is now sleeping."

"Stay with her," Carter instructed. "I'm heading back to Jarrod Benton's office."

Dmitry Yashkin hunkered down closer to his computer. "You could not make me leave," he trilled in Russian.

When Carter Dunleavy burst unannounced into Jarrod Benton's office, he was surprised to find Sharon Conner working on the final script for the press conference while Mr. Benton perused security feeds of the complex on his desk screen.

"Where's the Gale family?" he blurted.

"They felt it best to leave before the press conference got underway."

"How long ago? Do you think they're still on the premises?"

Tapping his screen, Mr. Benton divulged their whereabouts. "They're being led to the south gate away from the crowds as we speak."

"Call the gate. Don't let them leave."

"What's this all—"

"Kathleen is still alive! Olivia Cole disabled the cremation system days ago. Dr. Yashkin just confirmed it."

Jarrod Benton's face turned as red as hot coals. "How did we not catch this?"

"We can discuss that in a minute. Call the south gate and get the Gale family back up here."

Mr. Benton did as he was charged, then turned his attention back to the Pioneer program director. "Start talking fast, we've got some changes to make before the press conference begins."

Sharon Conner furiously reworked information within Mr. Benton's speech as Dr. Dunleavy relayed the details of the case. Jarrod stroked his salt and pepper beard while pondering the facts. Suddenly, he bolted forward in his chair. "What if Kathleen's life remains in danger? Isn't this what we feared from the beginning?"

Ms. Conner glanced up from her tablet, releasing a deep sigh. "I've already thought of that, but we can't hold back the tempest any longer. Now that the FBI is investigating, we'll have all the security we need on Kathleen Raines." She removed her glasses, a serious expression thinning her lips. "By no means are either of you to utter the name Victor Belkin in this press conference. Understood?"

Both men pledged their word.

"Stick to what we know about Kathleen's awakening on Mars and stay completely away from today's incident at the biomedical station. The FBI will reveal their facts of the case in due time."

"Any word from Dr. Utley?" Carter asked.

Jarrod Benton shook his head, worry lines creasing his forehead. "He checked in early this morning before his flight to Houston. We haven't been able to get hold of him and NASA says he's not scheduled for a meeting until five o'clock their time." After a long pause, he added, "I'm sure once he hears the news, he'll be on the first flight back."

Sitting in a private room at UISC, watching the press conference on a large screen, Marc couldn't help but feel enormous relief. Their family had been ushered onto an emotional roller coaster this afternoon that had finally pulled into the station. While they had yet to disembark the ride, at least it was standing still and they could relax their grip on the handles a bit.

Marc glanced at his wife and daughter still clinging to one another as they sat side-by-side on a small sofa. Streaks of dried tears stained their cheeks. Kari briefly met his gaze, a humorless smile tipping her mouth. It was obvious she was utterly spent.

Jarrod Benton's statement refocused his attention back to the screen. "On day twenty, after the landing of the Pioneer spacecraft, for lack of a better word, a miracle occurred—Coach Kathleen Raines awakened." Mr. Benton momentarily paused as a rumble of astonished voices inundated the large room. Raising his hand to the crowd, he continued. "According to our medical team, the effects of deep space and perhaps the gravitational pull of Mars itself, by some means rewired Kathleen's brain. Research shows that in certain circumstances, the human brain is able to create new cells. This process is called neurogenesis. There is no doubt that neurogenesis has taken place within Kathleen's brain."

"Why was the public not informed of this situation?" someone called from the crowd. The room erupted again with hundreds of questions hurled toward Jarrod Benton, who immediately appealed for order.

"Because of the international nature of Coach Raines's accident, we believed it best to keep this information private, primarily for security reasons. While I am not at liberty to discuss today's events, suffice it to say that our intel was correct on this matter."

One voice persisted above the din. "Will we be allowed to see Kathleen Raines for ourselves? Can you show us proof that what you're saying is true?"

"In a moment we'll be showing a video clip from two days ago, but unfortunately, our communications component has been badly damaged. While we have a capable team working to correct the problems, the situation has not been rectified at this time. However—" His statement was drowned out by another barrage from hungry reporters. "However," he persisted loudly, "we plan to introduce the world to the Pioneer Woman in real time as soon as communications are repaired."

"Is this the first time Coach Raines' family has heard about her revival? If so—"

"No," Mr. Benton asserted. "The Gale family was apprised of the situation not long after she awakened. They have had the privilege of communicating with her on a regular basis."

"An employee of UISC is in the hospital in critical condition," a veteran reporter shouted out. "What can you tell us about this morning's incident? And more importantly, was Coach Raines involved in an assassination plot against the Deputy Prime Minister of Russia?"

Ally leaned forward on the sofa, deeply disturbed by the reporter's inquiry. "Why would he ask that?"

Kari laid a cautioning hand on her daughter's arm. "You know we don't have to watch this, sweet girl."

"No, I want to hear it. But I thought they proved last year that it was all an accident?"

Marc knew down deep there was more to Kathleen's accident than they had first been told. He swallowed back the concerns he would share later with his wife. "We all know Granny K had nothing to do with any assassination plot," he assured. "Somehow she must've accidently got caught up in something beyond her control. We'll just have to let the FBI uncover the truth."

"They've hardly done *that* in the past year," Kari groused before realizing how that must have sounded. "I'm sorry, I know that was uncalled for. There's so much we simply don't understand."

"Which is why we need to trust the authorities, as hard as that may be," Marc said.

As the press conference continued, the FBI's director of Intelligence, Matthew Waites, took the podium. He successfully dodged every difficult question hurled his way. The Gale family, along with the rest of the world, was no closer to knowing the truth than when they first entered the premises of UISC.

"Dad, could we go by the hospital to see Olivia?" Ally begged.

Eager to get away from the frenzy of the press, Marc readily agreed. "If they'll allow us access, I think that would be a great idea. Have you all heard enough?"

Both Kari and Ally snatched at the opportunity to get away from the space center.

"We may be jumping from one frying pan into another," he told them. "But hopefully most of the reporters are in that room and we won't have to mess with them for a while."

Steven Utley pulled his car through security at the south gate away from the hub bub. It was by pure chance that his flight had been cancelled this morning due to a storm at his final destination. Shutting down all tech, he had settled into a traveler's lounge at the airport for several hours of much needed sleep. Researching the effects of deep space and neurogenesis had kept him up far too many nights. He and Dmitry Yashkin were very close to a major breakthrough.

When he awoke late in the afternoon he began checking his devices. Stunned, was a word far too mild to describe his emotions upon reading texts about this morning's events from Yashkin and Dunleavy. For a long moment his mind whirred with options until duty compelled him to return to the space center. Everything else would have to be temporarily sidelined.

Glancing to his left he was surprised to see the Gale family on their way out. Their daughter turned her head his direction but appeared not to notice him. He wondered how they were dealing with yet another shock in this improbable saga.

It took several long minutes to finally gain access into the medical lab. All of Dr. Utley's superiors were still tied up in the press conference, along with the FBI's Director of Intelligence. Apparently Director Waites was the one pulling all the strings on this investigation and his underlings were leery of making decisions without his approval. It was Dmitry who finally came to his rescue. "The life of Kathleen Raines depends on Dr. Utley," he had told the agents convincingly.

Under his breath, Steven thanked his colleague as they entered the lab together. "Tell me everything you know," he persisted.

Dmitry Yashkin urgently relayed vital information about the morning's events. "They have Victor Belkin in custody down the hall. I've heard him screaming his innocence on and off. Even the FSB has been interrogating him."

"The FBI has allowed it?" Dr. Utley was shocked that the Federal Security Service of the Russian Federation had been allowed access to their suspect so soon.

"I am astonished, as well. But that is no matter to us. We must make sure we do not lose our comrade on Mars."

"What about our comrade on Earth?" Steven asked as he logged into his medical computer. Olivia Cole was nearly as much a concern to him as Kathleen Raines.

"Victor nearly killed her. Even now, her life hangs in the balance. We can only hope for the best."

>>>

The Gale family peered from behind a large glass window into the room of Olivia Cole. Ally felt a rush of warm tears. Olivia had become her friend and confidante throughout this yearlong ordeal. She wondered who could've committed such a cruel act?

"May we go inside?" she asked the doctor, who stood beside them.

"I see no reason why not." Then he pointed toward the two FBI agents standing guard at the door. "But they have to make the final call."

"I'll talk to them," Marc said, and Ally watched as her dad quietly pleaded their case. A relieved breath escaped her lungs when the agents stepped aside for the family to enter.

Slowly Ally approached the bed, observing the ventilator tube running into Olivia's mouth. She remembered the same kind of tube in Granny K's mouth before her grandmother had ripped it out on Mars. It must be a terrible feeling to wake up with something so intrusive down your throat.

Ally turned around to Dr. Creighton, who lingered near the door. "Is it all right for me to talk to her?"

"Absolutely," he answered.

Without hesitation, Ally turned back to Olivia, suddenly noticing the terrible bruises encircling her neck. She briefly closed her eyes, shoving back the violent image of someone's hands crushing her throat. "Olivia," she said, a tremor in her voice. "It's me, Ally." She reached for her hand and held it lovingly.

"I'm here with you now…my mom and dad are right here, too. We just want you to know that you're not alone. I hope you can hear me."

All three family members took turns speaking to Olivia, trying to infuse her with as much reassurance as they could muster. Truthfully, the situation appeared to be grim, but they continued their constant encouragement.

Eventually, a nurse entered the room and told them they would need to exit to the waiting room. "You'll be able to come in one more time at eight o'clock if you like. That will be the last visitation hour for the night."

Passing the two FBI agents at the door, Marc expressed his thanks. "Will we be permitted to visit with her again this evening?" he asked. Ally was grateful her parents had no intention of leaving the hospital without seeing Olivia one more time. She was beyond relieved when the agents granted their permission.

Blowing out a breath of exhaustion, Marc lowered himself into a chair in the waiting room. "Come 'ere, Cupcake."

Ally took the chair beside his, dropping her head onto his shoulder. He gently wrapped his arm around her and asked how she was holding up.

"I'm okay," she breathed. "But what about Olivia's family and friends? Do you think there's someone we should contact?"

Kari had been wondering the same thing. A waiting room devoid of next of kin was a bit disconcerting. "You all wait here," she said. "I'm going to the nurses' station to see what I can find out."

While her mom was away, Ally napped on her dad's shoulder. It had been a very long and taxing day. When Kari returned a few minutes later, she did so empty handed. She and Marc talked quietly about Olivia's situation while their daughter slept. "The nurse told me they haven't been able to locate any of Olivia's family and no one from the space center is sharing any information. It all seems so bizarre."

"Maybe when the press conference is over, someone from UISC will come to the hospital. I'm with you, something doesn't seem right about this." After a long silence, Marc looked down at his sleeping daughter, a smile turning his lips. "She's gonna be hungry when she wakes up."

"Well, I'm awake and hungry right now," Kari mused. "Why don't I go down to the cafeteria and get us all something to eat."

"Sounds good. I'll eat anything you bring back."

Kari laughed quietly. "Be careful what you hope for," she said, before kissing him lightly and heading downstairs.

When Kari returned with three hamburgers and bags of chips, she was surprised to find the waiting room empty. Thinking Marc and Ally may have gone to the restroom, she laid everything out on the coffee table in front of their chairs. She started to eat without them, but something didn't seem right—at least one of them would've been back by now. She sent them both a text, but neither responded.

Leaving their meal, Kari quickly made her way to the nurses' station only to find it vacant. Glancing at the doors to the ICU she thought she heard a clamor down the hall. Without a thought for hospital rules, she waved her hand across the beam of the door-opener behind the desk and rushed in. Whatever was going on was happening inside Olivia's room.

Recognizing her daughter's panicked scream, Kari sprinted the length of the hallway. The scene inside Olivia Cole's room was an enigma—hectic, but somehow under control. Ally was not the only one holding onto Olivia, who appeared to have awakened. The doctor and two nurses held down her limbs while Marc and the FBI agents stood at the ready.

"What happened?" Kari asked.

Ally peered over her shoulder. "She woke up and is trying to get the tube out of her throat. She nearly managed it a second ago."

"We know this is difficult, but please try to relax," one of the nurses prevailed on Olivia. "You need the tube to help you breathe."

Dr. Creighton asked Marc to hold down Olivia's arm while he talked to the FBI agents. Kari stepped a little closer so she could hear their hushed conversation. "We're going to have to sedate her to keep her from pulling out the ventilator tube. She's experiencing a fairly common reaction."

One of the agents spoke quickly. "We need to get a statement from her first."

"You'll not be able to get a statement with that tube down her throat." The doctor's tone left no doubt that he was perturbed.

"Do you think it's possible for her to write something?"

Dr. Creighton rubbed the back of his neck. "She's obviously conscious, I just don't know what her state of mind is." He glanced back toward his patient. "If you're asking if it's possible for someone to communicate in writing while on a vent, the answer is, yes. Is it possible for Ms. Cole? I have no way of knowing at this point."

One of the agents took out his small, electronic tablet. "It's imperative that we try."

Dr. Creighton hesitantly nodded his head. "Give us a moment to calm her down, then you can proceed." He stepped back to the bed and relieved Marc of his duty.

"Ms. Cole," he said in a low voice. "My name is Adam Creighton. I'm your doctor." Olivia's panic-stricken eyes snapped to his. "I'm not going to let anything happen to you. The tube in your throat is hooked to a ventilator—it's helping you breathe. You have a severe injury to your neck and throat."

The wild look persisted. Ally lovingly stroked the arm that she held and Olivia's gaze switched to the other side of the bed. For a long moment the only sound in the room was the swish-poof, swish-poof of the breathing machine. "I'm here for you, Olivia. I'm not letting go," Ally pledged.

Kari stepped closer, amazed by the calming effect of her daughter's presence. Olivia's eyes emptied of anxiety and filled with tears. Ally gently erased them from her cheek with the back of her hand, then leaned in close. "We're here for you," she assured compassionately.

Both FBI agents crowded close to the bed. One of them held out the tablet toward Ally.

"I'm going to let go of your arm, Olivia, but you need to promise me you won't try to pull the tube out of your mouth." Astonished by the interaction, Kari watched Olivia's head nod ever so slightly.

"Thank you," Ally said softly, then took the tablet from the agent. "Who did this to you?"

While Ally held the tablet, Olivia painstakingly tapped out her answer. It was all Kari could do not to squeeze in behind the bed to see the name. The air in the room took on an ominous feel.

When Olivia's hand dropped to the bed, Ally turned the tablet around. Terror instantly seized her face. "Oh, no!" she cried. "I saw him at the space center today."

"Where did you see him?" one of the agents pressed.

"He was driving in the gate just as we were leaving."

>>Chapter 25

Agent Ryan McGuire, now stationed inside the biomedical lab, received a message summoning Dmitry Yashkin to the third floor conference room for questioning. Director Matthew Waites would lead the interrogation. Agent McGuire promptly stood and straightened his tie. "It's your turn, Dr. Yashkin. The director will see you now."

Dmitry Yashkin bent a wary glance toward his medical colleague. It was obvious he did not want to leave his work in the lab.

"It probably won't take long," Steven encouraged. "I'll hold down the fort while you're gone."

Agent McGuire held out his arm and motioned for Dr. Yashkin to take the lead. With a congenial grin he said, "I'm sure you'll be next, Dr. Utley."

Steven Utley's eyes flickered. "I'll be here," he assured, knowing he would be long gone before their return.

In a dream-like state, Kathleen Raines rose up into a sitting position. Her eyes meandered around the space module, then landed on the bio-bed's connection at her hip. It took a moment for the silver conduit ring to come into clear focus. When it did, she encircled the ring with her right hand. As the seconds ticked by her hand tightened, then gradually twisted the ring into the unlocked position. As if a puppet master controlled her movements, Kathleen pulled the tube free from the capsule bed.

A rush of air escaped her lungs as her body instantly felt the adverse effects. Now she was fully conscious, horrified by the tube resting in her hand. Her mind scrambled to make sense of what she'd just done and for what purpose. Sleep walking was the only logical explanation. The suit, which had sustained her life, now seemed to be crushing that life right out of her. It hung heavily upon her frame—she had to lay back down.

"Oh, God, what have I done?" she whimpered.

At one time Olivia had explained the importance of the tube at her hip. Should it ever come loose, simply plugging it back into the bed was not an option. The entire system would have to be rebooted.

"Precious Father, I don't really want to die."

While the bio-suit ebbed and dwindled, Kathleen's heart yearned for one last moment with her family. A burning ache cramped the muscles of her stomach. Without warning, heat rose to her cheeks and nausea replaced her angst. Grabbing the sides of the bed she pulled herself upward once more. There was no holding back the queasy tide. She leaned over the side of the bed and retched repeatedly, emptying the liquid contents of her stomach onto the capsule floor.

Steven Utley congratulated himself on eliminating Kathleen Raines for the second time today. Had it not been for the storm in Kiev, his clandestine mission would have failed. While he had no fear of the FBI, he desperately needed to avoid the FSB. If they were to capture him within the confines of the United States, his life would be forfeit. The FBI's means of interrogation were child's play compared to the FSB. He fingered the syringe in his pocket, eager to release Olivia Cole from this world and disappear into deep cover.

Inside the hospital he followed the signs to the intensive care unit. There, he asked at the desk for Olivia Cole. The nurse on duty gave him a sympathetic look. "Are you family?"

"No, I'm a colleague. May I please see her for just a moment?"

"I'm sorry to tell you this, Sir, but Ms. Cole passed away less than an hour ago."

Dr. Utley's chin dropped to his chest. He allowed a sigh to escape his throat. "That's terrible," he breathed, then turned away slowly. Inwardly he congratulated himself on a job well done as he headed down the hall at an unhurried pace. While waiting for the elevator he calculated his time of arrival in Kiev. He had already sent a coded message to the operative who would be waiting for him. Disappearing would be easy. And with patience, within the year he would reemerge with a new cover. He looked down at his feet, a half-smile crossing his lips—it would be hard to beat this assignment. How often do you get to eliminate a world leader and work on an historic mission to Mars? His cleverness was boundless.

When he lifted his gaze, Steven Utley was immediately wrenched from his egotistical reverie. It had only taken a few seconds of inattentiveness to cost him everything. Flanking him on both sides were two FBI agents. He felt the presence of others behind him. When the elevator door opened, four more were waiting. He instantly slid his right hand inside his pants pocket.

"Put your hands where we can see them." All four agents on the elevator drew their weapons.

Dr. Utley raised his left hand slowly while flicking the cap from the syringe with his right.

"Both hands. Now!"

A slow smile crept across his youthful features. Going out at the top of his game—what could be better? He jabbed the needle into his inner thigh and emptied the poisonous contents into the femoral artery. Leaving the syringe in his pocket, he slid his right hand out and into the air.

Immediately, the agent to his left yanked both arms behind his back and cuffed his wrists tightly before shoving him onto the elevator. Sweat dotted his forehead and his vision blurred. Before the doors slid shut, one of the agents disembarked. "I'll let them know that Ms. Cole is safe now."

Steven Utley's eyes grew wild. An angry snarl replaced his self-important smirk. His knees buckled and he dropped to the floor of the elevator. By the time the door opened on the ground floor, he was already dead.

Agent Terrell stopped by the ICU desk. "We got him. Thanks for your help."

The nurse let out a nervous breath. "That's great news."

"I'm going back to let them know."

Relieved that it was over, she swiped the ICU doors open for the agent.

Kari watched the three FBI agents speak in hushed tones in the doorway. Her heart beat an anxious rhythm. She and Marc and Ally continued surrounding Olivia's bed even after Dr. Creighton had ordered her sedation. He feared the damage she might cause if she succeeded in ripping out the ventilator tube.

Finally, Agent Terrell turned his attention to the Gale family. "It's over," he said. "We have Dr. Utley in custody." All three breathed a heavy sigh of relief.

"What about my mother?" Kari pleaded.

"I'm sorry, Ma'am, we don't have any information from the space center." Immediately he tapped his earpiece to receive a message. "I'm needed in the lobby," Agent Terrell told them, then urgently left the room.

After a short, yet arduous interrogation, Dmitry Yashkin returned to the medical lab. He was dismayed to find no bio readings on Kathleen Raines. Not even a blip on the screen. Terror struck his heart. He tapped his wrist band and Carter Dunleavy instantly responded. "What is it?"

"Lozhis' syuda nemedlenno!"

"In English, Doc!"

Dmitry could hardly think. "Come to the lab, now!" He looked around for Dr. Utley, but his comrade was nowhere in sight.

Within the minute, Carter Dunleavy ran into the lab. "What's happened?"

"We have nothing on Kathleen Raines," he spat. "No pulse. No heart rate. No readings whatsoever. They are all gone—and so is Dr. Utley."

Carter tapped his wrist band. "Locate Steven Utley." A text immediately flashed across his screen. *Dr. Steven Utley exited gate 3, 18:09PM.* Carter looked up. "He's not even on the premises."

Dr. Yashkin sat back in his chair, a sick feeling invading his gut. He wiped his hand across his mouth and released a curse word in Russian. "It wasn't Victor Belkin, after all," he whispered.

"What do you mean?"

Slamming his hand down on the table, Dr. Yashkin stood to face his program director. "Don't you see? Dr. Utley was left alone in the lab while I was taken to interrogation. He has finished what he came to do."

"That can't be," Carter muttered.

Feeling thoroughly deceived, Dmitry told him, "It all makes sense now. Did you know he could speak fluent Russian? We never discussed it, but there were times when I spoke in Russian *only* and he knew exactly what I was saying. There were other times when he spoke in my native tongue."

Carter Dunleavy wasted no more time. He tapped his wrist band once more. "Locate Director Matthew Waites." The incoming text read, *Matthew Waites—control room, communications station.* "Contact him directly." Within seconds the connection was made. "Director Waites, you're needed in the medical lab immediately."

"I'll be right there," he responded.

Seconds later he called back. "I'm sorry, Dr. Dunleavy, we've got a situation. I'll get back with you when I can."

"But this is important, it's about Steven Utley."

The director allowed a brief pause, Carter could tell he was on the move. "Yes, I'm afraid that's our situation. I'll send an agent to debrief you immediately. In the meantime, you might want to get to the communications lab. I think they've reestablished contact with Mars."

How many times would his family be put through the wringer today? The look on his wife and daughter's faces almost made Marc want to break down and cry. The day had started out so hopeful with Kari attending church, then dashed to pieces with news of Kathleen's cremation. Minutes later they were told she was still alive, and now, for all they knew, Dr. Utley had slipped back into the space center and finished the job he started early this morning. He didn't know how much more of this they could take.

"Daddy, we can't go home, not until we know for sure about Gran."

"I know, Cupcake." If school was starting tomorrow, he'd have second thoughts about taking them back to the space center tonight. But thankfully, it wouldn't start till the middle of the week. Either way, if Kathleen lost her life this evening, it would be a difficult way for Ally to start off her first week of high school.

It was nine o'clock before the Gale family found themselves with Sharon Conner. She met them at their final security check inside the south entrance to the building.

"We were expecting to see Dr. Dunleavy," Kari put forward, exhibiting very little patience.

"I understand." Sharon Conner was nothing if not forbearing. Twenty-three years in public relations had taught her how to deal with every sort of human emotion. While her day had been long and stressful, she still possessed an air of genuine concern and empathy. "I'll take you right to him."

A driver stood by with a tram to carry them swiftly through the space center.

Ms. Conner turned from the front seat to speak with the family. "I'm taking you directly to the communications lab, but there's a situation you need to be advised of."

"Is Gran still alive?" Ally blurted.

"Yes, she is. However, the connection from her bio-suit to the capsule has been terminated. I'll let Dr. Dunleavy explain the particulars to you when you arrive. Most likely you won't have the opportunity to speak with her tonight. A team of specialists is helping her reestablish the connection and reboot the system." Sharon gave her a warmhearted smile. "Your Gran is actually working very hard right now."

When arriving at the communications lab, Sharon Conner hustled the family inside. Immediately, all three froze in place, gawking at the video screen. Kari let an inappropriate phrase slip from her mouth with neither Marc nor Ally reacting, even when she apologized. Kathleen was no longer inside her bio-suit, she was wearing only the thin-layered shell from beneath. Small tubes and wires hung at odd angles all over her body. The bio-suit itself lay flat within the bed, still connected at various other points. But what grabbed their attention from the moment they entered the room was the fact that Granny K was standing upright!

"How is this possible?" Kari breathed.

Carter Dunleavy turned from where he stood near the control panel, nodding to the family. He raised an index finger indicating that he would join them shortly. Ms. Conner led them to a seating area at the back of the lab, but none of the three felt like sitting. As long as Gran was on her feet, they would be too.

A few times Kathleen's knees buckled, forcing her to the capsule floor. As eager as the team of specialists was to help her complete the mission, they patiently endured the short breaks. Kari felt certain they were on a tight timetable to get her bio-suit back online and promptly quizzed Dr. Dunleavy on that subject when he joined them.

Instead of answering right away he proclaimed, "This is amazing, isn't it!" He motioned toward the chairs. "Please sit down while I fill you in."

Hesitantly, the family took a seat while Carter Dunleavy told them what prompted such an extraordinary turn of events. "At 18:00 hours, that is six o'clock this evening, Kathleen disconnected her bio-suit from the conduit which supplies her nutrients—food, water, medications, and so on. She claims that it happened while she slept. Incredibly, that's about the same time Dr. Utley administered a lethal drug overdose. Unfortunately, some of the drug reached her system before the disconnection, but only enough to make her sick. Coincidentally, communications were reestablished with the Pioneer space capsule about that time, and we've been working with Kathleen since then to reboot her nutrient support systems."

When he paused, Kari asked, "How long can she survive without it?"

Releasing a long breath, Dr. Dunleavy told them she could survive for quite some time without it. "She's been breathing on her own for weeks, so that's not the issue. Hydration is our biggest concern. Without the suit, there's no way for her to receive water and food. It also provides warmth. She's been complaining about her hands feeling numb from the cold atmosphere."

"How cold?" Ally asked.

"Current temperature inside the cabin is 56 degrees. Not too terribly cold, but her body is not used to such an extreme drop."

Marc introduced a question of his own. "How is she standing? I mean, this is unbelievable."

"Truly. We're all amazed at her willpower. It took a good two hours to get her removed from the suit and out of the bio-bed. Obviously, she's very unsteady, but whatever the force is on Mars, it's indescribable."

Kari's face flushed pink. "It's God," she whispered under her breath. She knew at that moment her mother's life was directly in the hands of the all-powerful God of the universe. The very thought made her feel miniscule in His incomprehensible presence. All of these scientists could say what they like, but she knew within her spirit that God was the force behind it all.

Shortly after eleven o'clock, Kathleen knelt beside the bed and reintroduced the all-important tube into its conduit. Silence spread through the communications room like an ocean fog. When nothing appeared to be happening, Marc gathered his girls in tight and worded a quiet prayer, while everyone waited.

"Kathleen?" one of the engineers called. "Let's try one more thing." He guided her through a series of steps at the control panel on the side of the bed and suddenly, the suit took on a life of its own.

Cheers of relief set the team of specialists back into frenzied motion. "Let's get you back in that suit," Dr. Dunleavy spoke over the com.

Kathleen sat unmoving on the floor of the capsule. All eyes observed her limp hand slide down the outside of the bed. She had given every scrap of energy to the mission—there was nothing left to get her back in the bio-suit, much less the capsule bed.

"Kathleen, you've got to get up one more time," Carter encouraged. "You can do it."

Her spine slumped and a line of tears formed on her cheeks. She couldn't even raise her hands to wipe them away, much less stand up. Letting out a jagged breath she wheezed, "I can't."

Kari thought her heart was being ripped right out of her chest. She didn't care one bit about protocol and pushed her way to the control panel. "Mom! It's me, Kari, and you *can* do this. You always told me *can't* is not a part of our vocabulary. You can do *anything* you put your mind to…so, put your mind to it!"

Kathleen's head slowly raised.

"Do it for me, Gran…please!"

At the sound of Ally's voice, Kathleen's eyes turned to narrow slits. After several deep breaths, she propelled herself up to her knees. Clasping her hands to the side of the bed, she dropped her forehead against the cold surface. Every movement cost her dearly.

It took three earnest attempts to stand. Every specialist in the room winced when she fell headlong onto the bio-suit. "So much for easing into it," one of them muttered.

"How are the connections holding?" Dr. Dunleavy demanded.

"They're holding, Sir."

Time interminable passed before Kathleen turned herself over. When she finally fit her limbs into the suit she appeared to lose consciousness.

"Mom! Mom! Wake up!" Kari yelled.

Kathleen's mouth moved, but no words were forthcoming.

"Granny K, you're almost there. Finish what you started. Please!" Ally begged.

"I'll try," slid from between Kathleen's lips.

One of the specialists took control as soon as Kathleen opened her eyes. She pushed through one more burst of energy to sit up and connect every loose tube to the inside of her suit. Marc turned away as she reconnected the more sensitive areas. As hydration gained the threshold of her body, Kathleen began to revive a bit during the hour-long ordeal. By the time she finished fastening the suit closed she collapsed out of extreme fatigue. Within moments, her lids fluttered shut and her breathing evened out.

From the medical lab, Dr. Yashkin monitored her vitals. He had maintained an open com link with the team of specialists in the communications lab throughout the entire incident. "Goodnight, sweet princess," he crooned with a thick Russian accent.

To everyone's delight a quiet response returned from Mars. "Goodnight, my prince."

>>Chapter 26

Marc sat on the back patio drinking a cup of coffee, filtering through the early morning news feeds. Though he was exhausted from yesterday's events, sleep had managed to evade him for most of the night. Falling into bed after two o'clock in the morning, he couldn't help but worry over his family. Reporters were practically camped on their doorstep, and they didn't seem inclined to be leaving any time soon. Sharon Conner had already asked the family to come back to UISC this evening for another press conference. She told them she was working on a statement for them. Plans were also in the works to do a live feed from Mars with Kathleen. He was curious how his mother-in-law would feel about that. Did she have a choice, he wondered? It was all happening so fast. How could they get off this crazy ride?

Drawn out of his troubled thoughts by a gentle hand running the length of his neck, he grinned. "I didn't expect you to be up so soon." He slid his arm around Kari's waist and drew her down to his lap.

"I'm finding it hard to stay in bed if you're not in it." She laughed softly and leaned into his chest.

For a long moment they sat in contented silence, enjoying the comfort of each other's arms. Kari finally broke the hush. "Are you sure you have to go in today?"

Marc let out a deep sigh. "I'm afraid so. The cross country team has practice at ten and I have a department meeting after lunch. As soon as that's over, I'll come straight home." He rested his chin on the top of her head. "You and Cupcake need to stay inside today. Don't give the reporters anything until we have to."

Kari rose up and gave him a simmering smile. "I'd rather stay inside with you today."

Tightening his arm around her waist, Marc cupped the side of her face with his left hand. "I wish," he said, then drew her mouth to his.

> > >

The press conference was scheduled for seven, so the family arrived at UISC by five o'clock. Sharon Conner immediately brought them to a conference room to look over their statements. All three were handed a separate tablet.

Eyes wide, Ally glanced up. "You mean I'm going to say something, too?"

"Not if you don't want to." Kari turned a proprietary gaze toward Ms. Conner, ready to safeguard her daughter from the scrutiny of the press.

Sharon cleared her throat and rested her elbows on the tabletop. "Well, of course none of you absolutely have to make a statement, but we feel it would be in your best interest to be open for questions. We have two hours to go over the possibilities."

"Mine isn't really a statement, though," Ally observed.

"No, that's why I wanted you here so early. If you're willing, Ally, we'd like for you to have an interchange with your grandmother during the press conference."

Kari sat in stunned silence, watching the color flood to Ally's cheeks. "Sweet girl, you don't—"

"It's okay, Mom," Ally interrupted. "I actually think that would be pretty cool." She thrust her shoulders back. "I can do that."

Kari's emotions held a remnant of fear. She and Marc had worked so hard to protect Ally from the press. Their daughter was about to be placed in a vulnerable position within a self-absorbed and oft times malicious society. She wanted to protect her baby at all cost. "Marc, what do you think?" she pleaded.

Marc laid the tablet down and held his daughter's gaze. "Do you think you're ready for this?" he asked quietly. "The whole world's going to be watching."

Ally's chin tilted slightly to the right, her eyes took on a look of maturity beyond her fourteen years. "With Gran by my side," she smiled, "I can do anything."

"Then…it's settled?" Ms. Conner probed.

"Sure, I'll do it. But will it be possible for me to speak with Gran before the press conference?"

"Oh, yes, that's what I was hoping for. She's been awake for a bit and is looking forward to seeing you face to face."

"What do you mean?" all three inquired simultaneously.

Sharon Conner tapped her forehead and laughed. "With everything that's happened I guess we forgot to tell you—our communications specialists have established a two-way video feed with the Pioneer capsule. Kathleen will now be able to see you."

Ally immediately jumped up from the table. "May I go to her now?" Her excitement was contagious. Kari and Marc came to their feet, as well.

"You certainly may. I think your grandmother has waited long enough to *see* her family."

At seven o'clock the Gales were ushered into the enormous room in front of hundreds of members of the press. They took their seats behind the podium as cameras recorded their every move. Sharon Conner sat down beside Ally, who appeared to be a little anxious. "It's going to be all right," she whispered. "You and your grandmother are going to take the world by storm."

Ally grinned nervously. "I hope so."

Dr. Dunleavy began the press conference by way of profiling Olivia Cole. He recited her college degrees in bio-engineering and medical technologies from the University of Chicago. It was there that she had been recruited by the FBI. Kari turned to Marc and realized he was just as surprised as she was to learn that Olivia was an undercover agent, specifically assigned to the Pioneer medical team. As it turns out, Olivia had been the perfect person for the job, although it had nearly cost her her life and that of Kathleen's. UISC had no complicity in the matter and were unaware that Olivia had been assigned to surveil and protect Kathleen Raines.

Next on the podium was the FBI's Director of Intelligence, Matthew Waites. While he was not at liberty to share many details, he revealed that Dr. Steven Utley, now deceased, had been a Russian infiltrator inside the Universal Intergalactic Space Corporation. From what the FBI had uncovered to this point, Steven Utley had aided in the assassination of Deputy Prime Minister Pavel Vasiliev in September of last year. A holographic design of the parking area above the Ocean Terrace restaurant had been recovered among his effects.

"Earlier today," Director Waites continued, "our agents ran the program at the very spot of the accident. It appears that prior to Ms. Raines' arrival, the parking barrier and fence had been removed and the holographic program installed. It was by sheer chance that Kathleen Raines was the first person seeking access to the upper parking area. The hologram made it appear that the barriers were still in place, but it was actually projected several feet beyond the side of the cliff. This holographic program proves beyond a shadow of a doubt, the innocence of Kathleen Raines."

Director Waites paused as a round of applause and cheers erupted. Kari felt a rush of relief. Their family had carried an unimaginable burden ever since her mother's tragedy. While they had never doubted Kathleen's innocence, they had also never been able to provide proof otherwise. Marc reached over and squeezed her hand. He had tears in his eyes causing her to release a batch of her own.

When the room settled down Director Waites shared a few more details, then turned the program over to Sharon Conner. "Good evening, everyone. I have the pleasure of introducing the world to two extraordinary women. The first is Miss Ally Gale, who will be entering her freshman year at Malibu High School in just a few days. She has shared an incredible journey with her grandmother, Kathleen Raines, over the past eleven months."

Ms. Conner went on to describe Kathleen's awakening during the ninth month and the subsequent removal of her breathing apparatus. "For an entire month our medical team kept Coach Raines under sedation while her throat and esophagus healed. As you can imagine, she experienced a great deal of pain after ripping the tubes from her lungs and throat."

For the next few minutes, Sharon Conner gave credit to both Olivia Cole and Ally Gale for providing Kathleen with the psychological encouragement needed to cope with the solitude of Mars. And finally, with a broad smile, she pronounced, "The Universal Intergalactic Space Corporation proudly introduces you to Miss Ally Gale on planet Earth and Coach Kathleen Raines on planet Mars."

The enormous room took on an air of anticipation while Ally stood and moved to the giant screen at the front. She was wearing a microphone chip at the base of her V-neck blouse. "Gran, are you there?" she spoke, with surprising confidence.

"Yes, my angel," Kathleen responded as the screen lit up. "I don't have any other plans at the moment." A ripple of laughter pervaded the room. Everyone seemed to be on the edge of their seats in awe of this historic moment.

Kathleen was sitting up in her bio-bed. "I understand we have a few billion people eaves dropping on our little conversation."

Ally smiled sweetly. "As a matter of fact, we do. Would you like to see just a few hundred of them?"

The video communications operator turned his lens toward the press in the audience. Kathleen graced them with a wave before her granddaughter was projected back onto the flat surface at the end of her bed.

Sharon Conner had given Ally several conversation starters for her time with Kathleen. She wanted it to flow as naturally as possible. Ally felt exposed standing in front of such a large crowd but did her best to focus solely on her grandmother. "Gran, we haven't really had a chance to talk about what it was like for you during the storm. You weren't able to talk to anyone for seven days. How did you get through it all alone?"

Kathleen took in a deep breath and let it out slowly before answering. "The team at the space center really did a wonderful job getting me prepped for the storm. I felt pretty confident that I could handle being alone for a while. But I've just got to tell you, it was the hardest thing I've ever gone through. I kind of froze up when the capsule lost power. All of a sudden I couldn't remember what I was supposed to do."

"What happened, Granny K? How'd you get everything going again?"

"I'm ashamed to say I didn't do anything at first. As a matter of fact, I laid back down in the bed and prepared to meet the Lord. But after a few minutes in the dark, my mind started to clear and God gave me the strength to sit up and try. He's been sustaining me ever since."

"It's your faith that's gotten you through this, isn't it?"

"Yes, through a lot of prayer and focus on my Creator, I'm still here. And then, thinking I would be able to see you again kept me going, too."

The two continued chatting for a few more minutes before Sharon Conner intervened. "Coach Raines, I was wondering if you would do us the honor of answering a few questions from the reporters in the audience?"

"I'd be glad to," she agreed.

Sharon chose four random reporters to join them up front. She offered a small microphone to the first reporter, who promptly introduced himself as Jeff Crowder from a Los Angeles television station.

"Obviously, when you woke up, you had no idea where you were. Could you tell us what it was like when you first found out you were on the planet Mars?"

"As you can imagine, I couldn't quite wrap my mind around it. At that time, I didn't even remember being in an accident, so to find out I'd been in a coma for nine months was my first shock. But it took a lot longer for this Mars thing to really sink in. I remember asking Olivia to remind me where I was every now and then." She let out a soft laugh. "Even now I have my moments of doubt."

After two more reporters interacted with Kathleen, the final inquiry was made by a young woman from a New York based online magazine. "Coach Raines, Megan Trujillo with the Pulse of NY. I basically have one question. I think it's something everyone really wants to know. Have you asked to be rescued from Mars?"

Kathleen sat completely still save for the quickening of her breaths. After a prolonged silence, Ms. Trujillo stammered, "I mean, I'm sure it's very difficult for you to be on Mars alone. I thought you might've had some sort of discussion…about trying to get off the planet."

"Honestly," Kathleen began, her voice breaking slightly. "I don't believe there are any plans to rescue a sixty-five-year-old woman from Mars. I feel certain I'm here to stay."

Carter Dunleavy immediately came to the podium as the press conference took a heart-rending downturn. "Ladies and gentlemen, we are indebted to Coach Raines for speaking so candidly with us this evening. Coach, we bid you goodnight for now. Thank you for gracing us with your presence."

A few claps sounded from the large audience, then more followed until everyone was on their feet applauding Kathleen Raines. The video operator turned his camera for her to see the incredible response from those covering her story. Tears streaked her face as she waved and quietly thanked them for their venerable display. Many among the reporters were openly emotional.

When the viewing screen darkened, hands flew up and a frenzy of questions were launched from the audience. Nearly every single person wanted to know if UISC had plans for a rescue mission.

Raising both hands to the audience, Dr. Dunleavy tried to call for silence, but little by little a chant captured the hearts of the media personnel—*Bring Coach home, bring Coach home, bring Coach home!*

"Be careful. You don't want to run over anyone." Kari rested her hand on Marc's thigh, worry straining her brow.

Marc steered his jeep slowly through the thick crowd outside the gates of UISC. The press conference had ended less than two hours earlier, but in the falling dusk, hundreds of people had come out to show their support for Kathleen. It wasn't a raucous gathering, but one evoking solemnity. They lightly tapped the top and sides of the jeep as it passed by, leaning in with messages of encouragement. *We love Kathleen. Rescue the Pioneer Woman. Bring Coach home from Mars.* Kari and Ally nodded to the billowing crowd as Marc inched the vehicle forward.

Kari's mind wandered back to their time with her mother after the press conference ended. They were allowed to speak with her privately for several minutes inside the communications lab. It had been a subdued conversation, to say the least. All three did everything in their power to bolster Kathleen's hope and courage, while she in turn tried to convince them she would be fine. But Kari knew better. She feared the press conference had somehow damaged her psyche by forcing her to face the unwinnable predicament she was in. All throughout her long career as a coach, Kathleen had been known for her dogged determination. As long as the game was alive, hope carried the day. But tonight, despite the fact that the game was still on, Kari noticed the fire of hope had abandoned her mother's eyes.

A cold shiver travelled the length of her spine. Marc felt her tremble and dared a quick glance. "Are you okay, Babe?"

Kari nodded tentatively. "I'm fine. Just watch the crowd." She didn't want to put a voice to her troubled thoughts. Deep down she felt certain, that in the very near future, their family would be called on to make yet another crucial decision concerning the life of Kathleen Raines.

>>Chapter 27

The weeks following the press conference held moments of utter joy and extreme frustration. It seemed the Gale family could barely brush their teeth in privacy, much less go about their life as normal. With Marc and Ally starting a new school year, Kari took it upon herself to lead the hordes of reporters away from her husband and daughter. Being unemployed at the moment proved to be an unexpected serendipity. Her full-time position now consisted of ordering and controlling the invading forces around them. Making a few concessions to appease the relentless beast, she agreed to appear on several local morning shows and accepted invitations from two major television newsmagazines. When she wasn't running interference for her family, she spent every possible moment at UISC with her mother.

After a rare dinner together at home, Ally headed upstairs to work on a group project for environmental science. The other three students on her team were joining in on a holographic video conference at seven o'clock. Marc bounced his eyebrows across the table at Kari. "It's just you and me, Babe. Do you want to go watch your latest appearance on CrossFire?"

She rolled her eyes. "Are you kidding? That's the last thing I want to do. I can't stand seeing myself on screen."

With a wide grin he said, "I don't know why not. I think you're the hottest-looking woman on any screen."

She laughed, pushing back from the table. "Maybe you need to get an appointment for lens implants," Kari teased.

Marc cut her off before she could make it to the counter with her dishes. "Here, let me take those." Instead of carrying them to the sink, he set them right back down on the table.

"What are you—?"

He didn't give her a chance to finish before lowering his mouth to hers. After a long moment he whispered, "I forgot what you tasted like. I miss you when you're out of town."

Lingering in his arms she told him, "I'm hoping that's the last of it for a while. I plan to stay right here with you."

He gave her another quick kiss, then released her. "What do you say we sneak out for a walk on the beach this evening?"

A grateful sigh escaped her lips. "I can't think of anything better. Let's hurry and get this cleaned up."

"Leave it," he said. "I'll go tell Ally we'll be back by nine-thirty. This can wait."

Twenty minutes later Marc and Kari playfully strolled barefoot along the beach. At one point, Marc grabbed her up in his arms and ran toward the surf while she screamed.

"Marcus David Gale, so help me…"

Pretending to pitch her into the water he nearly lost his footing and thought they were both going in. He quickly set her feet on the wet sand and grabbed her hand to outrun the chilly incoming wave. Not letting go of him, Kari bumped him higher up on shore. "You just about ruined a perfectly good walk, buddy."

Marc's eyes held a mischievous gleam. "Yeah, that could've been disastrous." He released her hand and encircled her waist possessively. "Do you know how much I love you?" he asked, looking down at her. "I always have."

Kari fought to hold his gaze, but it seemed impossible as a guilt-ridden sentiment wound its way through her core. It seemed every time her husband professed his unshakable love, she was slapped in the face with her own shortcomings.

For a long time they didn't speak. Marc stayed silent as the sun made its unhurried dive toward the sea. Sensing her somber mood, he asked, "Everything okay?"

"Yes," she answered quietly.

"Wanna sit down a while?"

She nodded and they moved higher up on the beach before sitting side-by-side in the soft golden sand. It took a while for Kari to summon the words that mirrored her emotions. When she found her voice her eyes remained on the steady waves. "Marc, what if I can't be what you need?" She briefly met his gaze before looking away. "I mean, what if I hurt you again, somehow?"

"Kari," he said in an unwavering voice. "That's not going to happen."

"You don't know that. How can you possibly know?"

He swallowed hard, obviously pained by his wife's self-doubt. "Because I know Who you gave your life to, and once you set your mind to something, you don't back down. Kari, look at me." He took her hand and held it tenderly. "You're going to have to find a way to release the past. I have. I don't look at you and think about anything you might've done."

"But *I* do," she admitted.

"Come 'ere." He reached over and drew Kari in between his legs, her back against him. His arms crossed her chest and he held her shoulders tightly. "I get where you're coming from—honestly, I do. If you want to see a counselor, I'll go with you."

For the length of several breaths Kari acknowledged this was something bigger than herself. It wasn't simply going to vanish on its own.

His mouth was close to her ear. "I just wish you could trust me."

"I trust you, Marc. You've got to believe me. I don't doubt your love for me one bit." She squeezed her eyes shut and took in a sip of the ocean breeze. "I guess I don't trust myself. I'm scared I've got too much of my daddy in me."

When Marc said nothing, she turned to look back at him in the waning light. "I'm sorry. I didn't mean to put a damper on our time together. We've had so little of it lately."

"You didn't. But I think this actually proves you're nothing like your daddy. If you were, you never would've brought this subject up. You'd be running away from it as fast you could."

A faint smile touched her lips. "You think so?"

"I know so." He paused for a long moment, then said, "Kari, you've been dealt a hard blow where your dad is concerned. The man you thought was so perfect turned out to be terribly flawed. All of us earthly fathers are defective in one way or another, but you have a heavenly Father that's perfect. He loves you unconditionally. He looks at you and says, 'Daughter, you are enough just the way you are.' He'll never break your trust."

After taking in her husband's words, she leaned her head back into his shoulder and he kissed her neck. "I don't deserve you, Marcus Gale."

Instantly, he moved out from behind her and pushed her back in the sand. "Oh, yes you do," he said, leaning over her with a rascally grin. "You deserve every bit of me."

>>>

It had been five days since the doctors weaned Olivia from the ventilator and released her to a regular hospital room. She still suffered from deep tissue and organ bruises while undergoing rehab for her neck, throat, and vocal chords. Her voice was no more than a whisper and still painful to use. An intravenous diet was all that was on the menu, much to her chagrin.

She had welcomed many visitors since transferring out of the ICU—the Gale family on three occasions, her next door neighbors Warren and Jill, who reported Max was doing fine although pining for his mama daily, and several colleagues from the space center and FBI. Even Mason Hill and his wife Jolene had dropped by to visit just the day before. However, no visitor could've surprised her more than the one currently standing beside her bed holding a bouquet of fresh flowers.

"Victor," Olivia rasped, instantly clutching the brace around her throat. Her brow wrinkled deeply. Any use of her vocal chords produced immense pain.

He gently touched her arm. "Don't try to speak. I know how glad you must be to see me," he teased. He set the vase of flowers on the bedside table and pulled up a chair. Olivia was shocked by the glimmer of compassion in his eyes.

"I am sorry it took so long to come to you. Maybe no one has thought to tell you that I no longer work at the space center. I have a new assignment."

Olivia gave her bedside visitor a quizzical gaze.

"I was overly surprised to learn that you are FBI, as you may be just as surprised to learn that I am FSB. I was assigned by my government to monitor any developments in the Kathleen Raines case. My government knew as well as yours did, that Pavel Vasiliev was assassinated. We wanted to keep a close eye on the coach, just as you did. We even had her family followed in case they learned any pertinent information."

Letting her lids drop briefly, Olivia couldn't believe what Victor was saying. All along they had essentially been working on the same team and neither one was aware of the other's mission.

"I, of course, was blamed for what happened to you. Your FBI did not cut me any rope."

Slack, Olivia wanted to correct, but didn't dare risk it. Her eyes crinkled at the corners, amused by Victor's use of the English language.

"They formed many opinions of me before knowing all the facts. It was the FSB who set them straight." He leaned forward, a steely gaze changing his demeanor. "If I had known Dr. Utley would do this to you...I would've killed him myself."

Victor had spent so much time irritating her during their night shifts, she never would've guessed his intense loyalty. A twinge of guilt tightened her chest. Her opinion of him instantly took an upward turn.

"Tomorrow I leave for Russia, so I will bid you farewell." His eyes warmed and he reached into his back pocket pulling out a thin book. "Sometimes, when you were not looking, I removed my headphones and listened to you and Coach. I think maybe you would like this to remember me."

His chair scraped the floor as he stood and leaned over her bed, kissing both of her cheeks. Smiling, he pressed the gift into her hands. "Until we meet again, comrade," he said quietly, then left the room.

For a long moment Olivia stared at the empty doorway. She could've sworn Victor had been working against her all this time. If she had only known. Taking a slow, deep breath, she finally looked at the gift he had brought her. A sheen of tears filled her eyes and she drew it tightly to her chest. Victor, of all people, had brought her a brown leather volume of the book of Psalms.

> > >

While Kathleen missed Olivia immensely, she had been given little time alone in the past three weeks. Her days were filled with a steady stream of visitors. In Olivia's absence, Doctors Dunleavy and Yashkin, along with Sharon Conner, had set up a daily schedule for her to receive family, friends, and former players. Even a highly select group of reporters had been given access. Two, thirty-minute naps were built into her days and no more visitors were permitted after seven o'clock in the evening. A few exceptions were made for the Gale family when their schedules did not permit them to come any sooner.

This morning, the communications lab was filled with raucous laughter. Three of Kathleen's former volleyball players from Pepperdine had come to visit. Kari stood in the background amazed at the deep connection these players shared with their coach. Though all three had played on a national championship team, not one time was the game ever mentioned. It dawned on her that her mother's primary focus had never been on winning—it had always been about relationships. Kathleen wanted to know all about their lives. How were their husbands and children? Were they happy in their jobs? And most importantly, how was their spiritual walk? The two-hour session flew by and before anyone wanted it to end, Sharon Conner was telling them it was time to go. Tears began flowing unashamedly.

"You know I would hug each one of you tightly, if I could," Kathleen told them. "I love you dearly."

Each player professed their love and loyalty to her.

"Kari, honey, are you still there?"

"Right here, Mom. What can I do for you?"

"I want you to hold each one of my girls for me. Your arms will have to be my arms."

Kari's throat tightened with emotion. "Gladly," she breathed.

One by one Kari took the younger women in her arms and held them firmly to her, feeling the beat of their hearts. For the briefest of moments, God allowed her to grasp the enormity of her mother's influence on so many lives over the years. What a shame she herself had missed out on such richness and beauty.

When the room was clear, Sharon told Kathleen to lie down and rest. "That will be it for the day. Dr. Yashkin tells me you didn't sleep well last night and he wants you to settle in a little earlier." She turned to Kari. "Jarrod Benton would like to meet with you in a few minutes. Do you have time?"

Kari nodded. "Yes, I actually had planned to stay until early evening, but if Mom needs her rest…"

"Good. I have a tram waiting—there's something I want to show you on the way."

Kari turned to say good-bye to her mother, but from the medical station, Dr. Yashkin had lowered the lights. She appeared to already be asleep. Both women left the communications lab together.

Sharon stepped into the driver's seat of the tram and Kari got in beside her. They definitely were not headed to Jarrod Benton's office on the fifth floor. Stopping in front of two steel doors, Ms. Conner got out and pressed her palm to a small panel, then leaned in close for facial recognition. The doors immediately slid back.

"This tunnel goes to another part of the complex," she said, keeping to the right lane. Many trams and other types of vehicles passed them on their left. Kari was astounded at how little their family had actually seen of the space center.

After what seemed like a very long distance, Sharon pulled the tram over close to the cement wall. "You'll have to get out on my side, I'm afraid."

Kari slid across the bench seat and followed her companion through another door, down a hall, and into an elevator. Seven stories up, they disembarked onto an open promenade. Dozens of UISC workers bustled through the area, obviously engaged with important projects.

Sharon led her guest toward an enormous glass wall. Kari looked down from her vantage point and realized the massive chamber in front of them housed a rocket.

"This is only half of the rocket—the other half is in another building. As you can see by the tip in front of us, it's the top half. Are you afraid of heights, Mrs. Gale?"

Kari swallowed hard. Of course she was. But fascination had gotten the best of her. "No," she squeaked.

"Excellent. We'll take the lift." She opened a nearby box and handed Kari a hardhat. "These are required from here on out."

Sharon breezed them through another security checkpoint which led to a nine-story, open air elevator, enclosed by only a waist-high railing. Kari inched onto the platform and stopped. She was paralyzed to move any farther. Ms. Conner, however, walked to the front and rested her hands on the top rail. "It's breathtaking, isn't it?" When there was no response, she turned around, a slow smile tipping her lips. "If you'd rather take the real elevator…"

"No," Kari said a little too quickly. "I just need to stay close to the wall."

Dipping her chin, Sharon pressed the controls and the platform began a slow descent. After lowering a couple of stories it came to a stop.

"What's wrong?"

"Nothing. I merely wanted you to see the payload system of the rocket. This is where the crew lives and works during their mission."

"Sharon, if you don't mind…" Kari let out a nervous breath. "Could you walk me to the railing?"

"Of course." Sharon came to her side and clasped her elbow. "I know how you feel. I was a little shaky at first, too."

Kari somehow doubted it. She felt like such an idiot taking baby steps across the platform. Her knuckles turned from pink to white as she formed a death grip on the railing. Sharon explained a few more details about this section of the rocket before taking them all the way down to ground level. Kari exited the lift on rubbery legs.

"Mr. Benton is waiting in his working office. Right this way." She looked over her shoulder as they walked down the hall. "You can take off the hardhat now."

Surprised to see the CEO of the space corporation in coveralls, Kari almost didn't recognize him. The walls of this particular office were lined with computer screens, a large table served as Mr. Benton's work space. He jumped to his feet when the women entered the room.

"Please, Mrs. Gale, sit down." He rolled a chair away from the table and waited until she was seated before he did the same. Sharon also sat down and pulled out her electronic tablet.

"You may be wondering why I went to such great lengths to meet you down here," he began. "I'm not going to beat around the bush with you. I wanted you to see this rocket."

Kari was experiencing a sensation of déjà vu. She remembered the day she signed her mother's body away to Mars. Her heart quickened.

"Have you ever heard of the organization Heartbeat of Humanity?"

She nodded, picturing their logo, one hand pressed on top of a fist across a heart.

"They've stepped up in a major way to fund our next mission." Mr. Benton leaned forward, pressing his elbows on the table. "In the past month alone, over six-hundred million dollars have poured in from all over the world. Your mother has captured the hearts of an entire planet. They want to bring her home."

Stunned by his declaration, Kari remarked, "But I thought there was no way to get off the planet."

Pointing toward the rocket outside his door, he said, "In the time that your mother has been in the Pioneer capsule, we've perfected the technology to land and boost off the planet with the same rocket. A team has been in training for months." He shrugged. "We just didn't know it was going to be a rescue mission when we started."

Kari's mind struggled to decipher all of the information Mr. Benton was feeding her. "Is this a joke?" she finally asked.

Sharon Conner slid her tablet across the table. "It's no joke, Mrs. Gale. Here's what you couldn't see on the other side of the rocket."

Kari stared at the screen, her eyes instantly filling with tears. There on the rocket, clearly printed in bold letters, it read, *Pioneer Rescue One*.

>>Chapter 28

After her meeting with Jarrod Benton, Kari sent Marc a message letting him know she wouldn't be home in time for dinner. *You and Ally eat without me. I'll grab something on the way,* she texted. She didn't want to talk on the phone for fear she wouldn't be able to disguise the thrill in her voice regarding her mother's rescue mission. This kind of information should only be shared in person. She couldn't stop smiling in anticipation of her daughter's reaction.

True to form, Ally did not disappoint. When Kari arrived, she found her in the backyard kicking a soccer ball with Marc. The evening sun still warmed their small area of green space.

"Hey, you two."

Ally sent the soccer ball in Kari's direction. "Hi, Mom."

Kari quickly trapped the ball, kicked off her sandals, and stepped out into the grass. She passed the ball over to Marc.

"How was your visit?" he asked.

"Pretty amazing, actually." They kept the ball going around the triangle a few more times, before she announced, "I've got some news I think you're both going to want to hear."

Ally immediately kicked the ball toward the fence and trotted over to her mom. Kari moved into the shade where they could sit down on the cushioned chairs.

"I'll tell you about my visit with Gran in a minute, but first, I think you need to know about my meeting with Mr. Benton." She quickly told them about her ride with Sharon Conner and the top half of the rocket she was able to see up close and personal.

Before she could disclose the most important part, Ally was already animated. "Do you think they'll let me go on the lift? That sounds awesome!"

Kari let out a soft laugh. "I definitely think that could happen, considering the name of the rocket…Pioneer Rescue One."

For a moment Marc and Ally sat in dazed silence. She could almost see both of their brains whirling, until Marc asked, "Is that rocket going to Mars?"

Beaming with sheer delight, Kari nodded. "Yes, it's a rescue mission. They have plans to bring Gran home!"

Ally jumped to her feet, letting out a shriek the whole neighborhood could hear. She plastered her hands to her cheeks. "Mom, you're not kidding about this, are you? They're really going to Mars to get her?"

"Yes, sweet girl. Apparently they already have a team of astronauts that have trained for months. They were planning to do a first run landing on Mars and boosting back off the planet. But now—"

"They're going to rescue Granny K!" Ally squealed, her feet dancing gleefully. All of a sudden she grabbed Kari by the shoulders and planted a kiss on her cheek. Then she twirled out into the yard.

Marc leaned forward in his chair, eyes glowing. "Kari, this is incredible."

"I know. I still haven't fully wrapped my mind around it."

"When, Mom? When are they going?"

"Well, that's the thing. The mission is set for February and this particular rocket will take at least nine months to arrive. That means they won't get to Gran until October of next year."

Nearly all of Ally's exuberance dimmed. She slowly came back to the patio to sit down. Kari knew how her daughter's mind worked. She would now be contemplating every possible angle. "How long will they stay on Mars before they can come home?" she asked quietly.

Kari had voiced that exact question to Mr. Benton only a few hours earlier. This was the part she wasn't looking forward to revealing. "Because of the orbit of Mars, they're going to have to stay on the planet for another six months. That part was already planned from the beginning. They're actually going to start setting up pods for a colony to live on the surface. They'll also make some additions to the boosting station that orbits around the planet." She let out a heavy sigh. "All in all, the mission will take a little over three years."

Ally fell back in her chair. Her eyes glossed over with tears. "I'll be a senior by then," she said soberly.

Kari rested a gentle hand on her leg. "I know, sweet girl. This is going to try our patience."

Marc brought up something Kari had hoped to avoid, at least for now. "Do you think Kathleen will be able to hold on that long all alone?" As soon as it was out of his mouth, he grimaced. He wanted to take it back, but it was too late—like it or not, they were going to have to discuss it.

"Yeah," Ally pressed. "That's such a long time."

Kari filled her lungs deeply, exhaling slowly. "That's where we come in. They want us to have a discussion with Gran and see if she prefers to stay awake for all of this or be put into a deep sleep."

For a very long time no one spoke. Kari had shoved this little tidbit to the back of her mind, hoping to deal with it later. She wasn't looking forward to having this particular conversation with her mom. It was going to be a big decision for her to make, and truthfully, Kari wasn't sure which one her mother would choose.

Later that night after Ally was in bed, Kari came into the living room and discovered Marc asleep on the couch. She sat down on the edge and smoothed her hand across his chest. "Hey, sleepy head, it's ten o'clock. Do you want to go to bed?"

He opened his eyes and clasped her hand with both of his. "Not yet," he said, sustaining her gaze. "How about telling me what you didn't want to say in front of Ally?"

She snickered. "How do you know me so well?"

A slow grin tipped his mouth. "Because I've spent nearly half my life studying you."

For a long moment Kari weighed her words. When she had first heard them from Jarrod Benton, it had been like a blow to the stomach—the kind that leaves you gasping for breath. "You know how Mom's brain reacted to the effects of deep space, and in particular Mars?"

He nodded.

"Essentially, it caused her brain to completely rewire." Kari paused and looked away.

"And?"

"And apparently," she said, lowering her eyes back to his, "there's a possibility that coming back to Earth could reverse that process. Maybe even…cost her life."

A tear slid from the corner of her eye. Marc rose up on one elbow and gently wiped it away with his thumb. "They don't really know for sure, do they?"

"No," she answered. "They're only speculating at this point."

Marc sat up and gathered her in his arms. They agreed that it would be better not to share this information with their daughter. No need giving Ally something to worry about for the next three years.

With his unflappable optimism, Marc told his wife, "God is the only one who knows what's about to happen. He's already walked this incredible path ahead of us. We'll just have to trust Him for the outcome."

"Easy words to say—hard words to live by," she breathed.

He stood and pulled Kari to her feet, leading her toward the stairs. "But live by them we shall," he pronounced with conviction.

> > >

Saturday morning Kathleen drowsily welcomed her family. Last night's sleep had been as elusive as oxygen on Mars. Carter Dunleavy's news concerning a rescue mission had kept her mind churning for hours on end. The sight of Ally, however, perked her up a bit.

"How's my angel?"

"I'm doing fine, Gran," she answered. "What about you?"

Kathleen pressed her shoulders back, hoping to chase away the lethargic haze. "I'm trying to wrap my mind around this rescue mission." She shook her head. "I can't believe they're actually coming for me."

For several minutes Kathleen listened to Ally's excited chatter. It brought such joy and delight to her weary heart.

Eventually, Kari nudged her way into the conversation. "Mom?"

"Yeah, honey."

"There's something really important we need to talk about concerning this mission."

Kathleen felt her heart pick up speed. All the scenarios that had run through her mind the night before now emerged from her subconscious. It was time to get down to the nub. She released a deep breath through her parched lips. "Such as?"

"Did Dr. Dunleavy tell you how long this mission was going to take?"

"Over three years," she uttered quietly.

Kari took in a long breath, started to say something, then glanced at her husband. Marc scooted in a little closer to the screen.

"Hi, Kathleen."

"Hello, Marc. I was wondering if you were going to get a word in edgewise today."

He chuckled softly. "We need to ask you a question."

Her patience felt thin. "Just cut to the chase."

"Okay," he said in a toneless voice. "We need to know if you want to stay awake for the mission or be put into a deep sleep and wake up when it's all over."

Kathleen let out a dry laugh. "Believe it or not, I've already mulled that over in my mind about a hundred times." She fell silent for a few breaths, hands tightening on the side of her bio-bed. "These last few weeks have been incredibly fulfilling. My days have been packed with visits from so many people dear to my heart. Even the President of the United States himself!" She threw up a lighthearted salute. "I never dreamed I could last this long in solitude. But I know deep down, I can't make it for another year waiting for the mission crew to arrive. Truthfully, I've just been gutting it out." Her voice broke and tears glistened in her eyes. "It's so hard," she whispered.

Kari found her voice. "Mom, I'm so sorry. I can't even imagine what you're going through."

Sleep deprivation hindered Kathleen from mincing her words for the sake of her granddaughter. "I can't hang on much longer. My body works against me every waking moment." Letting out a faint moan she said, "I need to sleep through this mission."

The family sat in staggering silence. Kari thought she would be prepared for whatever her mother decided to do, but she wasn't. It struck her chest like a heavy-handed blow. "Are you sure?" she asked with deep emotion.

"I have no doubt it's the right thing to do. I hope you understand."

"Oh, Gran, we understand," Ally exclaimed teary-eyed. "Just think, time will go by so fast for you. You'll go to sleep one minute and wake up the next."

"But I'm afraid it will go by slowly for you," Kathleen countered.

All three agreed that it would, but they assured her they would be waiting for her when she woke up.

"And," Ally added emphatically, "you'll be home just in time to see me graduate from high school."

Beneath her weariness, Kathleen felt a sweet hope that brought a smile to her lips. "I won't make any promises, Angel girl, but I'll do everything within my power to be there."

>>Chapter 29

Marc, I thank God for you. You're my rock and my anchor in the storms of life. You hold my heart entirely, and there will never, *ever* be another. I promise my love and faithfulness to you for the rest of my days."

Kari slipped the new gold band, inscribed with two wedding dates, onto her husband's finger. He caressed her hand that displayed the new silver band he had placed on her finger moments earlier. His eyes held such unconditional love. She swallowed back the urge to weep with gratitude.

Marc's good friend Scott, the minister from their church, covered both of their hands with his and spoke a deeply moving prayer over their marriage. The small gathering inside the communications lab, along with the audience of one on Mars, added their assent at the end with an exuberant, "Amen."

Eyes gleaming, Scott brought the ceremony to its culmination. "I now pronounce you husband and wife…again. Marc, you may kiss your bride."

For a moment, Marc held her face tenderly, his grin ever widening. "I love you, Kari."

With deep emotion she responded, "Oh, Marc, you better."

Before she could profess her love to him, he pulled her close, and gave her a lingering kiss. Amidst the applause, he whispered something in her ear that no one else could hear, leaving her flushed.

Thanks to Sharon Conner, music filled the communications lab, and the guests were invited to a reception of cake and punch laid out on a table at the back. Ally, who had stood by her mother's side for the ceremony, threw her arms around both of her parents. They huddled together in each other's embrace, wishing Kathleen could make it a foursome.

"Congratulations, you two!" she exclaimed from her perch on Mars. "This day means more to me than the first one."

They all blew her a kiss but seemed reluctant to leave her side.

"Go on and cut the cake—enjoy your guests. I'll be here when you get back."

Ally leaned in close. "Granny K, I've got someone here who wants to sit with you during the reception. She's not allowed to eat cake, so she's going to keep you company."

Ally walked over to their special guest, seated in a wheelchair. Olivia Cole had a tablet in her lap, ready to type messages for Kathleen. Her throat was rapidly healing, but her voice was still nearly inaudible for even those right beside her.

When Olivia came into view, Kathleen choked back a sob. "Oh how I've prayed for you, my dear friend. I'm so thankful to see you again."

Olivia pressed her tablet screen, which contained a previously typed message. "Hello-Kat-dearest. I've-missed-you-so-much," her tablet read in a monotone voice.

"As I have missed you. They tell me you should make a complete recovery."

Olivia briefly shared her prognosis.

"That's wonderful news," Kathleen told her. "I'll keep praying for your healing."

For an extended moment, Olivia worked on her next message. When she pressed play and looked up, she did so with red-rimmed eyes. "I-now-know-what-you-went-through-when-you-first-pulled-the-tubes-from-your-throat. You-must-have-been-in-terrible-pain. I'm-so-sorry-for-all-that-you-have-had-to-endure-on-Mars."

"Not for much longer," Kathleen countered. "I've decided to take a very long nap."

Olivia simply nodded.

Kathleen cleared her dry throat. "I want to thank you, dear friend, for getting me through such a terrible ordeal. I know I wouldn't still be alive if it hadn't been for you. You coached me through so many grueling hours. For that, I will always be grateful. I hope you know how much you mean to me and how dearly I love you."

Tears now escaped freely from Olivia's eyes. They dampened her tablet as she wrote. "I-hope-someday-to-wrap-my-arms-around-you,-dearest-Kat,-as-I-have-often-longed-to-do. I'll-be-waiting-for-you-when-you-awaken."

"I know you will. I look forward to our meeting on Earth."

The reception soon came to an end, and the small gathering of friends began to leave. Scott and his wife Claire huddled together with Marc and Kari for a few moments.

"We want to have you both over for dinner," Scott told them. "Just the four of us. We'll send the kids off to their grandparents for the evening. Claire makes a mean brisket."

"Thank you," Marc responded with pleasure. "We look forward to it."

Claire reached out to Kari and hugged her tightly. Over the last few weeks their friendship was beginning to develop a close bond. Claire had brought Kari into a discipleship group that was giving her a strong base of support from a circle of women. She had never experienced anything like it before. Most of her friends at the law firm had been worldly and ambitious. These women were gently teaching Kari how to trust again.

"I'll call you soon," Claire promised.

Kari returned her new friend's hug. "Thank you. And thank you for being here for us today." She stepped back to Marc's side and he wasted no time drawing her close.

When the lab was nearly empty, Dr. Yashkin made an appearance. "I have come to take Olivia to the medical lab for a visit." He stiffly wished the Gales his best and waited for each family member to give Olivia a hug.

Finally, down to Sharon Conner and a few communications technicians working in the far corner, Kari turned her attention back to her mother. Kathleen was no longer sitting up.

"Are you feeling all right, Mom?"

"Never better, honey. I just needed to lie down for a while."

"Go ahead and rest. We'll stay with you as long as you like." Kari felt hesitant to leave, knowing they had such precious little time left with her.

"Honey, you all go on. I know you and Marc have plans, and truthfully, I'm pretty sleepy. I must've had too much punch," she giggled.

Marc chimed in with a laugh. "I can assure you, there was nothing in that punch that would make you sleepy."

Kathleen's smile faded as quickly as it appeared, her tone more serious. "Thank you for moving your wedding up for me. I know your fall break is not for another month, but I wouldn't have missed this for anything in the universe."

"We didn't want you to miss it, Mom. Besides, I'm getting two honeymoons out of Marc. We have a fancy hotel for the next couple of nights and then he's flying me to Victoria, Canada in October." Kari turned a sparkling gaze toward her husband. "I think it's a pretty good deal."

"I'd say so," Kathleen agreed.

"Gran, I'll be back tomorrow. I'm staying with Reagan while Mom and Dad are away, and her family has been given permission to come with me for a visit."

"That will give me something to look forward to, Angel girl." She smiled wearily, and a long pause ensued.

"You're fine to go on, now," she finally said. "I love you all the way to Earth and back."

"I love you all the way to Mars and back, Granny K."

"You better," she quietly uttered just before her eyelids dropped.

Ms. Conner stepped forward, shutting down the com system. "Is there anything else I can do for you today?" she asked.

Ally's brow rose excitedly. A sly grin captured her features. "There *is* one thing I'd like to do before we leave."

Half an hour later Kari found herself frozen outside the open air lift, wearing a hardhat with her dress. Ally already stood at the outer railing with Sharon Conner. They were both wrapped in an animated discussion. Marc vacillated between joining the conversation and checking on his wife. He finally stepped half way off the lift.

"What is it, Babe?"

Kari felt every muscle in her body tense. "I can't do it."

His brow knit tightly. "Why? I thought you did this the other day."

Her voice quavered. "I did."

"What makes this time any different?" He held out his hand, beckoning her to join them.

All she could do was shake her head.

He looked back at Sharon and Ally, still chattering away. "I don't understand," he said in a hushed tone.

"I don't either. But I can't."

Marc was obviously trying to hide his disappointment. She knew he had wanted to share this incredible experience with her.

"Do you want me to ride down in the elevator with you?"

"No," she answered quickly. "You need to do this."

He bent and kissed her lightly on the mouth. "Okay, we'll see you below."

As soon as her husband moved back onto the lift, Kari felt her heart plummet. She desperately wanted to go with them, but couldn't quite summon enough courage to do so.

"Only the two of you, then?" Sharon asked.

Marc pressed his lips together and nodded, but when she placed her hand on the controls, Kari seized their attention.

"Wait!"

All three turned to face her.

"I think this is an important moment," she said in a stilted voice. "I want to be a part of it."

Marc immediately moved back to the opening where she stood. Even while she wavered, he offered his hand. "Let's do this together, Kari."

The hint of a smile turned her lips and she reached for his hand, determined to relinquish her fatuous fear. Keeping her eyes on his alone, she took one bold step after another, exactly as she planned to do for the rest of their lives.

"Together," she breathed.

>>>

The space center was abuzz with energy when the Gales arrived. The public had turned out in droves. All along the thoroughfare to the main gate, well-wishers stood with one fist pressed to their hearts, their other hand splayed on top. It was a sign of respect for the coach. The world had fallen in love with an extraordinary woman. They would walk with her family until she was finally home. Reporters and cameras captured the scene, but on this day, none were allowed to enter inside the gates.

Kari felt her throat constrict the moment she stepped up to the screen. Her mother was lying prone, eyes closed. Marc nodded for Kari to speak first. Drawing a long breath she said, "Mom?"

Kathleen startled awake. She blinked several times before reaching for the sides of her bed, pulling herself into a sitting position. For a long time both women held each other steadily with their gaze—neither one in a hurry to speak.

It was Kathleen who finally broke the silence. "I've thought of a thousand things to say to you, Kari, but for the life of me, I can't remember one of them."

Kari laughed softly, warm tears filling her eyes. "That's all right. You can save it for our next conversation."

Kathleen's voice took on an emotional tone. "Oh, how I look forward to that one."

"Me too, Mom," Kari said, trying hard not to think that this could be the last words they would ever speak to one another. She took in a shuddered breath. "You know, if I had it to do all over again..."

"Kari, honey, I've tried to live my life with no regrets—that's my mantra, and I want you to do the same." A soft smile turned her lips. "It's quite possible if you had left me on Earth, I may have been long gone by now. I choose to believe that God gave us this precious time together to reconcile. As hard as this has been on both of us, I can't thank Him enough for such a gift. He gave you back to me."

"I thank Him for that every single day, Mom." Kari wiped the tears from her cheeks with the back of her hand. "I hope you know how much I love you."

"I do," she sighed. "And I hope you know how much I love you."

"Without a doubt, Mom."

Kari motioned Ally forward and witnessed a sweet conversation between grandmother and granddaughter. It was amazing how much these two were alike. Both were determined to keep it on the light side, playfully teasing one another.

"Gran, I'll be looking for you at graduation. You'll be there, right?"

"Wouldn't miss it for anything, Angel girl. Look for me in the front row."

For a few more minutes they bantered back and forth until Kathleen asked for Marc.

"I'm here, waiting my turn, as usual."

She snorted. "Marc, I know you've been taking care of my house and property all this time, but I'd like to suggest a proposal. Why don't you move the family in? There's no mortgage, you'll be close to school, and even closer to the beach. You have my permission to pack up all my coaching memorabilia and put it in the storage room."

Marc turned a tentative gaze toward Kari. They hadn't once given thought to doing such a thing.

"I'd feel a lot better knowing you all were taking care of my things until I get back."

"Are you sure about this?" he asked.

"Very. As a matter of fact, I insist. But there's one string attached." Her brow arched playfully. "Three years from now, I get the spare bedroom."

A slow smile spread across Marc's face. "You've got a deal."

"Good. Now I'll be able to sleep better."

They all laughed and talked until Kathleen's perky smile slipped away. It was obvious their time was drawing to a close.

"I guess that leaves one more thing for us to do," she breathed. "If you don't mind, I'll start and Marc can finish."

Marc drew Kari and Ally into his arms as Kathleen poured out her heart in prayer. Kari went next followed by Ally, and finally Marc finished their supplication with fervor. Remarkably, no tears were shed. A feeling of peace had settled over the family.

Kathleen lay back in her bed, a tranquil look on her face. "I'm ready now," she said. "See you soon."

Carter Dunleavy stepped close to the family, speaking in a low voice. "Would you like to leave before we do this?"

"No," Kari said softly, keeping her gaze on her mother. "We'll stay."

Carter solemnly nodded.

Half an hour later, he returned to the lab and confirmed that Kathleen was now in blissful sleep. Kari pressed her fingers to her lips and laid them gently over her mother's image on the screen. "See you soon," she whispered.

When the family left the space center, they did so beneath a blushing sky. "Look what Gran sent us," Ally declared reverently.

The trio came to a standstill on the sidewalk, basking in the beautiful hues of orange and pink. Kari drank it into her very soul. If her transformation had been the equivalent of one day, this would be a fitting close. She would never be able to look at another sunset without thinking of her mother's undying love. Kathleen had waited so patiently for her. What a strange twist their lives had taken. How could they have predicted that this horrific restitution had been the very path to Kari's redemption? God's grace was truly unfathomable.

Marc glanced down at his wife with a tender smile, encircling her with his arm. "Let's go home," he said.

Kari leaned in to him and reached for her daughter's hand. Together they walked away, not knowing what the future would hold, but trusting the One who did—echoes of a very long day fading with the evening sky.

A Note from the Author

Dear Reader,

If you were expecting my third book to be another historical fiction novel, well, join the crowd. I was too! But I've learned that when God gives me a story—just go with it. It all started on June 8, 2014, at 4:18 p.m. when my daughter sent me a message on Facebook with an instrumental song attached along with these words: "You have to hear this song. Gave me chills." By 4:32 p.m. *Restitution* was born in my head, start to finish. I'm what you call a "seat of the pants" writer, so I never really know where a story is going until I sit down at the computer and type the words, "Chapter One." While writing about the future took me way out of my comfort zone, I really enjoyed every moment of this story.

In Beth Moore's book *Audacious*, she writes, "I believe that God can use a book to mark a life. It doesn't even have to be a great book. It can just be well-timed. He can cause a set of pages to hit a pair of hands with the kind of timing that sparks a decision that marks a destiny. Something within those pages becomes a catalyst that shapes a calling." That is my hope for every book I write. My intention for this novel was not to simply create a work of entertaining fiction, it was meant to inspire its readers to become better people, to know the Father on a deeper level, and to walk more closely with Him. If that should happen in just one life, then these hours at the keyboard will have been worth it.

After my first novel, a reader once wrote, "God is glorified throughout her book…nice to have an author return the favor to the Author of our lives." That is my purpose and calling. I pray that it will always be so.

May the grace of the Lord Jesus Christ, and the love of God, and the fellowship of the Holy Spirit be with you all (2 Corinthians 13:14).

Love and blessings,
Kristy Shelton